W9-CFC-084

WALKS WITHOUT A SOUL

Also by Geo. W. Proctor

ENEMIES

Walks Without a Soul

Geo. W. Proctor

A DOUBLE D WESTERN
DOUBLEDAY
New York London Toronto Sydney Auckland

Western

A DOUBLE D WESTERN
PUBLISHED BY DOUBLEDAY
a division of Bantam Doubleday Dell Publishing Group, Inc.
666 Fifth Avenue, New York, New York 10103

DOUBLE D WESTERN, DOUBLEDAY,
and the portrayal of the letters DD
are trademarks of Doubleday, a division of
Bantam Doubleday Dell Publishing Group, Inc.

Library of Congress Cataloging-in-Publication Data

Proctor, George W.
    Walks without a soul/Geo. W. Proctor.—1st ed.
        p.   cm.—(A Double D Western)
    I. Title.
PS3566.R588W3   1990
813'.54—dc20   90-30683
                        CIP

7/90 Doubleday
$14.95

ISBN 0-385-24470-3
Copyright © 1990 by Geo. W. Proctor
All Rights Reserved
Printed in the United States of America
August 1990
First Edition

FOR LANA
Twenty years is a long time; thank you for being.

WALKS WITHOUT A SOUL

ONE

AN ICE FLOE born of more than the chilled nip of the early October morning shivered through Nate Wagoner's veins and shuddered down his spine.

In a dark niche along the lowest row of a neatly stacked cord of mesquite and cedar came a flash of copper, a shifting glint caught in the yellow light of an awakening sun.

Copperhead! The brief flash, the movement—Nate needed no more to identify the venomous snake coiled within the woodpile.

"Daniel!" Nate's gaze shot to his son, who stood a stride away from the hidden viper. "Freeze, Daniel! Don't you take another step, boy. Don't even twitch a muscle!"

The sternness of his father's command wrenched the ten-year-old boy upright. Like a statue of a child poised to take a tentative step, Daniel stood rigidly. Only his fear-rounded eyes moved, rolling to find his father, who stood at the doorway to a settler's shack twenty feet to the left.

"Don't move, son." Nate outstretched both arms, hands held palm out with fingers splayed to reinforce the caution in his voice. "There's a copperhead coiled in the wood two feet from your toes."

Daniel's throat bobbed as he swallowed hard. His eyes shifted again, this time to search the weathered gray of the split wood for the poisonous snake that remained concealed in its dark cubbyhole.

"Don't move, boy. He's just waking up and probably ain't even noticed you yet." A soothing calm replaced the sternness in Nate's voice while he eased a hoe from two wooden pegs embedded in the front of the shack. "He ain't going to bother you none 'less you give him reason. He just coiled himself up in that wood-pile last night to keep warm. He ain't going to pay you no never mind 'less you go moving about like some kind of fool."

Nate tried to believe his own words. In truth Daniel's approach and not the warmth of the rising sun probably had aroused the sleeping copperhead.

"Pa?" Daniel questioned, his eyes still probing the nooks and crannies of the woodpile. "I can run fast. I can . . ."

"Quiet, boy!" Nate cautiously stepped along the front of his home, hoe clenched tightly in his fists. "Don't you even think 'bout running. Just listen to your daddy. Everything's going to be all right, you hear?"

Daniel's Adam's apple bobbed again with the dryness of another hard swallow. The boy's head nodded ever so slightly, and he whispered, "I hear."

"Good, 'cause I'm right behind you with a hoe. Soon as that snake pokes his head out, I'll whack it off quick and clean." Nate's slow maneuvering brought him to within an arm's length of his youngest son's back. "Just draw in a breath slow and easy like then let it go the same way. And don't go moving on me now."

The pounding of Nate Wagoner's temples doubled its panicked pace. A flat triangular head of glinting copper scales pushed from the security of the woodpile. A black, forked tongue flicked from the poisonous snake's mouth to smell the cool morning air.

Sweet Jesus! Half raised, the hoe trembled in Nate's hands while fine beads of sweat prickled across his dark forehead. There was no possible way he could get at the snake from this angle—not without taking off one of Daniel's bare toes in the process!

"Easy, son," Nate whispered softly and steadily, ignoring visions of the copperhead abruptly lashing out, sinking curved fangs into his son's vulnerable flesh, and releasing a flood of deadly poison into Daniel's young body. "Take it nice and easy, boy. We got to let it come out a mite more before I can get at it with this here hoe."

Daniel's head tilted a fraction of an inch in acceptance while unspoken terror opened his saucer-round eyes even wider.

Atop a mottled patterned neck of cream, tan, and copper, the snake extended its head outward. That black tongue constantly flicked, nervously tasting the air around it. For a moment the copperhead paused, head arching upward, tongue stopping.

"Pa?" The softness of Daniel's voice could not conceal his trembling fear. "Pa, it's going to—"

Nate caught himself, whispering rather than snapping, "Quiet!" The last thing he wanted now was for a sudden outcry from either himself or Daniel to startle the snake. "Keep still, boy. He's been sleeping all night and is just taking a gander at the new day."

Daniel remained motionless, young eyes locked on the snake as its ugly head lowered once more. Outward the slender reptilian neck arched, pulling a thick, sinuous body from the pile of split firewood. A foot, two, three full feet from its triangular head to tapered tail the mottled killer undulated from side to side. The scales of its underbelly gripped the ground moving it forward toward the dusty ebon of Daniel's bare foot.

A piteous moan pushed from the ten-year-old boy's trembling lips. His board-straight body went as rigid as granite.

The copperhead's thick body writhed against the boy's right foot, paused a moment as though surprised by the warmth it found radiating from the strange-shaped mound that lay across its path. The snake's flat head wove right and then left before it rose to slither across Daniel's unprotected flesh.

"Pa?" That single word was the terrible plea of child to parent to save him from certain death.

"Hush!" was all Nate could say. Nor could he do more than stare down at the copperhead while his pounding heart lodged itself solidly in his throat. His mouth went cotton dry as a cold sweat prickled over his body in a horrible counterpoint.

Its thick body constantly shifting, the copperhead wove through the dusty sand between Daniel's spread legs. There was no hesitation in the snake's movement now. It crept forward as though it accepted man and boy as natural parts of the Texas terrain.

One . . . two . . . three . . . Nate judged the distance the copperhead inched past his son's left heel. He edged the hoe upward to extend it high above his head. The knuckles of his black hands strained with the power of his grip on the wooden handle. *Four . . .*

The hoe sliced downward in a whistling arc as every ounce of strength in Nate's muscular arms drove it home.

The hoe's blade found its mark. With a solid thud it struck. There was an instant of resistance as iron bit through scale, flesh, and bone to sever the snake's head cleanly from its coppery-hued body.

"Pa!" Unashamed relief voiced itself in Daniel's cry.

The hoe fell from Nate's quivering hands as he threw open his arms to Daniel, who ran into his father's sheltering embrace. Legs abruptly gone liquid and bladder suddenly aching, Nate sank to his knees and hugged his youngest son close.

"It's over." He desperately clung to Daniel's small, trembling body while his lips repeatedly kissed the side of the child's head. "Ain't nothin' goin' to hurt you. Not while I'm here. It's all right, boy, you hear me?"

Nate's walnut brown eyes rolled to the ground. The copperhead's body spasmodically coiled and flopped in the sand. The snake's still pumping heart futilely struggled against the inevitability of death while precious life spurted from its severed neck in an ever-weakening flow of crimson.

Anger flared to replace the relief that had left Nate atremble only a heartbeat before. His caressing right hand jerked into the air to firmly swat his son's backside three times in rapid succession. Daniel wailed in surprise; tears welled in his eyes and rolled down his dark cheeks.

Grasping the ten-year-old by the shoulders, Nate thrust him back at arm's length to shake him. "Don't you ever do that again. Your ma and me didn't birth you just to have you go and get yourself kilt by some damned copperhead. I cut you that cedar rod to prod the wood like I told you, and I expect you to use it. You understand?"

His cries diminishing to sobbing shudders, Daniel raised a small fist to his eyes and wiped away the tears. He drew a shaky breath, rolled his eyes to his father, and nodded.

"Then I'm takin' you at your word. 'Cause next time me and

that hoe might not be so close. Now go fetch that firewood like your ma asked." Nate released his son and sent him on his way with another swat to his bottom.

Daniel stiffly trotted to the side of the house and hefted a long, smooth cedar branch leaning against the wall. He then returned to the woodpile to probe the dark crannies between the split logs to make certain no other critters had taken up residence in the wood.

Better my hand than a snake's fangs. A twinge of parental guilt shot through Nate's chest as he stood. His son tentatively rubbed a hand over his buttocks in an attempt to remove the sting left by his father's palm.

Strappings were not Nate's way, nor were switchings. A man who had felt the bite of the white man's whip never wanted his sons or daughters to know even a hint of the pain and terror that was too often the lot of black-skinned men in this country. Yet, Daniel was young, and, if he were to grow to a man, had a lot to learn about Texas and her ways. A strong hand applied to the seat of his pants on occasion taught a lesson that could never be achieved with mere words.

"Nate? Nate, what's goin' on out here? What's got Daniel squallin'?"

Running a hand through the thick mat of his hair, Nate turned to the woman who stood in the doorway to the house. Concerned furrows deeply creased a high forehead that lay partially concealed by a red bandanna tied tightly about her hair.

"Our youngest son almost got hisself bit by a copperhead, Bessa." Nate pointed to the now-still snake.

"Daniel!" A mother's worry lined Bessa's delicate features as she stepped from the house and bustled toward the boy.

Arms opened wide, Nate caught his wife and hugged her closely to him. "Let him be. Ain't no damage done, 'cept maybe to his pride." He playfully swatted her backside to emphasize his meaning.

Bessa tilted her head to the side to avoid a kiss meant for her lips and raised a reprimanding eyebrow. "You ain't been beatin' the boy, have you, Nate Wagoner? I'll take my fry pan to the side of your head if'n you been switchin' Daniel."

Nate glanced at his son then back to his wife, his face splitting from ear to ear in an ivory grin. "Probably wear my handprint on his rump for the rest of his life—or at least until he gets into the house with that arm load of wood."

Bessa stamped a foot and tried to wiggle free of her husband's encompassing embrace. "For good measure I ought to whop you . . ."

Her protest died in a muffled sigh as Nate's mouth found hers. Her arms slid around his back, clutching to him as enthusiastically as he held her slim body.

When their lips parted, Bessa's eyelids fluttered open to reveal sparkling eyes as black as lumps of coal. A coy smile upturned the corners of her mouth. "That ain't always going to work with me, you know."

"Been workin' for nigh on to sixteen years now. Don't see no reason for things to be changin'." Nate's right hand rose, his fingertips tenderly caressing his wife's cheek. He lightly kissed her lips again. "You're still a mighty handsome woman, Bessa. As pretty as that skinny little gal Master Campbell first brought to my bed back in Galveston."

"Listen to you astandin' here sweet talkin' at this hour of the mornin'. You ought to be ashamed, Nate Wagoner. You a growed man with five childrens. Next thing you'll be suggestin' is that you and me should go trapsin' out to those bushes over yonder together!" There was a bite to her words, but her tone was sweet and purring like a fat cat getting her ears scratched.

"Mighty fine way to begin a day. Find us a bed of fresh, green clover . . ."

Grinning shyly like a young girl being courted by the first beau to catch her eye, she shoved away from her husband. "Go on with you. Ain't neither of us got the time to be rollin' in the clover. 'Specially me! I got a kettle of mush hung above the fire and five kids and a husband to feed."

"Then how about tonight when our sons and daughters are sleeping?"

Bessa's grin widened with obvious delight. "Now you're layin' plans for something that can't happen. You done told Ben y'all were goin' to set snares this eve."

"Them javelinos ain't goin' nowhere. They can wait until to-morrow night." Nate smiled. "A man and a woman needs their time together."

Bessa's dark eyes rose to her husband, and her lips parted hesitantly. "Then we'll see about tonight—*after* the childrens are sleepin'."

"That we will," Nate laughed, realizing the wordplay had concluded as it had always ended during their sixteen years together. "That we will!"

"Now you and Daniel come along inside, if you don't want your breakfast to scorch."

Bessa spun about on the balls of her bare feet, setting her gray sackcloth dress swishing rhythmically around her long legs, and walked back to the house. She paused outside to stoop and lift the pail of morning milk Nate had left by the door. Casting a beaming smile over a shoulder at her husband, she stood and disappeared inside.

Warmth nestled deep in Nate's chest while his gaze followed his wife. He had not lied to her; she *was* still as pretty as the day their former owner had brought the skinny fifteen-year-old girl to the cabin of a stout buck who had seen eighteen summers. Just watching the movement of her lithe body then had set his blood afire with desire. It still did.

Neither had expected that first night, when they had been no better than the white man's breeding stock, to stretch all the way from Galveston to their life here beside the Brazos River. Nor had they known that love would root itself firm and solid in their hearts, binding them as man and woman, husband and wife.

Waving Daniel ahead of him, Nate followed his son inside their home. Nate's gaze moved over the house's large main room. To be certain it was no better than other homes built on Texas's western frontier. Then it was no worse. Nate had seen to that with his own hands and his own sweat.

The walls were in fact two walls constructed from cedar and oak limbs woven among cedar posts set deep in the ground. The eight-inch space between the wooden barriers was filled with rock and dirt. While not the brick and board of Galveston mansions, the walls kept out the bitter winter wind while cooling the house beneath an unforgiving Texas sun during the long summer.

Bessa's pride was the single glass window, complete with curtains sewn from white flour sacks, that looked out from the front of the house toward the Brazos and the greenery that flourished along its banks. Nate had traded five plucked turkeys and four tanned deer hides for the frame and four plates of slightly blue-tinted glass. The steep price was well worth the contented smile he saw on Bessa's face each time his wife stood at the window.

Tables and chairs placed about the room had been hewed by Nate's hands, including Bessa's rocker that sat by the stone hearth. Once the floor had been laid with split logs. After a month he had consigned the logs to the woodpile. A well-packed earth floor contained far less splinters and offered no refuge for nesting scorpions.

A door at the back of the room opened onto two small bedrooms: one for the children, the other for Bessa and him. Like the chairs and the tables, the beds in those rooms had been shaped by Nate's hands.

"Come get your breakfast 'fore it gets cold." Bessa summoned him to a rough-hewn table set near the hearth. She placed a tin can beside his steaming bowl of mush. "This is the last of the ribbon-cane syrup we traded for last fall."

"Flowers's store still had a pail or two last time Ben and I rode in. I'll get one Saturday." He poured a dark layer of syrup over the cornmeal mush, then ladled a dipper of milk atop that, before pushing milk and syrup down the table. "Speaking of Mr. Flowers, Ben, I want you to skin that copperhead outside. It'll bring a few pennies in trade."

His oldest son Benjamin glanced up as he prepared his own bowl of mush. At fifteen, Ben was rapidly developing into a younger version of his father. He matched Nate's six-foot height and promised to sprout another inch before he reached his next birthday. The thick muscles that strained his shirt sleeves were already those of a man rather than a boy.

It was not just himself that Nate saw in his first-born. Those high cheeks and dark, clear eyes belonged to Bessa. Ben also had inherited his mother's thin nose and mouth.

Ben nodded. "I'll get to it before we head to the fields, Pa."

"You do that now. 'Cause it might bring enough to buy some peppermint sticks. Although I never knowned anybody in this house to have a taste for peppermint," Nate said.

"Peppermint!" was chorused by his daughters Mary and Eve, whose excited eyes rolled to their father.

"You're not just teasin' us, are you, Pa?" This from Mary, whose thirteen years had sobered her with the reality of their hard life. Like her mother, whom she favored more and more with each passing day, she knew money, even pennies, was difficult to come by.

"If'n you buy me a stick of candy, I'll even share it with Daniel," piped eight-year-old Eve, her wide, round eyes sparking with a touch of the devil. "I always share, just like Ma tells us. I ain't like Daniel, who ain't never given nobody a lick of his candy."

"I gave you a bite of my piece of cake last Christmas," Daniel answered sheepishly.

"Ain't the same thing, Daniel," Eve retorted. "Peppermint's *special.*"

"Children!" Bessa called her family to silence while she took her place at the table with her youngest daughter, eighteen-month-old Naomi, in her arms. "I thought when I gave y'all names from the good book some of that goodness would take on you."

Bessa's gaze crossed the table to her husband. "You ain't got no right talkin' about peppermint. It costs too much."

"Way I figured it, Daniel and I earned it this morning." Nate glanced at his youngest son and winked. " 'Sides, ain't none of us had peppermint in a month of blue moons."

"I thought we already decided what we's goin' do with all the money we make?" Bessa's words were a question, but her tone that of a final decision. "Have you talked with Master Turner yet? Ben's not getting any younger."

"I plan to talk with Master Turner after the oats are in, when I see what I get for them," Nate answered. "Until then a few pennies for stick candy ain't going to make any difference one way or the other."

Bessa said nothing as she poured milk and syrup into her bowl.

However, Nate noticed Ben carefully kept his eyes averted, staring at the table rather than looking at his mother or father.

He knows what we're talking about. Nate realized that his oldest had overheard Bessa and him talking about finding their son a wife. They would have to give Master Turner the hundred dollars they had saved over the years to buy a young girl for Ben. *I'll have to talk to Ben 'fore I speak to Master Turner. Maybe he's got his eye already set. He seemed to take a shine to Master Wilson's young house girl last Christmas.*

"Nate, it's your turn to give the blessin'," Bessa interrupted his thoughts. "Children, bow your heads while your daddy prays."

Nate watched while each of his sons and daughters did as their mother said, then saw Bessa smile approvingly and do the same. It was moments like this when he drank in his whole family, felt the love binding them to him and him to them that made life and all the trials it threw at a man worth the struggling.

Lowering his own head, Nate Wagoner gave thanks for the bounty the Lord had granted him. Each word he reverently uttered, he meant with all his soul.

TWO

NATE WAGONER slipped a forked oak branch beneath a cowpaddy to flip it over on the ground. Assured that the sun had baked the last moisture from the eight-inch-in-diameter manure paddy, he reached down, lifted it, and placed it inside a half-full burlap bag that he dragged on the ground behind him.

The cowpaddy, like the others in the sack, would be stored in the barn until winter. On an icy January day when a blue norther lashed across the plains like an invisible knife that cut man and beast to the bone, he would bring all the stored bags from the barn into the house. For a day, maybe two, he and his family would labor diligently to second harvest the undigested oats from the manure.

Grim distaste set the corners of his mouth at the thought of the unrelished dirty task that lay ahead. Yet, it was one that could not be shirked.

The grain handpicked from the dried manure, after being soaked in water for a day to awaken dormant kernels, would provide seed for his crop next year. The remaining manure would be spread across his field to enrich soil that was more rock and sand than fertile farming loam.

Five strides farther, Nate turned another paddy over and passed it by. A wet brown spot on its bottom warned that it needed at least another two days in the sun before it was ready to be collected. Placing a moist paddy into a sack would breed fuzzy, gray mold and taint both manure and seed. This natural bounty was too precious to be so thoughtlessly and recklessly ruined. Only when the Texas sun had sucked the last drop of moisture from the manure did he gather a paddy.

Walking on, he found another cowpaddy between two bone white limestone rocks that poked from the ground. He flipped it, deemed it dry, and lifted it from the ground. Oats, specks of yellow embedded in dusty brown, were scattered through the hardened manure.

Oats, Nate smiled. He had chosen wisely when he had selected oats as his money crop. In this harsh country a man and his family might endure the rumblings of half-filled stomachs throughout the hard winters, but livestock had to be fed. A man's horse, mule, and cows were the difference between life and death along the Brazos River. That meant oats could always be sold or bartered for necessities.

A smile spread across Nate's blue-black face. Not that oats had been his original choice for a crop. He, like every man who came to this rugged country, had tried to raise cotton. And he had watched it wither and die in the ground. This sun-baked land was not the rich soil of East Texas. The cotton fields he had worked until he was thirteen would never flourish here.

The idea to try oats had come from a tale he had heard spouted by two grizzled, old trappers who had passed through his first winter along the Brazos. They had told of Indian tribes who second-harvested grain from their horses' manure, cleaned it, then used it in their own food.

The realization human beings could eat such and survive had sent him scouring Master Turner's pastures for cowpaddys. He and Bessa had hauled water from the river daily to nurse their first crop into green life. Over the years, that first acre had swelled to twenty of the twenty-five Master Turner allotted him. Wooden barrels in a small mule-drawn cart had replaced the buckets of water his wife and he had hand-carried to the fields that first year.

"Pa!" Benjamin hailed his father.

Nate turned to the right, facing his oldest son, who approached with his younger brother in tow.

"Daniel got hisself into a paddy that was still a mite ripe." Ben hefted the boy's right hand to display fingers and palm covered with still-glistening green-brown manure.

Nate shook his head, thinking for the second time that day that his youngest boy had so much to learn about their life. If Daniel wasn't into one thing, it was another. With the dawning of each day, it was as though the boy awoke into a new world, having forgotten everything his father had taught the day before.

"It 'peared dry on the top!" Daniel loudly defended his messy mistake.

"That's what your stick's for. You're supposed to turn it over 'fore pickin' it up." Ben made no attempt to hide his exasperation. "Pa and I done told you that time and time again! You got ears, why don't you listen?"

"I forgot," the ten-year-old replied sheepishly. His eyes rolled downward to escape his older brother's harsh glare.

Amusement uplifted the corners of Nate's mouth. Not that many years ago, Ben had worried him as much as Daniel did now. And Ben had come along just fine—developed into a strong, young man who was capable of stepping into his father's shoes should anything happen to Nate.

"No need to get riled." Nate winked at his oldest son, then looked at Daniel. "The stink'll wash off. 'Sides it's time to take a break and get a cool drink of water."

"Hear that? The stink'll wash off." Daniel grinned from ear to ear and nudged his brother's side with an elbow.

Ben grunted, rolled his eyes in disgust, and stepped to his

father's side as they started over a rise toward a creek that separated Nate's land from that of his owner's property.

"Wait up for me!" Tugging his burlap bag behind him, Daniel ran after the two. He looked up at Nate when he reached his father's left side. "Ben says we're slaves, Pa. He said Master Turner owns us. That ain't true, is it?"

"I didn't raise Ben and you to tell lies, did I?" Nate rested his hand on the boy's shoulder.

"But it don't make no sense." Daniel shook his head. "How come we ain't got the same last name as Master Turner then? The black folks around here that are slaves all got their masters' names."

"All the black men in Texas are slaves, Daniel." Nate's chest constricted as though a steel band tightened around it.

He did not like to think about the past. Neither Bessa nor he talked about their former lives, even when they were alone in their bed at night. He glanced down at Daniel. The boy was old enough to hear the truth; he had a right to know about the chains that once bound his mother and father.

"Master Turner's a lot like the man who first owned me and your mother. They don't believe in givin' no niggers their last names. Master Campbell, who owned us back in Galveston, was a wagonmaker. He called all his guineas Wagoner. That's where we got the name. Master Turner kept it," Nate explained when he and his sons reached the stream.

"Then we're all slaves?" Daniel said softly when he squatted by the water.

Before the boy could shove his hands into the creek, Ben grabbed him by the collar and maneuvered him several feet to the right. "Wash your hands downstream from us. Pa and I ain't got no want to have our water seasoned with cow manure!"

Nate sat on his heels, cupped his palms, and pushed them under the cool water. He brought his hands to his lips and drank, washing the dust from his mouth and throat. It took two more handfuls before he quenched his thirst. Splashing water on his face, he stood to let the sun's evaporation cool his skin.

Silently Daniel squatted beside the stream, rinsing the manure from between his fingers. A frown furrowed his dark, young brow.

Nate's chest tautened again. It was not an easy weight for shoulders so young to carry. The knowledge that a man was the property of another was never a light burden.

"Sometimes a soul can't put too much faith in a name, boy." Nate walked to his son and settled on the ground beside him. "Slave—freeman ain't always what they sound like. They's just words that don't always tell things the way they really is."

Daniel looked at his father, his eyes silently questioning.

"I ain't goin' to lie to you, boy. Master Turner's got the papers on all of us. We're legally his," Nate explained. "But it don't mean the same as it would if we were still back in Galveston with Master Campbell ownin' us."

Daniel dipped a hand into the creek for a drink, then sat on the ground at his father's side. "You mean we're really free?"

"For all purposes." Nate grinned and rubbed a hand over his son's head. "It ain't no white man set us free. It's this land that give us our freedom."

While Daniel and Ben listened, Nate told how William Turner had purchased Bessa and him in Galveston. "They had come into Texas from Alabama. Just married they was and needing two niggers as house slaves. It was me and your ma they chose."

Nate chuckled remembering Bessa, her belly already swelling with Ben. The Turners had thought that they had struck quite a bargain, buying what would eventually be three slaves for the price of two. That was before they saw the land on which they were to build a new life.

"This land could barely support jackrabbits," Nate said. "Master Turner saw right off that he couldn't afford to keep no house or field slaves. So what he done was strike a bargain with me and Bessa. He marked off twenty-five acres for us to farm and build a home on. Said it was ours to do with as we please as long as he got a tenth of what we grew. And, of course, we had to help with the chores about his place on occasion."

"Which is why we help Master Turner bring in his crops," Ben added.

"And why your ma does some washin' and sewin' for Missus

Turner," Nate added. "And why we give Master Turner his portion of the game we trap."

"Then we are free," Daniel smiled.

"Just as good as." The tightness dissolved in Nate's breast, and his chest expanded with pride. "Don't need no paper out here to make a man free. It's the land. Hard and mean, it makes men equal—white or black."

He explained that all the settlers who brought slaves into this desolate portion of the Texas frontier found themselves faced with a similar situation. They could not afford to feed extra mouths so they gave their slaves land and a life of their own.

"That's why we tend our crops the way we do. It's hard work that can leave every muscle in your body achin', but it's freedom, Daniel. It's our freedom." Nate pushed from the ground and stood. "Speakin' of work, time we was gettin' back to ours."

His sons beside him, Nate strode back to the top of the rise where a mule and cart waited. Taking two long-barreled single shot rifles from the cart, he handed one to Ben, then tossed his manure sack within. The rifles were solid evidence of how free they were here, Nate thought proudly. In any other part of Texas a black man would have his flesh flayed from his back for even holding a firearm, let alone owning a rifle. But this was the western frontier, farmlands that pushed back the borders of Comanchería, the Comanche-held plains. A man without a rifle was as good as dead whether he was white, brown, or black.

Ben and Daniel deposited their own sacks, then stepped inside the cart behind their father. Nate lifted the mule's reins, holding them firmly in both his hands.

"We'll take this on down to the barn 'fore headin' to the field. Save your ma and the girls from havin' to bring us out our lunch." Nate clucked the mule to life. A painful, dry squeak of protest shot through his ears when the wheels began to roll. "Gonna have to grease 'em this evenin' . . ."

"Pa." Ben tapped his father's shoulder. "Master Turner's cows!"

Nate turned, his gaze following the line of his son's pointing finger. Twenty cows moved on a direct course toward the lush green of growing oats!

"Damn!"

Nate reined the mule around, lifted a rope whip tied to a cedar branch, and popped it against the animal's rounded, brown rump. With a protesting bray, the mule broke into a trot. Across rut and rock, the cart bounced and jostled. Each jarring vibration shot through Nate's legs upward along each bone of his body, threatening to rattle them apart.

"Ben, Daniel! Head 'em off!" He shouted back to his sons.

The two leaped from the wagon. Arms flailing the air and startling yowls whooping from their lungs, they ran straight for the errant herd.

A red-spotted cow with swollen udders that nearly dragged the ground and a black and white calf at her side led the assault on the oat field. Her thick, square head swung around to eye coolly the two humans who sprinted to intercede themselves between her and the rich grazing mere yards ahead. A low bellow rolled from her throat, and she hastened her pace.

"A rock!" Nate shouted. "Chunk a rock at her!"

Barely breaking his stride, Ben leaned down and scooped a stone from the ground. When his legs stretched again, his arm swung back then lashed forward. The rock hurled through the air to strike the red-spotted cow squarely on the end of her nose.

Ben lifted another stone from the ground, but there was no need for the second missile. The lead cow bellowed again, pivoted in a cloud of dust, and hastened away in the direction she had come. The remaining animals wheeled about in the next instant, following their leader and her calf back onto Master Turner's land.

"That was close!" Ben turned to his father when Nate pulled the mule to a halt beside his oldest son. "If they'd've gotten into the oats, we'd never run 'em out."

"Goin' to have to keep a sharp eye on Master Turner's herd until we harvest," Nate nodded in agreement as he turned back to proudly survey the acres of breeze-rippled green. "Grazin' gettin' sparse, and our oats are lookin' better every day to them cows. Wouldn't want to have to burn pear to keep our own stock alive this winter."

The stock he spoke of consisted of the mule harnessed to the cart and three milk cows and their calves. The bitter cold two winters ago had all but wiped out his animals. For months Ben and he had struggled to keep them alive by burning the needles off prickly pear cactus and feeding the animals the broad flat leaves. Although lacking in nutrients, the pear sustained mule and cows until spring rains brought grass pushing from the sandy soil.

"How many bushels an acre you reckon we'll get this year, Pa?" Ben asked while his own gaze moved over the field of oats.

"I smell somethin' burnin'." Daniel's nose wrinkled.

"Burnin'?" Nate's wide nostrils flared to draw in a deep breath. The smoky aroma of smoldering wood filled his nose. "Smells like Master Turner's fired up his smokehouse. Don't recall him doin' any slaughterin' lately, do you?"

He glanced eastward from his field. Beyond a cedar-sprinkled ridge, hidden from view, the Turner place lay nestled within a double curve of the Brazos. Greasy smoke curled in a cloud over the crest.

"Reckon I was mis . . ."

Nate's words trailed off. An icy chill shivered up his spine. There was too much smoke for curing meat! Farther to the east three other columns of black rose toward the clouds.

His head jerked around. A fifth column of smoke billowed above the rise behind him, blotting out half the sky.

"No," he mumbled aloud, his mind refusing to accept what his eyes saw.

The pouring smoke could come from only one place—his home!

THREE

FIRE!

Panic constricted Nate's throat. The Texas sun, the moisture-hungry heat, turned wood into brittle kindling. Flames could devour a house and all inside within a matter of seconds.

Bessa and the girls were still in the house!

His eyes darted back to the four other dark pillars rising in the east. The fires had not been sparked by nature. They had been set! Cold sweat prickled across his body like fiery needles. *Comanches!*

"Boys, in the wagon!"

He slapped the reins against the mule's hindquarters without waiting for his sons to scramble into the cart. By the time Ben manhandled his younger brother atop the manure sacks, Nate urged the mule forward with a pop of the rope whip to match each straining stride the animal took.

Above the rattle and groaning protests of the wooden cart rose high-pitched, ear-piercing yelping cries: coyote-imitating howls that left no doubt the still unseen attackers were a Comanche raiding party.

"Dear Lord, please protect them!" The desperate prayer mumbled over Nate's trembling lips as he cracked the whip to the mule's back three times in rapid succession.

The animal lunged forward against the leather harness, finding greater speed in its pumping legs.

"Pa?" Fear quavered in Ben's questioning voice.

"My rifle, boy!"

Nate tossed aside the makeshift whip. Without glancing back at his sons, he held out an open hand. Ben slapped a long barrel rifle into his father's waiting palm. Thumb arching to hammer, Nate cocked the weapon, then held it poised to swing to his shoulder the instant a target came into view.

As hard as he strained, he heard no gunfire mingled with the yipping battle cries that came from beyond the rise. It was a good sign; rifles were still a rarity among the Comanche bands, and he prayed he could turn that into an advantage.

Fierce and bloody warriors who for two centuries had defeated the English, French, Spanish, Mexicans, and Texicans in all their attempts to push the frontier westward, Comanche braves had one unpredictable weakness—superstition. They rode out of the plains on the backs of their mustang ponies only when they deemed good medicine protected their raiding party. The slightest hint of bad medicine often sent them reeling around, fleeing back into the desolation of the western plains.

Black smoke pillowed like a gathering thunderhead overhead as Nate popped the reins across the mule's back with his left hand. He heard the cracking and spitting of burning timbers, but the war cries were gone.

His grip tightened about the rifle. He had to make the single lead ball packed into the rifle barrel count. To kill, or even wound one of the attacking braves, might be all the bad medicine needed to drive away the raiders. Especially if the warriors were armed with only war lances and bows and arrows.

The right wheel of the cart jarred into a limestone rock embedded in the ground when the mule crested the hill. The small wagon flew a foot into the air.

Balance lost, Nate slammed into the wooden boards that formed the cart's side. Pain lanced hotly along his rib cage. He ignored it, struggling upward to regain his footing as the mule ran head-on down the gentle slope.

The clouds of smoke poured from the collapsed, flaming ruins of what had once been a low-roofed barn. The house stood untouched. Its front door lay open, swung inward like a gaping, toothless maw.

Dread twisted his gut. The marauding braves had vanished. Nor were Bessa and the girls to be seen.

Nate cautiously tugged the mule to a walk. Had Bessa driven the raiders away? Or was it a trap? Dropping the reins, he hefted the rifle's stock to the hollow of his shoulder ready to meet an attack.

"To the west!" Ben's arm snaked out, pointing down the narrow valley of the Brazos River.

Nate's head jerked around. Far beyond the range of his rifle, a half a mile upriver, twenty Comanche warriors, partially obscured by the dust that flew from their ponies' hooves, fled. As quickly and silently as they had struck, they retreated.

"Bessa!" Nate called out. "Bessa!"

No answer came.

The knots in his gut doubled.

"Pa, it's too quiet."

The fear Nate felt in every cell of his body was echoed in Daniel's words.

"Shhhhh." Nate hushed his youngest son and motioned for Ben to take the reins. "You and Daniel wait here. I'm goin' in for a look."

Rifle in his right hand, he used his left to vault over the side of the car. He hit the ground in a run that ended only when he stood pressed flat against the front of the house beside the open door. No sound came from within.

"Bessa? Mary? Eve?" he called. "It's me. They're gone. Y'all come out now."

There was no answer.

Rifle held level at his waist, he sucked in a steadying breath, then darted inside the house. A tornado had struck the main room. Tables and chairs were overturned and strewn across the earth floor. Bessa's pots and skillets had been torn from their wall pegs and thrown about the room. The half-cooked remnants of rabbit stew were spilled on now-cold logs in the hearth.

"Bessa?" he whispered while he moved toward the bedrooms, no longer expecting an answer.

The same red-skinned tornado had torn through his and Bessa's room. The bed lay overturned, its mattress slashed to shreds. Like a horrible blizzard, white and gray feathers covered the floor.

Trembling with fear of what he would find in the house's last room, he turned away and stepped to the threshold of the children's bedroom.

Confusion befuddled his brain. The butchered bodies of his wife and daughters that he expected to find were not here. Like the rest of the house, the Comanches had destroyed everything in sight, but Bessa and the girls were gone.

Captive! Realization came almost in relief; his wife and daughters still lived. *Not dead, but taken captive. They're alive . . .*

Half-formed, the thought died. Nate's heart pounded in his chest. To the left, moist crimson splattered the whiteness of the chicken down blanketing the floor.

"Pa?" Ben called from the front of the house. "Pa, you all right?"

"Ben, you and Daniel stay out of here!" Nate crept forward. "Stay out. Understand?"

A piteous, unintelligible moan pushed from Nate's throat when he stepped around an overturned bed. On the floor, her tiny arms and legs twisted at horrible angles, lay his infant daughter Naomi. A red pool spread about her fragile crushed skull.

"No, Lord. Please don't. Not my baby. Not my baby!" Tears welled from his eyes and rolled down his cheeks as he dropped to his knees beside Naomi's still body. "Why, Lord? Why my baby?"

Deny it as he tried. He knew the truth, the cold reason that explained the senseless butchery of a child who could barely toddle across the floor. A mere eighteen months, Naomi was too young to be of any value to the raiding braves. Her terrified cries had irritated them. So they had killed her, brutally smashing her head against the bedroom wall.

"Pa?" Ben called again.

"Stay out! Damn you, stay out!" Nate shouted, unable to contain the biting harshness in his voice.

He could not let his sons see their sister this way. Their memories of Naomi were all that remained now; he would not destroy those by allowing his sons to view her mangled body.

Pulling a knife-ripped blanket from the floor, he tenderly wrapped his daughter's small, still form in it. Nate then lifted the bundle to his chest, holding it close as he rocked back and forth on his knees and wept.

FOUR

BEN AND DANIEL gathered nails from the smoldering ashes of the barn and straightened them atop a flat rock with a hammer. They went about their task solemnly like old men who bore the weight of the world on their shoulders. The glistening tears that trickled down their dark cheeks told the painful truth. They were young, and as hard as life here was, it had not been hard enough to prepare them for this, nor would life ever be that hard as long as men remained men and held love in their hearts.

Nate watched his sons, wanting to reach out to them, to say that everything would be all right. He could not. A lie would only add to their pain. Ben and Daniel could see inside the house and the bundled blanket that held their sister.

Instead Nate rummaged through flat boards in a woodpile stacked at the side of the house. Lumber, real sawmill-cut boards, was rare along the Brazos River as were the iron nails needed to bind them. Over the years, Nate had hoarded those that had come his way, even if their ends were broken or splintered. He had idly daydreamed of one day shaping them into a fine table on which his family could dine.

The table was never built. Boards mentally set aside for such frivolity were stolen away time and again for far weightier matters. Patching holes in roofs and walls to keep out winter's winds and spring's rains came before something as luxurious as a simple table.

Selecting the four best boards he found, he used a handsaw to cut eight two-foot pieces and four one-foot pieces. With the nails Ben and Daniel brought him and the wood, he constructed a rectangular box, leaving it open. The two remaining two-foot pieces of board, he set aside while he carried the box inside.

There he gathered the scattered white chicken down and placed a thick layer on the bottom of the box. Atop this snowy bed, he lay the bundle that contained the broken body of his youngest daughter. Outside he took the last two boards and securely nailed the box shut.

It was not a proper coffin, not like those Nate had seen white folks buried in back in Galveston. But then this land was not Texas's populated Gulf Coast, nor was he or the eighteen-month-old girl he buried today white. He mentally whispered a prayer of thanksgiving that he had the needed wood for the simple box. Merely laying Naomi in the ground unprotected would not have been right.

He lifted the tiny coffin in both arms, then turned to his sons. "Ben, you bring the shovel. Daniel, fetch the Bible from the house."

Ben obeyed without question, but Daniel stood looking up at his father. Doubt furrowed his young brow. For a moment the boy's expression puzzled Nate. This was no time for Daniel to have one of his memory lapses.

"Do like I said, Daniel," Nate said sternly.

Puzzlement still clouded the boy's face. "But you and Ma said we was to never touch the Bible—that no black folks was suppose to have no book."

A sad, little smile of understanding hung at the corners of Nate's mouth. Daniel reacted only to what he had been taught. Slaves were not taught to read or allowed to possess books, even a Bible. Should a white man discover a black could read, Texas law said the black man could be put to death in whatever manner the white man saw fit.

The Bible, Bessa's most prized possession, was kept hidden behind a loose stone in the hearth. At night, when she was certain that no one beyond her family could see, she would reverently take the Bible from its concealed pigeonhole and teach her children to read just as her mother had taught her own children before her.

When they had first come to Brazos, Bessa had given Nate lessons from the Bible's thin pages. Somewhat to his embarrassment he had been less than a prized student. With great difficulty, he could struggle his way through the awkwardly constructed chapters and verses if Bessa pressed him. He preferred to listen while she read to him. The words somehow seemed to make more sense that way. He did take pride in his ability to write his own name and those of his wife and children. However, he had little need to do so since a black man's punishment for writing was the same as for reading.

"Go on ahead," Nate nodded to his younger son. "It's only right that we should read over Naomi."

Daniel returned the nod, pivoted, and disappeared into the house. He ducked back outside with Bible in hand by the time Ben appeared with the shovel.

With his sons following behind him, Nate walked to a massive cottonwood that stood a hundred feet from the river. Here he placed Naomi's coffin on the green grass that was fed by the

Brazos's water. He took the shovel from Ben's hands and began to dig, carefully preserving the top layer of sod and the grass rooted in it.

When Master Turner had given them these twenty-five acres to make their own, Bessa and he had spent their first night bundled in blankets beneath the cottonwood's branches with an infant Ben protectively held between their bodies.

"We's as good as free here, Nate, what with this land Master Turner's give us," she had whispered to him with wonderment brimming in her voice. "It's like a dream I've always been afraid to dream for us—a big, bright, beautiful dream!"

He had tried to tell her that making a life for them and their son would be hard, that they would have the work of ten field slaves back in East Texas thrust on their backs just to scrape a living from this inhospitable soil. She did not listen. All that mattered to her was that they were free of the Turner house and had land on which to build their own home and raise their son. Such freedom had been beyond their imagining back in Galveston.

"If I should pass over before I wake come morning, you know like it says in the prayer, I want you to see that I'm buried right here under this big ol' cottonwood, Nate," she had said. "You'll do that, won't you? 'Cause I want to be here on our own land for all of eternity."

He had promised her that. During the fourteen years that had passed since that night, Nate and Bessa had come to view the grassy shade beneath the cottonwood as the spot where they would eventually share their final rest, together, side by side, as they had shared their lives. Neither he nor Bessa had ever foreseen the possibility that one of their own children would proceed them to the cottonwood's cool shade.

The grave Nate dug was small but deep to make certain that coyotes would not be able to get at the precious coffin he lowered into the ground. He then gathered his sons to each side of him and stared down at the box so far below them. The tears he had managed to contain since covering Naomi's body in the blanket now welled in his eyes.

"I ain't certain exactly what the words are a man's supposed to say right now. All I know is that this is my daughter alayin' here, and that she was loved by me and her mother as much as any two people can love one of their own flesh and blood." His throat constricted, squeezing off the words, when an image of his daughter's mangled body pushed into his mind. He swallowed and struggled past the pain and anger that twisted knots in his gut. "I don't know why today was her time to be called or why her going had to be—"

Nate's voice trailed off. He did not have the words in him to go on. This was not a stranger lying in the ground. It was his own daughter, his Naomi, who had gurgled, laughed, and cried only this morning while Bessa had held her in her arms during breakfast.

He swallowed again and drew a steadying breath that he released in a quavering sigh. He then took the Bible from Daniel's hands and opened it. Although he stared at the pages, he could not read the words through the tears blurring his eyes. Instead he spoke the Twenty-third Psalm from rote; the Lord's Prayer was the only passage of the Bible he knew by memory. When he uttered "amen" to complete the prayer, he knelt. He scooped up a handful of loose dirt and slowly sprinkled it on the casket below.

"Boys, is there any last words either of you want to speak to your sister?" he asked, without looking up at Ben or Daniel.

Ben knelt beside the grave and imitated his father by casting a handful of dirt atop the coffin. "Baby sister, I loved you."

"Naomi, I'm going to miss you, even if you did cry a lot and keep me awake at night." Tears streamed down Daniel's cheeks while he added another handful of dirt to the grave.

"Ain't none of us never goin' to forget you, li'l one," Nate whispered softly when he stood and turned to his sons. "I'll do what's left to be done here. Y'all put the Bible back where it belongs and see what you can find to use for flowers. If your ma was here, she'd want there to be flowers, as many as we could find."

"Yes, Pa." Ben nodded while he took his brother's hand and led Daniel toward the house.

Picking up the shovel, Nate worked as fast as he could make his muscles move. The task at hand tasted bitter like sulfur powder mixed with molasses and whiskey. Only when the grave he had dug but minutes ago was filled did he pause. He dropped to his knees once again and carefully arranged the grassy sod he had saved atop the small mound. Next he found two cedar limbs and nailed them together in the form of a cross, which he shoved into the ground at the head of the grave. He wanted to carve his daughter's name into the wood along with her date of birth and death, but he could not. Nate Wagoner was a slave, and in Texas, writing was considered above a lowly slave. Because of that his daughter was denied her name on a simple cross.

"Pa, these was all we could find."

Nate glanced over a shoulder. Ben and Daniel walked from the riverbank with bunches of red inkberry and blue gay feather blossoms in their hands.

"They ain't much." Ben shook his head when he squatted beside his father and placed the flowers atop Naomi's grave. "Ain't much more than weeds."

"October's too chilled for real flowers to bloom." Nate took the bunches from Daniel and arranged the poor blossoms beneath the makeshift cross. "Won't even be these after the first frost, but we'll put fresh flowers here every day until then."

"Pa!" Daniel nudged his father's shoulder. "Pa, there's riders acomin'!"

Nate wearily pushed to his feet and stared eastward, following his younger son's pointing finger. Riders, at least twenty men, reined their mounts toward his home.

"Boys, we'd better get back to the house." He hastened his sons from beneath the cottonwood. He was not certain what the men wanted, but they were all white and they all had rifles in their hands. Both those things usually bespoke of trouble for a black man.

FIVE

NATE CAREFULLY LEANED the two rifles against the wall just inside the door. His dark eyes shot to the east and the approaching riders. If needed, he could easily reach the two weapons.

He lied to himself. The rifles were a ritual he performed each time anyone rode toward his home. Their presence was like a false boast. He never would use the rifles, not against whites.

"Pa, what'd they want?" Daniel poked his head out the door to stare at the horsemen. "We ain't done nothin'."

"They's comin' right for the house." Ben pressed behind his younger brother to get a better look at the men. "Ain't no doubt, but that they's headin' right for us."

Nate outstretched an arm and edged his sons back into the house. "You two stand back in the shadows. Stay out of sight. Understand? Ain't no need for either of you young'uns to go stickin' your noses into this. Let your pa handle everything."

Ben's eyes flared with proud defiance, and his facial features went rigid.

Nate caught his breath; his temples pounded. The last thing he needed was his oldest picking this moment to assert his manhood, not with half the white men in this country riding down on their house. "Ben?"

The edge to his father's voice snapped Ben's head around. He stared at Nate, then glanced back at the riders before nodding acceptance. He grasped Daniel's shoulders while he edged back into the interior shadows, pulling his younger brother after him.

A soft sigh of relief escaped Nate's lips when he stepped across the threshold to greet the riders, who yanked back on their reins. Twenty horses came to an abrupt halt with a cloud of dust and stone flying from their hooves.

"Looks like they hit your nigger's place, Will, the same as they done ours." This from a red-bearded man Nate recognized as Jeb

Ewell, a farmer who worked land ten miles down the Brazos. Mounted beside him was a younger man with a scraggly attempt at a beard splotching his cheeks and chin, Jeb's son Tatum.

Nate knew all the men. There, to the left, was Cal Jenkins and his two sons. Milt Steward and his brother Brewster rode in the middle of the pack. On the right were the Alseps and the Newmans. Next to Master Turner rode Howard Rawlins. Twenty men in all—each of them dirt farmers.

"Nate"—William Turner leaned forward in the saddle and stared at his slave—"reckon I ain't got to tell you 'bout the Comanches." His eyes cut to the smoking pile of cinders that had once been Nate's barn as though to emphasize his words. "They cut themselves a wide swath along the river. Hit most of these men's places as they went. They took captives and left dead behind them at each farm they hit. Struck my place, too. Burnt my barn like they done yours, and they made off—"

The man's voice broke, and tears welled in his eyes. He wiped them away with a shirt sleeve and sucked in a steadying breath. "They made off with Missus Elizabeth and my daughters Terry and Rachel."

"I'm sorry." Nate closed his eyes. Master Turner's wife was no older than his Bessa, and his daughters were fifteen and eleven. "They weren't no kinder here. Me and the boys was out in the fields when they hit. Took Bessa, Mary, and Eve." He pointed to the tiny grave beneath the cottonwood. "Killed my baby Naomi."

Nate listened to the others mutter the names of their womenfolk, seventeen taken captive, including Nate's wife and daughters, and another ten killed. Like him and his sons, all the men had been in the fields when the Comanche raiders had struck.

"We ain't come here to commiserate with no pickaninny. We're after another kind of nigger—red-skinned niggers. That is if we want to get our womenfolk back." Jeb Ewell nudged his horse forward, forcing Nate to backstep before the man halted his mount. "What we want to know is did you see which way them Comanches went?"

Nate nodded and pointed to the west. "They rode straight up the river. 'Bout twenty of 'em in all. Ridin' like the devil hisself was on their tails."

Ewell swung his horse around to face the other men. "You heard him. They lit out along the river. We goin' after 'em or are we goin' to sit here jawin' all day?"

Riding a surge of courage that broke within his breast, Nate stepped forward. If there was a chance of getting Bessa and his girls back, he wanted to be there. He owed the Comanches as much as any of these men for what they did to Naomi. "Master Turner, I'd like to go with you. I have a rifle and a mule."

Turner tilted his head in acceptance. "Ain't no harm in havin' another gun when goin' up against—"

"If you want your nigger along, tell him to mount up, Will." Ewell cut Turner short. "But he's gonna have to catch up with us, 'cause we ain't doin' nothin' but burnin' daylight here."

Ewell yanked his mount's head around and slammed his boot heels into the animal's sides. The horse grunted and bounded forward. On his father's heels, Tatum reined westward. Seconds later the rest of the men followed suit.

Turner looked at Nate and shrugged. "You heard Jeb. If you're comin', best climb on that mule and catch up with us." Turner swung his horse around and spurred after the men.

Nate stood there, blinking against the dust stirred by the horses as he stared after the riders. He had not expected to be allowed to ride with them. It took several seconds for Master Turner's approval to penetrate his brain. When it did, Nate pivoted and called into the house, "Ben, get me my saddle and bridle while I unhitch the mule. I'm goin' after your ma and your sisters!"

He was halfway to the wagon with rifle in hand when Ben's voice brought him to a skidding halt.

"Pa, you ain't got no saddle or bridle. They was in the barn. They's burnt up along with everything else."

"Damn!" Nate glanced at his son and then at the mule. "Then help me get that mule out of harness. I'll ride him bareback if that's all I got."

Ben did not question his father, but rushed to his side and began unhitching the animal from the cart.

The bridle was nothing more than a hackamore Nate had braided out of hair from the mule's tail and the saddle something he had jury-rigged with deer hide and an old blanket. He hated losing both, but in truth there was no great loss. Even when he used them, sitting astride the mule had been little better than riding bareback.

"Pa, I want to go with you. I can handle a rifle good enough." Ben pulled the harness from the mule, leaving only the headgear and long leather reins. "I could be of help."

Nate gathered the reins and knotted them together to shorten their length. He climbed atop the mule and looked down at his son. "Hand me my rifle."

Ben did. "Pa, I want to go," he repeated.

"I know you do, son." Nate pursed his lips and glanced around. "But I need you here to take care of Daniel and the house. It ain't the way you or me want it, but that's the way of it. You understand?"

Ben's chest gave a labored heave, and he nodded. "I understand, but I don't like it none."

Nate squeezed his son's shoulder. "I ain't askin' you to like it, just do it—for me and your ma."

Again Ben nodded. Nate's fingers squeezed into the firmness of his son's muscular shoulder once more. "I knew I could count on you. Now, you do what you can 'round here. I ain't certain when I'll be back so you might have to stake out the cows for the night so that they don't go wanderin' off."

"I'll take care of everything." Ben's eyes rolled up to his father. "You ain't got nothin' to worry about 'cept gettin' Ma, Mary, and Eve back."

"I'll do my best to do that," Nate assured him, reined the mule westward, clucked the animal into a bouncy jog, then used his heels against its sides to lengthen its strides into a rhythmic gallop.

Reining the mule to the Brazos, Nate headed westward. A quarter of a mile ahead, he saw the cloud of dust that marked the riders' lead on him. His heels tapped the mule's flanks, urging the animal into a run. Nate covered a full mile before reaching the others and might not have done that so quickly had the twenty men not suddenly pulled up their horses. Howard Rawlins had dismounted and knelt on the ground when Nate eased the mule to a halt.

"It's startin' to make sense." Rawlins stood; his gaze moved over the faces of his companions. "I saw fifty, maybe as many as seventy-five Comanche bucks high-tailin' it from my place, but Nate there only saw twenty."

Rawlins paused and pointed back down the river. "We ain't been followin' but twenty horses since Will's farms. But if you look here, ten other horses just joined up with them twenty."

"What's you gittin' at, Howie?" Jeb Ewell pressed.

"That them Comanches struck in one band, then splintered off with our womenfolk after they hit each of our places." Rawlins stepped into a stirrup and swung back to the saddle. "Them tracks angling in from the north say that a splinter group joined up here. We'll probably see other tracks comin' in the farther we ride upriver."

A high whistle escaped Tatum Ewell's lips. "Sixty warriors— that's three of them to one of us!"

"We got rifles and pistols, and they ain't." Jeb Ewell glared at his son, apparently interpreting the comment as a display of cowardice.

"But them signs is good, ain't they, Howie?" William Turner asked. "We want all them heathens in one group when we catch up with 'em, don't we?"

"As long as they join up ahead of us." Rawlins tugged the brim of a sweat-stained, creaseless hat low to his forehead. "What we don't want is one of them groups comin' in behind us."

"You tryin' to make a point?" Ewell asked.

"That we slow our pace a mite to make certain that we ain't hit from the rear," Rawlins answered. "We'll also save our horses until we got a real need to ride 'em hard."

Ewell grunted, but did not protest when Rawlins took the lead, keeping his horse at an easy lope.

Nate fell in behind the others. His gaze shifted around him, expecting to see howling Comanche warriors burst from stunted red oaks and cedars each time they rounded a bend in the river. He was scared, and did not try to convince himself otherwise. Comanches and their allies the Kiowas were part of the harsh

reality of the Texas frontier. That Nate owned no horses, a Comanche's most prized possession, was the only reason, he was
certain, his home had been attacked only twice over all the years
he had spent on the Brazos.

As frightened as he was, the terror he knew Bessa and his
daughters now felt kept him riding westward. It was well known
how Comanches used their female captives. Those they killed
outright were the lucky ones.

Three miles upriver, Rawlins pointed to tracks that showed
where another one of the splinter groups of raiders had rejoined
the main band. Within another two miles, he located the tracks of
two other small groups joining the larger. He urged his mount
forward in a long-strided gallop after announcing that all the
Comanches and their captives rode together again.

The trail they followed was an easy one. The high grass and
weeds that grew along the Brazos's bank had been trampled by
the passage of at least sixty mustang ponies. Even Nate, who had
only tracked deer for meat, found no difficulty in keeping to the
tracks.

Until they abruptly stopped.

Rawlins drew up his horse and raised a hand high to signal the
others to do the same. He pulled off his hat and scratched at his
head in puzzlement. "They're gone. The tracks just disappeared."

"Don't be stupid, Howie," Jeb Ewell said, disgust thick on his
tongue. "Sign don't just up and disappear."

Yet that's exactly what had happened. After following the deep
hoofprints left in the soft soil of the river's bank for ten miles, the
tracks had swung northward onto rocky ground. There the trail
ended as though it had been erased from the earth.

Which is what Howard Rawlins finally suggested. "They done
cut themselves some brush and are draggin' it behind their ponies to hide the tracks. We might be able to pick them up again, if
we spread out and head thataway." He pointed north where the
tracks indicated the band had ridden.

Nate followed the others' lead. With fifty yards separating each
rider, they moved forward at a walk. Nate scanned the ground,
searching for a broken weed or an overturned stone that would

confirm the Comanches had traveled this way. He found nothing, nor did any of the other men.

After an hour Rawlins once more called a halt and waved the men to him. "It ain't no good. We ain't never gonna find sign of them."

"You sayin' we should give up?" This from Jeb Ewell.

"I'm sayin' that I can't help no more," Rawlins answered, a sense of futility hanging in his words. "I ain't no ranging man. I done all I know how. It'll be dark come another hour, and it won't do any one of us no good bein' out here at night."

Milt Steward spoke up. "But we can't give up. They got my wife with 'em."

A wave of disgruntled mumbles and curses rolled through the men. Howard Rawlins's head lowered, and he stared at the ground. Nate studied the man, feeling sympathy for him. Rawlins's daughter also had been taken by the Comanches. But as much as he pitied Rawlins, he feared more for Bessa and his daughters. If the others pushed on, so would he. There was nothing else they could do.

"Howie's right."

Every head turned to William Turner, who swallowed hard and continued, "This job ain't for no farmers like us. Ain't one of us knows the first thing about Comanche ways. What we need is somebody who does."

Jeb Ewell spat to the ground in obvious contempt. "Will, there ain't a ranging company nowhere here about for a hundred miles or more."

"No," Turner agreed. "But we got us a man who used to be a Ranger not more than five miles from here."

The men looked at one another as though Turner were insane, until Milt Steward exclaimed the name, "Harlan Crouch!"

"That's who I had in mind." Turner nodded his head. "If I ride hard, I can have him fetched back to my house not too long after dark."

Again the men looked at one another before giving their approval. Turner glanced at Nate and signaled him to ride with him. Together they reined their mounts about and rode south for the Brazos River.

SIX

THE MEN flirted with death. Whether they did so as a display of united bravado after suffering the day's soul-crushing loss or they felt that lightning would not strike twice in the same place within the space of twenty-four hours, Nate was unsure. Perhaps the Comanche raid had numbed their minds and dulled their wits. Or maybe in their grief, they simply no longer cared. Whatever the rationale, it did not erase the fact that the farmers invited disaster while they huddled around the flickering flames of a fire built twenty strides from the front stoop of the Turner home.

That the men congregated to share their mutual anguish as much as to await Harlan Crouch's arrival at the Turner farm was not their method of trifling with a very real danger held in the heart of this night. It was the fire they clustered about to edge aside the encroaching chill of an October night that flaunted a perilous disregard of the common sense necessary for survival in the Cross Timbers region of Texas.

Tonight a moon three days' shy of full hung in the sky. It was the time of the Blood Moon, that two-week cycle each month from spring's thawing warmth to winter's hard freezes when the moon provided enough light for the Comanches and their allies the Kiowas to sweep out of the plains and terrorize the land all the way from the Red River in the north to the Rio Grande at its southernmost boundary. Comanche warriors raided in either day or night, but they traveled only by moonlight.

The orange glow of a night fire, visible for miles in all directions even among the long-running, oak- and cedar-covered ridges of the Cross Timbers, drew raiding parties like candlebugs to a flame.

Along the Brazos settlers were few and far between. Their sparse numbers were not enough to warrant ranging companies such as those that protected the farms and ranches to the south in distant Bexar and Travis counties. While the Blood Moon reigned, dusk signaled a man to end his day and gather his family behind the barred door to his house. No candle was lit against the darkness and embers in the hearth were doused in fear that the light of a single cherry-red spark might find its way through a crack in a wall and serve as a beacon to marauding war parties.

Sleep did not come easy during the Blood Moon. Man, woman, and child rested like napping cats with ears atwitching for sounds that might alert them to approaching danger. At the back of the mind, even in tranquil dreams, were the overriding thoughts of where rifles were placed and balls and powder cached so that in the first waking instant one was prepared to stand against an attack.

Nate's gaze shifted to the Turner home. The fireplace inside was much safer than the open blaze. However, the structure was little more than a soddy with three additional rooms built on it. The house was not large enough to hold all the men gathered here. Even that was no excuse for the needless risk of a fire.

Hiking the collar of his coat high about his neck, Nate hung back in the shadows away from the blaze. He found himself unable to sort through the tangled feelings that the flames evoked. Was his reaction a defense to the obvious threat the fire presented or was it because he had no place among the white men tightly ringing the flames? Not knowing only increased his discomfort.

"Will, you certain Crouch said he was comin'?" Seth Alsep broke the silence. "It's gettin' nigh on eight o'clock."

"He allowed how he'd meet us here at my place." William Turner spat a dark stream of tobacco juice and spittle into the flames. The fire sizzled and hissed.

Jeb Ewell shook his head. "I don't reckon Crouch allowed just when he'd grace us with his presence, did he?"

"Harlan Crouch is a man of his word, Jeb. He served under John Coffee Hays down in San Antonio. He'll be here," Turner answered with more faith than certainty. "He said he had to see after something, then he'd ride here."

The mention of the legendary Ranger captain Hays apparently was enough for Ewell. Which was just as well; Nate could not verify his owner's claim. Minding Turner's mount, he had sat outside Harlan Crouch's home while Turner met with the ex-Ranger inside. What passed between the two men had gone unheard by his ears.

Even if he had stood with his head pressed against the door, eavesdropping, Nate doubted that he would have been able to catch what the men had said. In all of the Cross Timbers, he had never seen a house built like Crouch's soddy.

The term soddy or house did not rightly describe the fortress the former Texas Ranger had constructed for himself. Nate had once heard Crouch warn his neighbors that they built their homes too flimsily and covered them with roofs that were little more than tinder awaiting a spark.

"A Comanche or Kiowa don't like walls when it comes to a fight. They like to hit fast and dirty. Ninety-nine times out of a hundred, they'll shy away from a man who's built good, strong walls for hisself and his family. They'll ride on to easier pickin's," Crouch had said.

The man built to his word. His house was cut into the side of a hill like many settlers' homes. There its resemblance to other soddies ended. The walls were laid with triple-wide sod and faced with stone. There was a full three-foot thickness to each of the walls. The same care was taken with doors and shutters. All were triple thick. Mud plugs, which could easily be knocked out to accommodate rifle and pistol muzzles in case of attack, filled loopholes in each.

Even the numerous tanning frames about Crouch's home, stretched with the hides of deer, wolf, bear, and antelope, were placed in such a manner that they provided no defense or cover for marauding Indians.

The clack of hooves on stone jerked the men's heads up. From side to side their eyes shifted, searching the darkness for the source of the sound, while their hands found rifles resting beside them on the ground. Apprehension lined each of their faces.

"Two men." Nate located the shadowy silhouettes of the riders and pointed. "They're comin' up from my place."

Every man turned to the approaching horsemen with rifles held ready. The wide-brimmed hats the riders wore provided no guarantees they were friendly. Hostiles were known to wear the hats, as well as other articles of clothing, they stripped from victims. Comanches, especially the braves, were partial to the bright hues of women's garments.

"William Turner?" a resonating voice called out when the riders stopped two hundred yards from the fire. "It's Harlan Crouch. I got me a friend here, and we'd like to ride in without getting our heads shot off."

Turner lifted an arm and waved the two forward. "Come on in."

Relief washed over the faces of twenty men as they lowered the muzzles of their single-shot longrifles. The two riders reined their mounts into the fire's light and halted at a hitching post beside the Turner home. Crouch, a wiry-built man standing no more than five-six, stepped down from the saddle, nodding to the men while he walked to the fire. Behind him came a man of equal height who wore an undecorated, black sombrero. Nate had never seen the second man or shiny, black leather breeches like those he wore.

"Boys, this here's Joaquín DeRosa." Crouch casually waved an arm to his companion. However, his disapproving glare focused on the blaze. Nate prepared himself for a reprimanding tirade from the former Ranger. Instead Crouch said, "I told Joaquín about y'all's grief and thought he might be able to help out."

Jeb Ewell leaned to his son's ear, and Nate heard his dubious whisper. "A Meskin?"

Apparently Crouch overheard the comment, too. His gray eyes darted to the farmer for an instant. He idly stroked the end of a dark brown mustache that drooped far below the corners of his mouth as though considering how to answer. He sucked at his teeth and let the remark pass while he sat on his heels by the fire and held his hands to the flames, rubbing them. Joaquín DeRosa did the same.

To Nate's left, on the periphery of the yellow glow cast by the fire, a blur of motion darted through the night. Nate caught his breath. Out of the corner of an eye, he discerned the familiar form of his older son Ben as the boy squatted behind the leafy concealment of a stunted persimmon bush. He had probably seen Crouch's approach and followed the ex-Ranger and De-Rosa.

Nate's gaze shot to the circle of men congregated around the fire. He released his overly held breath in a soft sigh. None noticed Ben. Their attention hung on the former Ranger and DeRosa.

Nate considered stepping to the persimmon, yanking Ben from his hiding place, and giving his backside a good dusting for leaving Daniel alone at home after he had been told to watch over his younger brother. Nate repressed the urge. White men frowned on blacks spying on them. The mood of these men was dangerous. The slightest provocation would be an excuse to take out their frustration on Ben's back.

Later, when he returned home, Nate would see that Ben received a proper tongue-lashing for his transgression. For now Ben could hide and listen. After all, he was a young man, not a child, who had lost his mother and sisters. He deserved to hear what was said here tonight.

"Joaquín here originally hails from Santa Fe." Crouch's voice brought Nate's attention back to the circle of men. "He came east two years back. Before that he traded with the Comanches in New Mexico."

"What?" Turner's head snapped up. Horror and disgust twisted his face.

The reaction was repeated by each man around the fire. Hate glared in their eyes as they stared at the Mexican.

"Goddamned, red-nigger lovin' son-of-a-bitch!" Venom spewed as Jeb Ewell spoke.

Howard Rawlins gave a name to the anger that knotted in Nate's breast, "Comanchero!"

Hated and despised as much as the Comanches themselves by every Texian who lived in fear of the Blood Moon were the Comancheros. These were men who profited from their commerce with the Comanche bands, often providing the heathens with rifles, powder, and lead balls. Placing a single firearm in the hands of hostiles was a hanging offense in Texas. However, in New Mexico such activities were a means to a fortune.

"Harlan, we come to you askin' for help"—disbelief brimmed in Turner's tone—"and you bring a Comanchero to my home!"

Joaquín DeRosa stiffened, but Crouch remained calm, his fingertips now toying with the opposite end of his dark mustache. Again the former Ranger sucked at his teeth. "Men have a way of givin' names to things. Sometimes they ain't exactly sure what them names mean—"

Nate knew what Comanchero meant. They were supposedly civilized men who aided bloodthirsty savages. They deserved no better than—

"—The Comanches have a word they consider the most vile pronouncement they can make." Crouch's words wedged through Nate's bitter thoughts. The man looked at William Turner. "The word's *tejano*. Know what that means, Will?"

Turner shook his head. Crouch glanced at Ewell and Rawlins. Both men diverted their eyes from Crouch's gaze and shook their heads.

"Any of you know what *tejano* means?" Crouch asked of the group. When he received no answer, he said, "It means Texian. Plain and simple, it means Texian."

He paused as though to let his words sink in. "Texian—something all of us are proud to call ourselves. I reckon it depends on whose boots, or moccasins, a man's standin' in that says what a name means."

"Every man here knows what a Comanchero is." Ewell made no attempt to disguise his contempt.

"Reckon we know what we see it to be." Crouch conceded with a tilt of his head. "But in New Mexico there ain't no Comancheros, just men who earn a livin' to feed their families by tradin' with the Comanches. And them traders can do something no Texian can do—they can ride into the plains and move among the Comanche and Kiowa bands without gettin' themselves kilt."

Again Crouch paused. His words rolled around in Nate's head; the ex-Ranger's meaning was inescapable. A man like Joaquín DeRosa, once a Comanchero, was far more likely to cut deep into Comanchería, the Comanche-controlled prairies and plains, than was a *tejano,* a man the Comanches hated above all others.

Although none of the farmers voiced a recognition of this fact,

Nate could see realization on their faces. Crouch had made his point.

"You just said more'n a mouth full." This from Cal Jenkins, whose eyes moved over the faces of his companions before returning to Crouch. "You're tryin' to tell us there ain't no way we can get our womenfolk back, aren't you?"

Crouch ignored every head that turned to him; he pursed his lips and gave a heavy nod. "Ain't no way *y'all* can do it. Besides bein' white, there's too many of you."

"Even with you and *him* leadin' us?" Jeb Ewell asked.

"If a Comanche band saw twenty white men ridin' up to their camp, they'd take it to be an attack." Crouch rubbed a hand over his throat. "Like as not, they'd kill any captives they was holdin' 'fore we was a mile from their village. I've seen 'em do that before, when I was rangin'."

Nate swallowed hard. The way Crouch described it, would-be rescuers could be the very cause of the deaths of those they sought to free. Nate glanced around. Apparently the others understood the gist of what the former Ranger said. Their expressions were long and lined.

"You ain't sayin' we should give up and forget them heathens took our womenfolk are you?" Turner asked. " 'Cause there ain't a man here tonight that's willin' to do that."

A rumble of agreement moved through the men.

Crouch held up a hand to quiet the farmers. "What I'm tryin' to say is that two men—Joaquín and myself—might be able to get done what twenty can't."

Before the men could comment, DeRosa spoke. "Two men leading pack animals heavy with goods and acting as traders can ride into Comanche camps. I have done it before, and I have brought back captives for others. But those men will need trade goods to bargain with—blankets, coffee, tobacco, bright cloth. Horses would be best. A Comanche warrior measures his wealth by the number of horses he can claim as his own."

"I got a seven-year-old roan geldin' I've been lookin' to sell. You can have him to take with you," Cal Jenkins offered. Then Jeb Ewell added, "I'll throw in a hundred pounds of flour and twenty-five of coffee."

One by one the men pledged for the items they could offer in trade for the release of their women and children. Crouch and DeRosa approved or disapproved each item. Only Nate remained silent, unable to recall a possession suitable for use.

"I'm willin' to sweeten the pot some," Turner said. "You bring back any of my womenfolk, and I'll pay you fifty dollars in gold— American coin."

Nate noticed a pleased smile slip across Joaquín DeRosa's lips. The Mexican's expression was that of a man who had sat and waited to hear those exact words. His smile grew as each of the farmers matched the reward Turner offered. "You gentlemen are more than generous."

Crouch pushed to his feet. "I think we've said all that can be said. Have your goods and animals here at Will's house by sunup tomorrow. Joaquín and me will be here then. We'll ride west soon as we're loaded."

While the men voiced their agreement, Nate drew a deep breath to bolster his courage. In spite of his pounding heart and the dryness in his throat, he managed to say, "Master Crouch, you said the Comanches would shy from white men ridin' up to their camp, but you didn't say nothin' about no black man. I ain't got no horses or dry goods to offer in trade like the others, but I can offer me—that is if'n it's all right with Master Turner. I got a strong back, and I'm good when it comes to tendin' stock."

A shocked moment of silence quieted the farmers. Each of their faces wore an expression of disbelief. They stared at Nate as though they did not trust their ears, as if they had heard wrong.

Tatum Ewell let loose with a high whistle. "Whoooeeee, will you listen to that nigger boy!"

"What's you been feedin' your nigger, Will?" Jeb Ewell laughed. "Whatever it is, it's done gone and made him think he's a god-almighty Indian fighter! Maybe he thinks himself a Ranger like Harlan here?"

Nate winced when the rest of the men chorused Ewell's laughter, punctuating their mirth with catcalls. His eyes rolled downward to stare at his feet, and his head hung chin to chest as he endured each of their crude jokes and chuckles. He had not made his offer in jest. Why didn't they see that? All he had to offer was himself. What few possessions of value Bessa and he had accumulated had been tools and farm implements. Those had been in the barn and were now ash and cinder.

"Nate, I think you're forgettin' that your place is here, workin' that oat field." William Turner stared at his slave with obvious disdain and embarrassment. "I think it would be best if you went on back to your shack and tended to your boys and let them that knows handle this. We'll talk about this tomorrow."

Nate's head lifted and his lips parted as he prepared to explain himself. One glance at the disgust on the face of his owner was all it took for him to realize that he had overstepped the invisible boundary that separated him from these men. He swallowed back the unspoken words, abandoned his wounded pride, nodded, and started for his home.

"Hold it, boy," Harlan Crouch called out. When Nate stopped and turned to the former Ranger, Crouch said, "I got use for you, if you're sure about wantin' to go."

"I want to go." Nate confirmed with a determined tilt of his head.

Crouch's gaze shifted to William Turner. "I'll take him with me, if it's all right with you, Will."

Turner's lower jaw sagged while he searched Crouch's face. "You ain't funnin' are you? You don't want no white men with you, but you'll take a darkie?"

Crouch shrugged as though he was not certain why he agreed to take Nate. "Comanches don't pay too much mind to a black-skinned man. They wouldn't even notice he's with Joaquín and me. 'Sides, it won't do no harm to have another pair of hands along. If we run down the band them warriors were out of, Nate there can watch out for our goods while we do what palaverin' that needs doin'."

Turner hiked his eyebrows high, edged back his hat, and scratched at his head. "If you can use Nate, then I reckon I got nothin' agin him goin' along with you." Turner looked at Nate. "You heard the man. You're goin' with him."

"Be here at sunup like I told the others," Crouch added. "Be ready to ride. I don't want no slacker."

"No, sir!" Nate assured him. "The one thing I ain't is no slacker. I'll be waitin' for you come sunup."

When Crouch's attention returned to the farmers, Nate hastened toward his home. Ahead in the darkness, he saw Ben scampering to reach the house before him. No longer did he consider reprimanding his son for his boldness. Nate's thoughts now centered on the coming morning and the task that stretched before him. He was going to ride into Comanche territory where few men had traveled before. Whether he wanted to admit it or not, he was scared—cold sweat and shaking hands scared.

As much as he was frightened for himself, the fear he held for his wife and two daughters was double that. If they could just hold on, he would find them.

SEVEN

BEN BROKE a cardinal rule of the Blood Moon; he lit a fire, small though it was, in the hearth before grays and purples of predawn had edged back the night's blackness. Above the flickering flames, he heated a pan of coffee and baked a covered skillet of biscuits.

While Nate dressed by the fire's paltry warmth, he bit back the reprimand that formed on his tongue. What Ben did, he did for his father's comfort on this morning. Neither mentioned how Ben knew that Nate would be riding west with the sunrise. Such matters were no longer of importance.

"How long you reckon you'll be gone?" Ben poured a cup of coffee, handed it to Nate, then poured a second cup for himself.

"Don't rightly know." Nate sipped the steaming brew. Its warmth settled in his belly and remained there, refusing to drive the chill from the rest of his body. "I've never done nothin' like this 'fore."

"No need for you to worry about Daniel and me—or the farm." Ben settled cross-legged on the packed dirt floor beside his father's chair. "I know what to do, and I'll take care of things just like you was here."

Nate squeezed his older son's shoulder firmly. "I know you will. Me and your momma done raised us a son to be proud of."

The compliment brought a weak smile to the corners of Ben's mouth. It quickly dissolved when worried lines returned to his young brow like the deep furrows of a newly plowed field. "What I want is for you to take care of yourself and come back to us. Daniel and me ain't old enough to be orphans."

Nate's hand once more tightened on his son's shoulder. "I'll do my best to do just that." He was going to add that he felt too young to be a dead man, but the image of tiny Naomi's crushed body edged the jest aside. In this country, death paid little heed to age. Instead he drained the coffee in hasty gulps, then stood. "Fetch me my rifle. It's time I headed for Master Turner's."

While Ben retrieved the longrifle, Nate took a powder horn and a leather pouch packed with lead balls and cotton wadding from a wooden peg embedded in the wall to his right. He slipped the looped strap to each over his head and arm so that the horn and pouch dangled on his left hip.

"Want me to wake Daniel so you can say good-bye?" Ben asked when he handed his father the rifle.

Nate shook his head. "Sleep will do him more good than kissin' his pa's cheek." He wanted to enfold Ben in his arms and hug the boy tightly to his chest, but Ben was too old for such parental foolishness. For a long, heavy moment, Nate just stared at Ben, then said, "You know where I keep the money hidden, if you and Daniel should need somethin' 'fore I get back."

"We won't need nothin'," Ben assured him.

"Just in case," Nate answered, then started for the door.

"The biscuits!" Ben called after him. "You'll be needin' somethin' in your belly."

Nate paused long enough to grab half a dozen biscuits from the skillet Ben took off the fire. With one in hand and five stuffed into his coat pockets he paused long enough to say, "You take care, understand?" turned, and walked outside, closing the door behind him.

He stopped beyond the threshold to raise his coat collar

against the morning chill and allow his eyes to accustom them-selves to the darkness. He then found his mule beside the house where he had tied it last night. Mounting, he tugged the animal's head around and rode toward the orange glow of a fire that radiated from the Turner house while he nibbled at the still warm biscuit.

Five minutes later, he drew the mule to a halt outside his owner's home and dismounted. Turner and three other farmers glanced up at his arrival, then returned to unpacking the trade goods the farmers had brought on their horses. Uncertain what was expected of him, Nate silently remained by his mule and waited.

All the farmers except Jeb Ewell arrived with their promised offerings by the time false dawn transformed the eastern horizon to a dusky gray and Harlan Crouch and Joaquín DeRosa rode in from the south on a buckskin and a black. Their mounts' bellies still dripped from crossing the Brazos River. Crouch's gaze alighted on Nate for an instant. Nate thought he saw a flicker of surprise in the man's eyes as though he had not expected a slave to make good on his promise to venture into Comanche territory.

"Everything here?" Crouch asked the farmers, who clustered around the small mountain of trade goods piled on the ground.

"Three horses and everything 'cept what Jeb Ewell promised." Turner waved a hand to the sacks and bundles. "Jeb and his boy ought to be along shortly."

"If he makes it, he makes it. We ain't got time to wait on him." Crouch shifted in the saddle and leaned back to look at Nate. "Boy, can you pack a horse?"

"Yes, sir," Nate answered with a nod.

"Then get to work on them three horses while I have a word with these men. The sooner they're carryin' loads, the sooner we can get about what has to be done." Without waiting for Nate to reply, the former Texas Ranger turned back to William Turner and pointed to the house. "If you got coffee on, I could use a cup while we talk."

The men moved to the house. Those who could not squeeze inside hovered around the open front door.

Nate was left with three pack saddles, three horses, and a small fortune of foodstuffs, blankets, knives, and pots and pans with which to ransom seventeen kidnapped wives and daughters. He had secured packs on the backs of two of the animals by the time the first yellow rays of the new dawn broke to the east and Jeb and Tatum Ewell rode up. They dropped the sacks of flour and coffee they carried behind their saddles at his feet without a word, then reined to the house.

The sun stood a full four fingers above the horizon when Nate tied the last of the trade goods on the back of the third horse. In spite of the morning's coolness, he wiped a sheen of sweat from his forehead with a coat sleeve while he walked back to the mule to wait for the congregation at the house to disperse. He dug one of Ben's biscuits from a pocket and took a bite. Even cold it tasted good.

An increase in the rumble of voices coming from the house drew Nate's attention. Crouch and Joaquín DeRosa made their way through the farmers to mount and rein their horses beside the waiting pack animals. Crouch studied the three horses for a moment before his head snapped around. "Boy, get your black ass over here!"

His brow knitting in question, Nate walked to the man. "Yes, sir?"

"I thought I told you to get them horses ready?" Crouch rested an elbow on his saddlehorn and leaned down toward Nate.

A hasty glance at the animals assured Nate that the packs were tightly secured to the horses' backs. "I packed 'em just like you said."

"But they ain't ready. They ain't all tied to a rope lead. How in hell we supposed to take 'em with us if they ain't all hitched on lead?" The man pointed to a rope coiled on the ground near the horses that had gone unnoticed until this moment.

As Nate took a step toward the rope, Crouch's left hand snaked out, his fingers grasping the shoulder of Nate's coat. "Boy, I want you to listen up and listen good. The only reason I agreed to take you along with me is because you went and bragged about havin' a strong back and bein' good with stock. If you expect to travel with me, you'd damned well better live up to what you said. If there's somethin' that needs doin', I expect you to do it and not stand around worryin' 'bout your own belly. Understand?"

Nate swallowed hard. The man's outburst was unexpected, nor had he deserved to bear its brunt. "Yes, sir. I understand."

Crouch released the coat. "Good, 'cause I ain't gonna tell you a second time. Now get them horses on lead. You've caused us to waste enough daylight as it is."

Nate walked to the rope, bent, and lifted it from the ground. What had the others spoken of inside the house to cause such a reaction from the former Ranger, he wondered while he hastily tied each of the three horses' halters to the lead. When the task was completed neither Crouch nor the Mexican displayed any interest in taking the rope. Nate, leading the pack animals behind him, walked to the mule and swung to its bare back.

The instant Nate sat upright, Crouch and DeRosa tapped spurs to their mounts' sides and headed southward for the Brazos River to pick up the Comanches' west-running tracks. Nate clucked the mule after them as he tugged at the horses he led.

Without a saddle's stirrups to maintain his balance and a broad saddlehorn to wrap the end of the rope around, Nate wobbled atop the mule like a drunkard. A full half an hour passed before he discovered the correct combination of leg pressure, tautness of rope, and rifle position that allowed him to rein the mule, lead the packhorses, and carry a longrifle all at the same time, and still keep his seat atop an animal that was more accustomed to harness than carrying a rider on its back.

Even then Nate's position was precarious. Should one of the horses snatch its head to the side to nip at a blowfly or decide to try for a tempting clump of grass, the sudden motion left Nate struggling to stay atop the mule.

His awkward seat astride the bareback mule went unnoticed by Crouch and DeRosa. Neither man glanced back to check Nate's progress until they reached the rocky bank where the raiding party's tracks had so mysteriously disappeared the day before. There Joaquín dismounted, handed his reins to his companion, and began to examine the ground on foot.

"Best give them horses a drink." Crouch twisted around in the saddle and motioned to Nate. "We ain't got no guarantee when we'll see water again."

Nate did as ordered, then followed Crouch when he nudged his buckskin after the Mexican, who moved westward along the Brazos's bank rather than heading northward as Nate and the others had done yesterday. A mile farther upriver, Joaquín stood straight and grinned back at Crouch.

"They came this way." He pointed to the ground. "There are tracks here. They left the water because it grew too deep for their ponies."

Nate stared at the sun-baked mud the Mexican indicated. It was difficult to discern the scufflike tracks of unshod hooves, but they were there. He found it hard to believe they had been overlooked by Turner and the others. On the other hand, it was not that puzzling to understand. Like himself, the others had ridden hard, driven by fear and near panic for their loved ones. Besides, they were farmers and not trackers; their livelihood came from tilling the soil, not reading it.

"We will lose the tracks again." Joaquín took his reins from Crouch, tossed them over his black gelding's head, stepped into a stirrup, and rose back to the saddle. "They used the river to cover their tracks. Soon as the Brazos shallowed again, they took to it once more."

A quarter of a mile upstream, Joaquín's prediction proved true. The faint tracks once more disappeared; this time it was obvious the Comanches' mustangs had moved into the river. Uncertain on which side of the Brazos the war party had chosen to leave the water farther upriver, Crouch ordered Joaquín to cross the river and watch for signs on the southern bank.

"It is a waste of time," Joaquín protested, apparently caring little for the prospect of a second soaking in the river that morning. "The band rode northwest when they abandoned the water."

"Like as not you're right," Crouch agreed with a nod. "But we ain't takin' no chances it might be otherwise. Get your backside across the river."

Joaquín grunted in disgust and shot the former Ranger a glare to match, but he did as ordered. When he reached the far bank, and his black had shaken away the water that ran in rivulets from its body, Joaquín lifted a hand and pointed to the west signaling he was ready to proceed.

"Let's get a move on, boy." Crouch shot a glance over a shoulder to Nate before nudging the buckskin forward.

Even when he hunted deer in winter, when the bitter cold kept Comanches near the warm fires within their tipis, Nate had never ventured this far up the Brazos. The river bent itself in long easy curves to conform to the valleys that ran between the oversized hills that Texians were wont to call mountains.

Oaks, red and pin, and bushy, conical-shaped junipers were the most prolific denizens of the stunted forest that was the Cross Timbers. Patches of rust marked the sprawling woods—leaves drying and turning color with autumn's approach. Closer to the river grew cottonwoods, black willows, persimmons, hackberries, and pecan trees.

Now and then a jackrabbit darted from the brush and sprinted across their trail or a covey of quail took wing to escape the mounted invaders who pushed into their quiet domain. Rather than the horse tracks they searched for, they found small, cloven hoofprints that told of the numerous deer populating the forest. They heard the cooing of doves and the occasional gobble of wild turkeys.

The noonday sun reached the meridian and edged toward the western horizon, but Crouch ordered no halt. Doggedly he rode, keeping his buckskin at a brisk walk.

Nate felt the weight of biscuits filling his coat pockets, but with hands occupied by rifle, reins, and rope lead, it was impossible to dig one out and silence the rumbling complaints of his stomach. He tried once and nearly found himself on the ground. After that, he pushed thoughts of hunger aside. If Crouch and Joaquín rode without eating, so could he.

A full fifteen miles from where the Comanches' trail had vanished into the Brazos, mustang hoofprints emerged from the water—on the north bank as Joaquín had said they would. At Crouch's command the Mexican once more crossed the river. Nate's knowledge of Spanish was limited to a sprinkling of words, mostly common curses. However, he understood enough to garner that Joaquín belittled Crouch's parental lineage, gave augury to the eternal destination of the former Ranger's immortal soul, and minimized the physical proportions and potency of his companion's manhood.

From Crouch's dark expression, Nate suspected the man also understood the gist of Joaquín's string of rapid-fire phrases. However, Crouch said nothing, except to order, "We'll take a break here and give the animals a rest."

Not waiting to be told, Nate dismounted, then led packhorses and mule to the river to allow them to drink.

"Might as well stake 'em out over yonder and let 'em graze." Crouch pointed to a thick patch of grass while he and Joaquín settled to the ground and passed a pouch of jerked beef between them.

Nate nodded and did as he was told. Two broken oak branches served as stakes, which easily sank into the soft soil near the river's bank, to secure rein and rope. Nate walked to where his companions sat and started to sink to the ground beside them.

"You are forgetting something, are you not, *esclavo?*" Joaquín leaned back, his weight resting on an elbow while he gnawed at a piece of jerky.

Nate halted in a half-squat and frowned in question.

"Our horses, boy." Crouch made no attempt to hide the contempt in his voice. "You think that damned flea-bitten mule of yours is more important than our horses, nigger?"

A cold, cringing shiver worked along Nate's spine. The almost forgotten sensation left his stomach churning. "No, sir. But I thought that—"

"God didn't mean for no black man to think. Just to do like he's told," Crouch cut him off. "Now take care of our horses."

Nate bit his lower lip to hold back the words that tried to leap from his tongue. Neither Crouch nor Joaquín had legal claim to him, but they were white—at least Crouch was—and Nate was black. A black man who disobeyed a white did not live long, not in Texas.

Diverting his dark eyes to hide the anger he knew flared there, Nate mumbled a "yes, sir," and once more complied with the order by leading the black and buckskin geldings to the other patch of grass and staking them there. He covered half the distance back to the two men when Crouch called out:

"Boy, see them trees over to the right. Well, them's pecan trees. Fetch the saddlebags from my horse and take 'em over there and fill a pouch with pecans. And you make sure there ain't one green hull among the lot, you understand?"

"Yes, sir," Nate answered, barely able to keep the enmity out of his tone. Not since the day Master Turner had given him twenty-five acres had a man—white, brown, or black—treated him thusly. It galled him, rubbing like a burr under a saddle blanket.

Still, he did as directed. He untied Crouch's saddlebags and carried them over his left arm while he walked beneath the yellowing leaves of the pecan trees. For a half hour he bent and stooped to pick the required nuts from the ground. Several times he selected pecans still cloaked in a green outer husk. He used a thumbnail to remove this and dropped the pecan it held within the bag, assuring that Crouch would eat the meat of an occasional green pecan.

When the saddlebag's pouch was brimming with nuts, Nate once more turned and started toward the men—he no longer considered them companions, they had already drawn too sharp a line for that. For a second time, he covered half the distance before Crouch called to him.

"Boy, it's time we was back in the saddle. Bring us our horses. And made damn sure you don't spill them pecans when you tie 'em back on my horse."

The curses Joaquín had shouted when he last forded the Brazos were mild and gentle compared with the ones that raged like a storm in Nate's mind while he gathered the men's mounts and led the horses to where they still sat on the bank.

"Get your mule and the packhorses," Crouch ordered when he took the buckskin's reins. "We can do another fifteen miles or so before sundown, if you get a move on."

Nate trotted to the remaining animals, pulled up their stakes, and remounted, riding after the two men who already followed the Comanche sign northwest away from the river.

THE BRIEF BREAK by the Brazos was but a sample of what lay in store for Nate when Crouch finally ordered a camp be made for the night near a trickle of clear-running water barely wide enough to earn the name creek. After Nate tended the stock, both Crouch and Joaquín kept him busy by having him fetch jerky from their saddlebags, as well as their canteens, pipes, and pouches of tobacco. Not once did they ask for more than one item at a time, seeming to delight in watching him scurry between where they had settled for the night and their saddles twenty feet away. Their final request was to bring their sleeping rolls and spread them on the ground. Only then did they leave Nate to himself.

He settled back against the trunk of a pin oak and slipped one of Ben's morning biscuits from a pocket. He ate it and another, washing them down with water from the stream. The two remaining biscuits felt heavy in his pocket, but he left them there for tomorrow. As dry and tough as jerky was, he would have gladly gnawed his way through a dozen of the strips Crouch and Joaquín had shared. However, neither man offered him even a single twist of the smoked meat.

Stretching out beneath the oak, he covered himself with fallen leaves as best he could—he had not considered the need of a bedroll—and folded an arm beneath his head as a pillow. He closed his eyes, but could not sleep, in spite of the weariness that settled all the way to his bones. His mind was filled with old fears and angers—ones he thought left far behind him on Texas's distant Gulf Coast.

He had ridden with these two men to help them. But he was no more than another packhorse to them—something to be used—a beast of burden. Nate had lived that life once, and thought it years in his past. Now in a matter of a single day Crouch and Joaquín had—

It doesn't matter, Nate thrust the bitterness aside. He had endured far worse at the hands of men whose orders were enforced with the bite of a whip. How or why Crouch and Joaquín treated him the way they did was of little consequence. All that mattered was the reason he was here—to find Bessa and his daughters.

A hollow ache welled inside him, swelled up as though intent on swallowing him. How he missed them! How he hurt to have them back with him! When he found them, they would return home and to the life that had been theirs. Until then, nothing Crouch and Joaquín could do would keep him from his task. *Nothing!*

EIGHT

THEY RODE upon the Comanche camp without realizing that it was there. Nate was not certain how it occurred. Two hours into their second day on the raiding party's trail, he followed Crouch and Joaquín as they wove through stunted pin oaks that covered an easy sloping hill. Crouch spoke of the mustang ponies Comanche warriors rode—how the range-bred horses had thrice the endurance of the white man's thoroughbreds.

"They ain't got speed, at least not in the short haul. But over the distance a mustang will be still fresh and runnin' when a fancy-bred is dead on the ground," Crouch said. "Hell, a Comach buck ridin' one pony with a spare on lead can cover a full hundred miles in a night. He'll ride the first pony till it drops, then leap to the back of the other and—"

Crouch's words died in a strangled little gasp as the buckskin and black topped the hill. Nate saw both men's faces pale visibly as their eyes bulged slightly and they stared below. Their Adam's apples twitched when they swallowed hard.

An instant later Nate's own gaze found the source of their consternation. Below them at the northwestern foot of the hill stood the Comanche camp. A gentle, warm breeze out of the south carried the gray smoke that rose from tipis and cooking fires northward, so that not even the scent of burning wood had betrayed the camp's proximity.

"I do believe we done stepped knee-deep in it, my friend," Crouch whispered.

"*Sí,*" Joaquin managed to answer after another laborious swallow. "This is not good. It is not good at all. There is no way we have not been seen."

"You have a gift for understating the obvious." Crouch glanced from side to side as though making certain the woods did not conceal hidden braves. He drew a deep breath and slowly released it when he saw no concealed warriors. "Looks like we've surprised them as much as they surprised us. Ain't certain how good that is."

Squaws tending the fires below abandoned their tasks and scurried through the small camp of ten tipis. Nate saw their arms shoot up to jab pointing fingers at the hill. He heard their voices as they summoned braves carrying war lances and bows and arrows from the conical, hide tents. The men stood, weapons raised and ready, staring at the three unexpected visitors who sat on the bluff above them.

"Whether we like it or not, I guess we'd best ride down like that's what we meant to do all along," Crouch said with a sideways glance at Joaquín.

"It is too late to turn away." Joaquín's nod confirmed his companion's plan.

Crouch lifted the reins from the buckskin's neck as though preparing to descend the hill. Instead he shifted around in the saddle and stared back at Nate. "Boy, I don't know what you was expectin', but this is it. All you gotta know about what's gonna happen is that if you wanna stay alive you do exactly what I say. Understand?"

"Yes, sir." Nate had no intention of doing anything else. His fear was as great as the fear he saw on the two men's faces.

"That's good, 'cause if you do somethin' stupid and git us in trouble, I promise you that I'll personally take your scalp—providin' them Comach don't take it first." Crouch turned to Joaquín. "Let's head on down. It ain't makin' them any easier with us sittin' up here."

Nate tapped his heels to the mule's sides and moved after the two men when they reined down the slope. The war whoops and charge he expected from the Comanches below did not come. The braves stood their ground with eyes locked on the approaching riders.

"These are not the ones we seek." Joaquín spoke in a whisper out of the side of his mouth. "They are too old. And there are not enough tipis."

Crouch gave a slight tilt of his head in acknowledgment. "The raidin' party's tracks came this way. For now, that's good enough."

Fifty yards from the line of ten braves and twice as many squaws, who held bared knives clutched in their hands, Crouch drew to a halt. However, it was not the ex-Ranger who called to the Comanches; it was Joaquín, speaking to them in their own tongue. When he finished, he again whispered out of a corner of his mouth. "I told them we come in peace to trade with them. That we have many fine goods for great warriors."

While Crouch gave another approving nod, Nate stared at the line of copper-skinned Indians. They were shorter and more heavy-set than he'd expected. On the ground, rather than astride the backs of racing mustang ponies, the Comanches appeared awkward and strangely out of place in this woodland wilderness.

He then saw what Joaquín had first noticed. Both braves and squaws wore faces lined with long years. These braves, although not ancient, were far too old to endure the hard, demanding rides of war parties.

One of the braves, the oldest-appearing of the lot, took a step forward and spoke in a rhythmic singsong voice. When he concluded, he stepped back in line.

"His name is Fears-Not-the-Owl," Joaquín translated, noting the name signified powerful medicine among the Comanches since the owl was a taboo bird to be avoided. "He invited us into the village to share tobacco in his tipi."

"Can we trust him?" Crouch asked.

"A Comanche is honorable in his own way. He would never kill someone he has offered the hospitality of his tipi, at least not while that man was still in the village—as he rode away, maybe, but not within the village. We are safe for now." A twisted little smile hung at the corners of Joaquín's mouth.

"Tell him we accept his offer."

Joaquín did. The line of Indians lowered their weapons and opened to allow the three men to ride through. Fears-Not-the-Owl led them to a tipi at the center of the camp, spoke again, held open a flap, and motioned them inside. When Crouch started to step from the saddle, Joaquín shook his head. "Only I am invited. The old man says you'll be safe outside, but he does not want a *tejano* in his home."

Crouch cursed beneath his breath, but remained in the saddle while Joaquín dismounted and followed the brave into the tipi.

Having been given no specific orders, Nate remained on the back of the mule, holding tight to rifle and the packhorses. In spite of his fear of the Indians, which he barely kept in rein, the Comanches did not seem to notice either him or Crouch. Apparently they had accepted the presence of white, brown, and black men and returned to the tasks that had occupied them before the strangers' approach.

A full half hour passed before he realized his observation was wrong. Those who walked past stared at Crouch with intense interest, but neither brave nor squaw so much as glanced in Nate's direction. He thought their behavior strange, but accepted it as a matter of luck. After all, these were Comanches, known for their barbaric cruelty; he preferred to be ignored. One lived longer that way.

"I don't like this, don't like it at all," Crouch muttered, but Nate was not certain whether the man spoke to him or merely gave voice to his concerns. "The stink of this place is enough to turn your stomach. Don't know how the Meskin can stand sittin' in that tipi."

Nate silently admitted the smell of the camp was an overpowering assault on his nostrils. Beneath the aroma of burning oak was the scent of rancid grease—bear and buffalo, both used by the Comanches to adorn their long black hair. Mixed in was the sour smell of stale sweat. The rank odor of human waste, urine and feces, was heavy in the air as well.

While Crouch grumbled to himself about being left outside the tipi and his uncertainty about what was happening, Nate kept a careful eye on the movement throughout the camp. Time and again, he was struck by how vulnerable these people were without mounts beneath them. Nate's gaze played over their faces. Neither man nor woman displayed a single trace of facial hair. Even their eyebrows had been plucked clean from their faces.

"What's takin' that pepper-belly so long." Crouch slipped a watch from a pocket and thumbed it open. "He's been in there at least a half hour if it's been a minute. It don't take that long for a smoke."

As Crouch shoved the watch back into his pocket, the tipi's flap opened. Joaquín and Fears-Not-the-Owl stepped out. For a moment, the Mexican stood and stared about the camp, then he walked to Crouch's side and looked up.

"I am not certain exactly what the situation is here. Much of what I gathered comes from what Fears-Not-the-Owl did not say while we smoked his pipe," Joaquín said. "I think that this is all that remains of his band. Not long ago there were younger braves, but they rode on a raid and did not return. These old ones stay alive by making weapons and trading them with other bands. They are as afraid of the rifles we carry as we are of them."

"What about the Comach we've been followin'?" Crouch glanced around. "Did they see them?"

Joaquín nodded. "Two nights ago they rode in with their captives. A Comanche warrior is very generous with the spoils of his raids. When the raiders saw the poor state of this band, they gave them three captives to be used for slaves or traded for other wealth."

Nate's heart raced at the pronouncement.

Crouch smiled. "And that old buzzard is willing to work a trade, right?"

"He wants us to talk with the other men in the village. The three captives are not his, but belong to the whole band. A decision to trade must be made by all the men."

"Tell him I'm ready to talk," Crouch said.

While the former Ranger dismounted and passed the buckskin's and black's reins to Nate, Fears-Not-the-Owl hailed the camp's other braves. Slowly the men moved into the tipi with Crouch and Joaquín at their heels. The flap fell once again, leaving Nate alone.

If he had been uncomfortable before, he was doubly so now. However, the village squaws paid him no more heed than they had done before their men had disappeared into the tipi. Those who walked by his position paused and scrutinized the packs held by each of the three horses, often letting their fingers covetously brush the bright bundles of fabric. Yet, when they passed by him, they did so without glancing in his direction. It was as though he didn't exist. Although more than one of the wrinkle-faced women did stop to pat the neck of his mule and carefully examine the animal.

Nate could only guess at the reason for their interest. Perhaps a people so attached to the horse found the long-eared mule a rarely seen curiosity—a cousin to the accustomed mustangs, but strangely different.

The half hour Joaquín had originally spent within the tipi tripled before the flap once more rose and Crouch and the Mexican emerged. Fears-Not-the-Owl and the camp's braves filed out after them. Crouch walked to Nate, took the reins and rope lead from him, and ordered him from the mule.

"They say they've got three captives that come from the bucks we've been followin'—an old woman and two little girls," Crouch said. "One of them girls is black."

"Black!" Nate's pulse pounded. "That has to be one of my girls! Where is she?" His head jerked from side to side, searching the village. "Where is she?"

"Hold on. Take it easy, boy." Crouch grasped Nate's arm. "We ain't got no guarantee these three are part of the ones we're lookin' for. Comanches don't lie, but often as not they only tell half truths."

Nate's eyes narrowed as he stared at the man. "What are you tryin' to say—that the girl might not be one of my daughters?"

"It's a possibility. Comanches have been taking captives since the Spaniards first settled Texas—'fore that if you count the other Injun tribes. That's a lot of captives. It ain't likely, but these three they got here could've come from somewhere else."

Nate had never considered that. "Then we'll take a look at them and see who they are."

Crouch shook his head. "It don't work that way, boy. If we want the three they got, we buy 'em sight unseen."

Furrows cut deeply across Nate's brow. Had Crouch said something that he missed? "Why you tellin' me this?"

"Take a look around you, boy. You don't see no ponies, 'cause this band is dirt poor. A Comanche village is usually filled with yapping mongrels, but not here. They done ate every dog they had," Crouch said. "What they want for their captives is food. Flour and sugar is nice, but what they are really after is meat. Most of these men are too old to hunt with a bow and arrow and they ain't got young bucks to do it for 'em."

"Meat?" Nate still did not know what the man was getting at. Then he noticed Crouch's eyes roll to the mule. "My mule? They want to eat my mule?"

The former Ranger nodded. "Ain't nothin' a Comach likes to sink his teeth into better than broiled mule, unless it's buffalo. Either we give 'em the mule or they won't trade for the captives."

"Sight unseen?" Nate asked, watching Crouch nod. Nate swallowed hard. "I guess I ain't got no way around it, do I?"

"We could take 'em in a fight, what with our rifles I reckon," Crouch replied. "But the first thing they'd do was kill the captives."

Nate thought of the years Bessa and he had sweated and saved pennies to set aside the money to buy the mule. Yet, if there was a possibility that the black girl held in the camp was Mary or Eve—

"Give 'em the mule."

Crouch tilted his head. "You done right, boy. Now get the flour and sugar off that roan while the Meskin and me get the three."

In the space of a heartbeat the ex-Ranger had once again relegated Nate back to his station as slave, but Nate paid it little heed. Instead he went about unloading the horse while watching Crouch and Joaquín follow Fears-Not-the-Owl to a nearby tipi and duck inside.

Moments later a woman, her dress rent in several places, and terror on her face, stepped out. She stared straight ahead, her gaze never shifting to Indians or their tipis. At first Nate feared the woman was blind, then he realized he had seen that dazed distant look in her eyes once before—in the eyes of a crazy man who had lost all contact with the world around him.

The old woman—it took Nate a few moments to recognize her —was Jeb Ewell's fifty-year-old wife Mariah. The captives had come from the Brazos raid! Behind the woman came a redheaded girl of no more than six years—Seth Alsep's daughter Callie. An instant before Crouch and Joaquín exited the tipi, Eve stepped outside.

"Eve!" The name trembled from Nate's lips. "Eve!"

The eight-year-old girl's head snapped up and jerked from side to side before her gaze alighted on her father. "Pa!" Tears streamed down her face as she ran through the camp with open arms.

Nate knelt, his own arms opening to scoop his daughter into them. He enclosed her in his embrace, drawing her to him, reveling in the life he felt in her sob-racked body. "It's all right, baby. It's all right now, your pappy's here to take care of you. Ain't nothin' more bad gonna happen to you."

Eve's small arms tightened around his neck as he kissed her cheek.

"Boy, this ain't no place for no family reunion. We got to get this woman and girl back home to their families," Crouch said while he helped Mrs. Ewell atop the buckskin, then climbed onto the horse behind her.

"Back?" Nate stood, still clutching tightly to his daughter. "What about the others? Aren't we goin' after them?"

"Not today. Old Fears-Not-the-Owl said the raiding party rode west from here, headed for the Llano Estacado." Crouch motioned for Nate to place Eve on the back of one of the packhorses as Joaquín had done with the Alsep girl. "Ain't no man gonna travel that deep into Comach territory with a woman and two children—not if he wants to stay alive."

"But—" Nate started to protest.

"Remember what I said about your scalp, boy?" Crouch glared at him. "I was dead serious. Now let's get the hell out of here while we can!"

Nate placed Eve atop a packhorse and walked beside her as Crouch led them from the Comanche camp, heading southeast, back toward the Brazos River. Nate glanced over a shoulder, to the west beyond the small Indian village. Somewhere out there was a place called Llano Estacado. His Bessa and daughter Mary were there, and these men were turning their backs on them and twelve other women.

NINE

NATE SAT in a chair beside his daughter's bed crooning a soft lullaby and holding her small hand entwined in his own. Her leadened eyelids gradually closed, and her breathing deepened to a gentle rhythm of sleep. Extracting his fingers from hers, Nate rose, bent over the bed, and lightly kissed her forehead. He tucked a quilt Ben had crudely mended under her chin before quietly slipping from the bedroom. Ben and Daniel still sat at the table although the supper dishes had been removed, cleaned, and stored on their shelf.

"Is she all right?" Daniel looked up at his father; concern shadowed his young face.

"She's sleeping soundly. That's the best thing for her right now. It'll help her forget all that happened." Nate walked to the cabin's open door and stared outside. Another autumn evening rapidly approached, and with it the Blood Moon.

"What about Mama and Mary? Why didn't you bring them back with you?" Daniel asked.

"Shhhh." Ben hushed his younger brother. "You ask too many questions."

Nate smiled. He had returned home with Eve less than two hours ago. After feeding his daughter and bathing her, he had tucked Eve away in her bed. There had been no time for the myriad of questions he was certain filled both Daniel's and Ben's heads. The boys had waited patiently; now was the time for him to explain all that had occurred.

"Your ma and Mary weren't with Eve at the Comanche camp we came upon," he said, detailing all that had happened in Fears-Not-the-Owl's village. "Joaquín DeRosa, the Mexican with us, said they were taken farther west to a place called Llano Estacado. We had to bring Eve and Mrs. Ewell and Callie Alsep back to their families."

"Llano Estacado?" Ben's tongue stumbled over the unfamiliar words. "I never heard of it."

"Me neither till back at that Comanche camp," Nate admitted. "I still ain't none too sure where it is, just west somewheres."

Daniel squirmed in his chair and frowned. "But you're going there, ain't you? You got to get Mama and Mary the way you done with Eve."

"I want to at least try." Nate turned away from the boy. How could he explain that the choice of whether he rode to this Llano Estacado rested not with him, but with a man who owned a paper that said Nate Wagoner was nothing more than a piece of property the same as a plow or a mule?

"Daniel, how come you're so full of questions?" Nate heard embarrassment in Ben's tone—embarrassment for his father. "Let Pa do the talkin'."

"But I want to know." Daniel refused to be silenced.

"So do I." Nate turned and smiled weakly at his younger son. "If there's a way to go after your ma and Mary, I'll be goin', even if I have to go on foot."

Distant hooves drew Nate's gaze back outside. Riders reined their mounts toward the Turner house. Although he could not discern them by face or form, Nate knew each of the men—the farmers who had suffered from the Comanche raid. The men rode to learn what Crouch had found out about the kidnapped women.

"Ben, fetch me fifty dollars from the hidey-hole," he said without taking his eyes off the riders. "I've a debt to pay this night."

Ben handed his father two twenty-dollar gold pieces and one ten that he took from a pouch concealed behind a loose stone in the hearth. Nate tested the weight of the coins in a palm. Bessa and he had saved each dollar with the thought of buying their oldest son a wife. Fifty dollars was the bounty the men had placed on the return of each captive. Bessa would not balk at paying the stiff price for having Eve safely home, he told himself.

Nate glanced at his younger son. "Daniel, I want you to stay here and watch over your little sister. Ben and me have business to attend. Latch the door after us, and don't go lightin' no candles. Just put yourself to bed. You can do that, can't you?"

"I'd rather go with you and Ben," Daniel answered, his expression a pout of disappointment.

"Next time maybe." Nate looked at Ben and motioned him out the door with a tilt of his head.

"You certain you want me along?" Ben made no attempt to hide his doubt.

"You're a growed man, gone hair all over," Nate replied. "You have a right to hear what's said this night. It'll be your ma and sister we'll be talkin' about—them and the others that was taken."

Ben did not answer, but Nate noticed his son's chest swell and a hint of pride dance at the corners of his mouth. Nate scratched at the three-day growth of whiskers sprouted on his chin, using his hand to hide a smile of amusement.

They reached the Turner house as Tatum Ewell walked his mother to a horse and helped her into the saddle. Jeb came out of the house next, swung astride his own horse, took Mariah's mount's bridle, and led his wife east to their home with their son following at their heels.

Nate drew a heavy breath and released it in a soft sigh. The woman looked as gaunt and terrified as she had when she first stepped from that Comanche tipi. During the ride back home, she had not uttered a single word, nor did he expect that she would for a long time. Nate had never seen a woman returned from the Comanches before, but he had heard countless tales of how female captives were used.

Reaching the split-log stoop that led to a narrow gallery at the front of the Turner house, Nate turned to Ben. "You wait here and stay out of the way. You'll be able to hear all that goes on inside."

He excused his way through the men who crowded around the doorway and entered the house. Crouch and Joaquín sat at a table with cups of steaming coffee in their hands. Tobacco smoke from several pipes shrouded the house's interior in a blue-gray fog. The men crowded around the two looked up to see who intruded their inner circle.

It was William Turner who spoke. "Nate, is there anything you wanted?"

"I brung this for Mr. Crouch." As Nate stepped to the table to place the gold coins before Crouch, he saw Seth Alsep in the corner of the room hugging tightly to his returned daughter. Tears rolled down the man's cheeks.

Crouch stared at the fifty dollars a moment, then eased them back to Nate. "Ain't no need for that. You done more'n your share, 'specially since it was your mule that bought 'em free."

Nate lifted the coins from the table and dropped them into a pocket. Inwardly he cringed when every eye in the house turned to him. He told himself to be grateful that the man had not taken the money, but he could not ignore the hint of contempt in Crouch's tone and the twist of his mouth, as though taking money from a slave was beneath him.

"You still ain't answered Howard's question." Cal Jenkins's head shifted to Crouch. "What plans you got for goin' after the rest of the womenfolk?"

The former Ranger lifted his cup and took a long draw of coffee. "I was tryin' to explain 'fore the boy there interrupted. That old Comach said the rest of the women was taken west upon the Llano Estacado—the Staked Plains. Any you men know exactly what that means?"

Crouch paused, letting his gaze move over each of the farmers' faces. When none of the men answered, he sucked at his teeth and shook his head. "I didn't think so. Let me tell you, it ain't the Cross Timbers or the rolling plains just beyond. It's the high plains, sittin' way up on a cap rock. And it ain't like anythin' any of you ever seen or want to see in your lives. I only been up there once and that's more'n enough for any God-fearin' man."

Nate listened while the man described an eight-hundred-foot escarpment of limestone that had to be climbed to reach the flattest land ever beheld by man or beast. The faceless plain was an ocean of grass that stretched hundreds of miles, all the way to the New Mexico brakes. Water was limited to a few streams that ran only in the rainy season, and trees were nonexistent.

"If there's water, there's game—buffalo and pronghorn antelope," Crouch continued. "But food and water are only minor concerns. The worse thing a man's got to face is the *Kwerhar-rehnuh* Comanche—the Antelope bands. Ain't no meaner redskins alive on God's green earth than the *Kwerhar-rehnuh*. Even the other Comach bands, the Kiowas, and the Kiowa Apaches leave them to themselves. Ain't nobody wants to tangle with 'em."

Crouch paused again to let his words sink in. " 'Course 'fore you reach the *Kwerhar-rehnuh,* a man's got to get himself and his scalp through the *Tehnawa,* the *Tahneemuh,* and the *Nawkohnee* bands. If that ain't enough to worry you gray in a night, there's the *Kuhtsoo-ehkuh* and Kiowas that drop down below the Red River whenever the mood takes 'em."

"Y'all need to take heed of what it means for a female to fall into Comanche hands." Crouch nodded to Callie still bundled in her father's arms. "The little 'un over there was lucky. She ain't growed teats yet. The others you lost were older. The bucks in the raidin' party will use 'em again and again like they did with Mariah Ewell. When they're through, they'll sell 'em to another brave who'll use 'em till he tires of 'em and then he'll sell 'em. They might still be your womenfolk by name, but they won't be the women you knew."

Nate closed his eyes as a cold shudder ran up his spine. An image of Mariah Ewell wedged into his mind. Had his Bessa been transformed into a haunted ghost of a woman like Mrs. Ewell?

Downing another swallow of coffee, Crouch shook his head. *"Kwerhar-rehnuh, Tahneemuh, Nawkohnee*—no, I won't go into that for you or any man. Only a fool wantin' to lose his hair and his hide would go that deep into Comanche lands. Even then he might as well put a gun upside his head and pull the trigger. It would be quicker and a damned site easier."

A silence as thick as the smoke clouding the house hung over the men when Crouch concluded. Each man's eyes rolled to the floor as though he were ashamed to meet the gaze of the man he asked to perform a task he was too frightened to consider himself or even as part of a group.

"I must be a fool then." Nate could not escape the vision of Bessa and Mary being repeatedly used to sate the lust of red-skinned savages. "I'll go after them. On my own if need be. And on foot, if I can't get myself another mule." Nate's eyes lifted to William Turner. "Master Turner?"

Crouch grunted with disgust. "Nigger, you don't know what

you're sayin'. If Joaquín and me don't see no chance of makin' it, what makes you think you can?"

Joaquín chuckled and circled a finger in the air near his right temple. "He is *loco en la cabeza!*"

No other man in the house laughed. However, their gazes shifted to Nate.

"You're serious, ain't you?" William Turner asked of his slave.

"I'll go on foot if I have to," Nate answered, standing straight with shoulders back.

"Your black nigger's as crazy as the red ones he's wantin' to go after." Crouch tossed down the remainder of his coffee. "And y'all are twice as crazy for listenin' to him."

If Cal Jenkins heard the ex-Ranger, he paid him no heed. "No need for you burnin' boot leather. I got a horse and saddle that's yours."

"The rest of us will see that you have the pack animals you need and the trade goods, if you'll try for our womenfolk." This from Howard Rawlins.

Milt Steward added, "Figure out what you need and when you want it, and we'll all see that you get it."

Crouch's eyes rolled back in his head. "Damned fools!"

Except for Nate no one appeared to hear the man, and Nate ignored him. Although he might not know a *Kwerhar-rehnuh* from a *Nawkohnee* Comanche, someone had go after the women. If Master Turner and the others were willing to give him the chance, then he was willing to try.

"Nate, I ain't expectin' you to do this thing for nothin'," Turner said. "If you get me back my wife and daughters, the papers I got on you will be yours."

Turner eyed his companions. "I say this before God and every man here as a witness—on the day you return my wife and daughters to this house, I make you a free man, Nate Wagoner. And the acreage you work, it'll be yours free and clear."

Turner's words left Nate in a daze. He had never hoped for freedom. To be his own man was beyond his wildest imaginings! And land that was truly his!

Howard Rawlins held up his hands to draw Nate's attention.

"Bring back my Caroline, and there'll be a hundred dollars' reward waitin' for you."

Each of the men chorused Rawlins, offering an equal weight in gold coin for the return of their loved ones.

It was then that Joaquín DeRosa pushed from the table and stood. "The *luto* raises your hope falsely. How can you expect a *negro*—a mere slave—to bring your women back to you safely? He has not a chance."

Joaquín's taunt quieted the farmers. Nate's heart pounded and uncertainty balled cotton in his throat and mouth. What was the Mexican doing?

A thin smile played over Joaquín's lips when he knew he held the men's attention. "However, if the offer of a hundred dollars a woman stands, I, Joaquín Manuel DeRosa, will gladly aid you—"

Money. Now Nate understood what Joaquín was after. Even if only half the women were returned to their homes, the Mexican would pocket a sum considered princely in a land where a dollar was as hard to come by as a raindrop during summer's drought.

"—Señor Crouch previously has told you of my experiences among the Comanches, so there is no need for me to repeat them. If you wish, I will ride west for you," Joaquín continued. "I will even allow the *esclavo* to come with me, if that is your desire."

It took only a single glance at the men's faces for Nate to realize that Joaquin had sold them on his plan. A sense of relief trembled through Nate's body. He would not have to venture into Comanche territory alone. Someone experienced would take up the search for the kidnapped women.

"YOU KNOW why I have to go, don't you, Ben?" In the moonlight that lit their way home, Nate saw his son nod. "It's a heavy burden I'm puttin' on your shoulders. You'll have to be ma and pa to Daniel and Eve while I'm gone, and you'll have the fields to take care of."

"Daniel will help some," Ben said. "We can take care of everything."

"You can use me and Bessa's bedroom to store the oats when they're harvested," Nate said. "But you'll have to build a shelter

for the cows and calves 'fore cold weather comes. I ain't expecting a barn, but—''

"I've been thinkin' 'bout a lean-to," Ben said, to his father's
surprise. "I could cut cedars—use the trunks for poles and the
branches for a roof and walls. It should last out the winter, until
you get back and we can work on a real barn."

"You done thought this through, ain't you?" Nate looked at his
oldest, once again struck by the realization his first baby had
become a man.

"Since I heard you say you was goin' after Ma and Mary."

"Have you thought about sellin' our oats?"

"I've been with you when you did it for the past five years," Ben
answered. "I know how it's done."

"What about a new mule?" Nate asked. "You're goin' to need a
mule."

Ben's frown indicated he had not considered buying a mule.

Nate dug the fifty dollars from his pocket and placed it in his
son's hand. "Here, you take that and ask Master Turner to help
find you a mule. Don't go no more than thirty dollars. If you can't
find a mule, then buy an ox for ten, but a mule's better in this
country. A man can ride a mule as well as use it to work the
fields."

Ben's ebony hand squeezed around the coins, and he nodded
solemnly as they reached the house. Nate tested the door with his
fingertips; it swung inward. Daniel had forgotten to latch it as he
had been told.

"I'll have a word with Daniel about that in the morning," Ben
said when he entered the house's dark interior. When his father
did not follow across the threshold, he stopped and turned back.
"Ain't you comin' to bed?"

"In a piece," Nate answered. "I got a mite on my mind. I need
to sift through 'fore I can sleep."

Ben bit at his lower lip and stared at his father for several
moments before tilting his head in acceptance. "Wake me when
you get up in the mornin'."

"I'll do that," Nate assured him.

When Ben disappeared into the house's darkness, Nate settled
to the ground and leaned his back against the doorframe. His

gaze slowly traced over the land that stretched before him. The fields of oats appeared black beneath the full moon that rode high in the sky.

He closed his eyes. Had only four days passed since the Comanche attack? It seemed like an eternity had slid by since he had sat with his sons, explaining how a black, even though a slave, was a free man in this country. Only now did he realize how wrong he had been. He had been born a slave—had been the property of other men all his life. He had fooled himself into believing he was free here in the Cross Timbers.

But I can change that, he thought. When he brought back Master Turner's wife and two daughters, he would own his papers. And when Bessa and Mary were once more home, they could begin their lives together again.

Crouch's words, the ways he said Comanches treated their women captives, tried to thrust into Nate's mind. He pushed the Ranger's comments aside, telling himself whatever happened to Bessa and Mary would not matter, not when they were back home, surrounded by their family.

He drifted into sleep assured by that last thought.

TEN

"HI, HITES." Nate approached the five *Kwerhar-rehnuh* squaws who sat on the ground softening buffalo hides by chewing them with their teeth. *"Nei te-bitze hites."*

He used the few words of Comanche he had learned from Joaquín DeRosa during their two months on the trail together. He called the women friends and identified himself as a friend. He then added that he sought his daughter and wife. *"Nei habbe nei mah-tao-yo, nei ner-pa-tahr. Nei habbe nei mah-ocu-ah."*

None of the women paused in their chewing. In truth they did not look up or so much as blink when he spoke. Nate sucked in a breath to contain his frustration and tried a second time. *"Nei habbe nei mah-tao-yo, nei ner-pa-tahr. Nei habbe nei mah-ocu-ah."*

The squaws continued to gnaw at the hides.

He had hoped for at least an uncomfortable wince in reaction to the way his tongue badly mangled their language. Surely the awkward utterances grated on their ears. There was nothing. Nor did repeating the words again bring a nod of the head or even the slightest acknowledgment of his presence.

The women's behavior dealt him no surprise. He tilted his hat to the squaws, turned, and walked toward the mounts and the packhorses that stood on the edge of the twenty-five tipi camp. In the ten Comanche villages Joaquín and he had visited since leaving the Cross Timbers, the squaws and braves had treated him with the same indifference.

Nawkohnee, Tahneemuh, or *Kwerhar-rehnuh,* the Comanche band did not matter; they allowed him to walk among them without a glance in his direction. Only the children, who stood at a distance, half-hidden behind tipis, appeared to notice his presence. Nate shook his head. Should his own gaze move in the direction of those children, they would duck from sight or run away laughing and chattering among themselves.

Reaching the animals, Nate gave the packs a hasty inspection and found no indication that the trade goods had been touched. In three of the previous Indian camps, he had caught children attempting to pilfer the packs, and in one camp a brave had tried to slip a sheathed hunting knife from under the canvas that covered the goods. Although a Comanche would never steal from a member of his own band, thievery from all others was considered an honorable and highly praised virtue.

Two braves, one young and the other with streaks of gray in his long, unbraided mane, halted near Nate's and Joaquín's mounts. The two spoke to each other as their fingertips explored the feel of the saddles and bridles. Now and then, they chuckled as though the horses' tack was a source of amusement. Nate had seen the reaction before. To warriors who rode stirrupless saddles made from blankets and rawhide and used simple, single-rein bridles that fitted over their mustangs' lower jaw, leather saddles and bridles appeared to be massive and awkward.

Nate cared little about how the two viewed the tack. Their interest provided an opening for him. He walked to the opposite side of the mounts and said, *"Hi, hites."* Although his greeting went ignored, he repeated the phrases he had used with the squaws, this time using a smattering of sign language to emphasize the words, to say he sought his wife and daughter.

The two braves continued to discuss the saddles and bridles without glancing up. When Nate tried again, the Comanches abruptly grew bored with the tack and strolled into the camp.

A soft curse slipped from Nate's lips while he watched the two disappear into a tipi near the center of the village. Pulling the hat from his head, Nate used a shirt sleeve to wipe away the beads of sweat dotting his dark brow. He glanced at the sun that rode in the southern sky against a cloudless field of blue. In spite of the fact that the first week of December was almost gone, the temperature edged toward eighty degrees.

Some might call the warm spell that had continued for weeks Indian summer—not Nate. To him it was simply Texas. Tomorrow, or even by this evening, a blue norther might blow in, and he would be standing in a foot of wet snow. The weather, like Texas and the people who inhabited her, was unpredictable and likely to kill a man if he faced it unprepared.

Nate glanced to a tipi with a lodge pole decorated with twenty scalps standing at its entrance. Joaquín and five *Kwerhar-rehnuh* braves had entered the hide tent two hours ago. None had exited during that time. That Joaquín had explained that Comanches were not to be rushed, that they would speak only after sharing several pipe bowls of tobacco and when they felt the time was right, did nothing to relieve Nate's antsy feeling.

This was their second day in the camp and though the Indians were more than willing to trade buffalo robes and antelope hides for coffee and tempered-steel hunting knives, they had given no hint that they held captives in the village.

Nate closed his eyes as a cold shiver worked its way up his spine. Since reaching the Staked Plains, they had found fifteen captives. None of the faces that had been brought before them belonged to the women they sought. That did nothing to erase those faces of women and children from Nate's memories. Many had been abused and tortured, their features cut with knives or scarred with burning coals.

The Comanches were as cruel to those they took as slaves as were the white men who called their practices barbaric. He kept his sanity by refusing to believe his Bessa and Mary could ever be treated so. Yet, niggling at the back of his mind was the hard reality that when and if he found his wife and daughter, they, too, might be thusly disfigured, if not worse.

Nate opened his eyes to see the flap beside the scalp-adorned lodge pole open. Joaquín ducked out, followed by the five braves. They spoke for several moments; the only word Nate caught was *"suvate."* It meant "that is all" and was often used as a farewell, which was its exact meaning at that moment. Joaquín motioned with his hands that he was riding north, then turned and walked to Nate.

"They hold no captives." He swung to the saddle and waited for Nate to mount before he urged his horse forward. "They suggested we ride north to the Kiowa lands between the Red and the Canadian rivers. They said they knew of white women who had been traded to the Kiowas a month ago. Those women had been taken from *tejanos* along the Brazos."

Nate wanted to ask if a black woman and girl had been among the women, but did not. If he had, Joaquín would have been likely to hold back the information, knowing that it tormented his companion. And the Mexican had displayed a decided relish for tormenting Nate with whatever means he could devise as a constant reminder that while Joaquín might be a Comanchero, he was a free man while Nate was a slave. Nate kept quiet, knowing Joaquín would tell him what he needed to know when it suited Joaquín.

"Damn!" Joaquín slapped his saddlehorn with a palm. "I had hoped to swing to the west, maybe to Santa Fe, and trade some of these hides for more goods."

Nate glanced over a shoulder. The warning he received when he had ridden upon his first Indian camp back in the Cross Timbers echoed in his mind—a Comanche would never kill a man he had extended hospitality to while in camp, but might take his scalp as he rode away. Nate saw no movement in the village.

"Kiowas!" Joaquín spat to the ground. "I hate the Kiowas. They are a sneaky lot. They would rather defeat a man by trickery than in a fair fight. My uncle Jesús was killed by Kiowas three years ago—Kiowas he had been trading with all his life."

Joaquín glanced forlornly to the west, then grimaced as his gaze moved to the northeast. He grunted and gave his mount's side a determined tap with his spurs as though it was the horse that had no desire to ride into Kiowa territory and he had to convince the stubborn animal.

For two hours they rode without another word uttered. When Joaquín did speak it was to order Nate to, "Dismount and gather buffalo chips, or we will not have a fire for dinner."

Unlooping the lead rope from his saddlehorn, Nate passed it to Joaquín. He then dismounted and untied a burlap bag from one of the pack animals. The sack was a quarter full with dried buffalo chips, the only fuel a man was likely to find on the Llano Estacado where wood was as scarce as hen's teeth.

"I don't understand them Comanches." Nate scanned the prairie for buffalo and antelope droppings while he walked beside the Mexican with a bag in one hand and his horse's reins in the other. "We been to ten villages now, and I haven't got so much as a howdy-do in none of 'em. I know Mr. Crouch said a Comanche don't pay a black man much mind, but these Indians act like I don't exist."

Joaquín chuckled a throaty, little laugh that sounded like half meanness when Nate bent to retrieve a dry buffalo paddy. "What did you expect? You are *esclavo*. To the Comanche, you don't exist."

Dropping the chip into the sack, Nate stood and squinted up at the Mexican. "How's that?"

"You don't exist," Joaquín repeated with another chuckle. "The way a Comanche looks at this world, there is room for men of red, brown, and white skin. But he does not see a place for a *luto* with black skin. A black man does not fit into what he sees as a balance of nature. Because he cannot find a niche for the black man, he believes those like you are not real men and not worth his attention. To the Comanche, black men are merely—"

Nate frowned when Joaquín spoke a Comanche phrase he had never heard before.

"—A man who walks without a soul," the Mexican explained

with obvious delight. "A man who has no soul is not real and cannot exist, so the Comanche ignores him. You are less than a man. It would be a waste of time for a brave or a squaw to even glance at you. A woman with black skin is still a woman and has a woman's uses. But a black man—"

Joaquín continued to talk, but Nate no longer listened. For the first time he understood why Crouch originally had been willing to take him along, why Joaquín offered no protest over Nate's riding with him to the Texas high plains. He offered no threat to the Comanche; he was a nothing.

Something twisted within Nate's breast and broke. To both white- and brown-skinned men he was a piece of property, not a man, a beast of burden to be used like a mule or an ox. Not even the Comanches, the ones who had stolen his wife and daughter, saw him as a man. To those red men he was a soulless being who walked the earth to no purpose. For the first time in his life, that was exactly what Nate felt like, something less than a man.

He bent down and picked up another buffalo chip. He did not notice or care that the paddy was wet and oozed its dirt between his fingers. Was there any place in this world where a man with black skin was truly a man—any place?

THE SUN HOVERED a hand's width above the western horizon when they reached the Red River, or what Joaquín thought was the Red. There were no maps of this country, and they relied on Joaquín's memories of past journeys into Comanchería to place landmarks they reached—more often than not vague memories.

They made camp in a shallow arroyo that fed runoff water into the river when it rained—although river was an exaggerated description of the narrow band of water that cut through the plains. Here, so near its headwaters, the Red River was no more than a creek a horse could ford in a half-dozen strides.

"Tomorrow we head northeast into what Americans call the Indian Territory." Joaquín stretched out on the ground, directing Nate while he prepared a supper of pinto beans, fried bacon, and corn bread. "Your two women make it easy to follow the others. Black women are still rare among these bands."

They're alive! Nate's heart quickened. Without saying it directly, the Mexican had revealed that Bessa and Mary were known in the Indian camp they had left that noon. They might be a month behind the captive women, but they were on the right trail!

While Nate dished out two tin plates of bacon and beans, Joaquín rose, walked to his horse, and pulled a bundle of dirty and wrinkled clothes from a saddlebag. He tossed the clothes to Nate's feet just as Nate lifted a forkful of beans to his mouth.

"Wash those in the river before it gets too dark for you to see." Joaquín tilted his head to the stream. "You might consider doing the same with your own. You are carrying a stink around as bad as the camp we just left."

A dark shadow crossed Nate's face when he glanced down at the pile of clothing. He might be less than a man to white, brown, and red man, but somewhere within his chest flickered a flame of something called spirit. Though he was no more than an animal to the rest of this world, he remained a man to himself. It was time Joaquín realized that.

Chewing the mouthful of beans, he swallowed and placed the fork and plate on the ground beside him. He then reached down to gather the dirty clothing and wad them into a ball. "Wash your own clothes. I ain't no washer woman." He threw the clothing back at the Mexican. "And if you want my clothes washed, you can do them too!"

There was a blur at the corner of Nate's eye as he reached for the plate of beans. His head jerked around in time to see blue and yellow flame belch from the Walker Colt Joaquín wrenched from his belt. Nate cried out in surprise when a white-hot brand of pain lanced over his left cheek. The pistol's ball grazed his skin! His hand slapped against the side of his face; warm blood trickled from the wound.

"You crazy or somethin'?" Nate started to shove from the ground, then froze.

The muzzle of Joaquín's pistol inched to the right until it pointed directly at Nate's face. "The next one I place right between your eyes, unless you crawl over and get these clothes, *luto.*"

Nate swallowed back the words that formed on his tongue.

There was no bluff in Joaquín's narrowed eyes, nor in the metallic click when the Mexican's thumb arched up to the Colt's hammer and tugged it back. The man intended to kill him!

The vestiges of Nate's flickering spirit fizzled out. On hand and knees, with head hung down, Nate crawled through the dirt to Joaquín's feet and picked up the clothing. While the Mexican leered with contempt, he crawled to the river and began to wash the clothes.

I'm a man! Nate's mind screamed as his hands plunged into the cold water. The mental defiance was not enough to convince himself. The Comanches were right; he was something less than a man. He had been robbed of his soul and left to walk the earth to serve those who claimed him as their property.

For an instant a vision of slipping from his sleeping roll that night and cutting Joaquín's throat flashed in his head. In the next instant, he thrust the thought away. Killing a man would not give him what he ached to possess.

To be a man in Texas required freedom. He had been given the opportunity to obtain that. All he had to do was return Master Turner's wife and daughters. To do that he could endure whatever degradation was heaped upon his shoulders. He would find Turner's womenfolk or die trying.

The thought of recovering his own wife and daughter no longer burned within his mind. Nor did he even notice.

ELEVEN

NATE WORKED AN ARM FREE of the sleeping roll and buffalo robe bundled around him and scratched his fingers through the untrimmed whiskers that bushed wildly over his cheeks, chin, and neck. His grime-dirtied fingernails relieved one spot of irritation beneath the three-month growth of facial hair only to have another itch pop up on the opposite side of his face. Rolling to his back he muttered a perfunctory curse at the fleas that infested the beard and robbed him of needed sleep.

Eyes wide open now, he stared at the moonless night sky over-head. Wisps of barely visible clouds drifted across a black field of stars—diamond-bright points of blinking light. He knew a few of the constellations such as Leo the Lion with its sickle-shaped stars for a head and triangle for a rump. Leo edged upward toward the zenith following a soft, fuzzy patch of light some called the Beehive and others named the Manger. To the west the unmistakable belt and sword of Orion sank toward the horizon.

Nate blinked at Orion as though seeing the starry hunter for the first time. What he actually saw was the message the setting constellation revealed. Orion ruled the winter skies; Leo was master of the spring heavens.

He scratched his fingers through his beard again, once more cussing the mites that had staked a claim there. It was not fleas at the heart of his cursing; it was the stark truth of time that stared him in the face.

In early October, he had left his home on the Brazos River. Now it was—

Nate frowned. He no longer knew the day or even the month. Since that night on the Red River when Joaquín had drawn down on him, neither had seemed important. He could recall the long days and cold nights spent in the Indian Territory, often holed up in a makeshift lean-to, huddled around a sputtering fire to escape the freezing snows that swept out of the north. There had been the Indian camps—hundreds of them it seemed now. Coman-ches, Kiowas, Cherokees, Osages, and the names of others that blurred into one another—all gathered to weather out the winter on government beef distributed by the Society of Friends, await-ing the return of spring so that they could once again ride onto the plains and return to the ways of the Blood Moon.

In the countless camps there had been rumors that led them north onto the prairies of Kansas. Where in Kansas, Nate had no idea, but Joaquín had assured him they had ridden north of the Indian Territory. In truth, Nate no longer cared. Since that eve-ning beside the Red River, little had mattered to him.

To be sure, he often thought of Master Turner's promise of freedom. It resonated in his memory like a half-forgotten dream. It was as distant as Texas—hundreds of miles and months behind him. It was as vague as his hope of ever finding Turner's wife and daughters—or the chance that he would someday in an eternity of tomorrows discover his own wife and daughter.

Turner and his vow were part of a life that was no longer his. He recognized that on paper he still was the property of a Texas farmer, but he now thought of himself as Joaquín DeRosa's nigger. He rode beside the Mexican not as an equal, but as a slave that jumped to fulfill the man's every command. Other than that, he ate, slept, and occasionally allowed himself the luxury of brooding over the fate life had dealt him. What else was there to expect for a man who walked without a soul?

March. As he recalled the month that positioned Leo so high in the sky, Nate's fingertips found a hairline scar on his left cheek beneath the thick whiskers. December, January, February—had so many months passed since they had camped on the Red River? How many lifetimes had slipped through his fingers in those same months?

It did not matter. Tucking his arm back into the warmth of the sleeping blankets, he rolled to a side and closed his eyes. There was nothing to be gained from dwelling on the past or the future —nothing, nothing at all.

The crack of a rifle shot rent the night's stillness. Nate's eyes flew wide; his heart hammered.

A volley of shots thundered to the north.

Joaquín came from a hard sleep, throwing his bedding aside and leaping to his feet with rifle in hand. A chorus of howling war cries rose to mingle with the rifle reports. The Mexican's head jerked around to Nate. "Get on your feet, you stupid son-of-a-bitch! There are Indians near! Are you deaf? Get your rifle."

Wearily, Nate did as he was ordered. Joaquín's fear amused him. The Mexican might fear an attack, but that was not Nate's worry. A man who walked without a soul had nothing to fear from hostiles; he did not exist for them.

The thunder of rifles fell away as did the bloodcurdling cries. Now and then a sporadic rifle barked, but the report remained distant. Eventually the night's silence returned.

"Whatever it was, it is over." Joaquín lowered his rifle, although he stood staring into the darkness for a half an hour before he returned to his bedroll.

Nate also climbed back into his blankets. Within minutes he slept, warmed by the thought of the fear he knew would keep his new master awake through the night.

THE GULLY, a six-foot-deep and thirty-foot-wide ditch cut into the flat prairie by years of eroding rains, went unnoticed until they almost rode their horses into it. At the bottom of the trench they found the site of the battle that had shattered last night's silence. The bodies of twenty buckskin-clad Indians lay strewn within the arroyo.

Joaquín stepped from the saddle and signaled Nate to do the same as he picked his way down the gully's sandy side. "They're Comanches." He knelt beside a dead brave and fingered one of three arrows that feathered his back. "But these have Kiowa markings. The Comanches are wearing no war paint. It looks like they were ambushed by the Kiowas."

"Thought you said Comanche and Kiowa was allies?" Nate wandered among the dead. All the bodies were riddled with arrows, and bloody holes marked where lead slugs had torn into the warriors' flesh.

"And I have told you a thousand times that Kiowas are not to be trusted." Joaquín stood and walked to another of the Comanches, toeing him over with a boot. "Kiowas are like snakes. They are not to be trusted by those they call friends. They are as sneaky as a coyote."

A moan caught Nate's ear. He turned in a circle trying to find its source. Nothing—he saw nothing except the dead.

"I wonder why the Kiowas did not take their scalps?" Joaquín shook his head when he squatted by another brave. "If we were in Texas, I would take all their scalps and claim the reward on them, but this is not Texas." He made no attempt to conceal his disappointment. "It is such a waste."

Nate had no doubt the waste the Mexican meant was the lost Texan bounty on Comanche scalps and not the lives of twenty braves. Joaquín's financial setback was of no concern to Nate. He frowned; he could still not find the moan's source.

"This makes no sense." Joaquín's fingertips traced over the colorful beadwork that adorned the buckskins of yet another slaughtered Comanche. "This is *Kwerhar-rehnuh* work. Only the *Yampahreekuh,* the Yap-Eaters, make this land theirs. Why would *Kwerhar-rehnuh* be this far to the north and east with winter still on this land?"

Nate had dismissed the moan as a trick of the morning wind when he heard it again. He glanced at Joaquín. The Mexican apparently did not notice the sound; he was too perplexed by the problem of discovering *Kwerhar-rehnuh* so far from their home on Texas's high plains.

The third moan came from Nate's right: of this he was certain. In a crouch, he moved among the Comanche bodies. With the fourth moan, he found its source. A brave lay on his back near the far wall of the gully. A scabbed gash ran across his unpainted forehead and a single Kiowa shaft jutted from his right shoulder.

Rifle ready for attack, Nate crept beside the wounded warrior. The brave neither stirred at Nate's approach nor when Nate lowered himself to his knees. Another moan came from the Comanche's lips as Nate lightly touched the brave's cheeks with an open palm. The Indian was afire with fever.

"What have you found, *luto?*" Joaquín stood and peered at Nate.

"This one's still got life in him." Nate examined the feathered shaft protruding from the brave's shoulder. The arrow was embedded only head-deep in the flesh. Grasping the shaft, Nate gave one quick yank. The arrow came free with little resistance, bringing another groan from the Comanche.

"A live one?" Joaquín's dark eyes narrowed as he pushed back his black sombrero and stared at the warrior. "Are you certain he still lives?"

"He's breathin' strong, and I can feel his pulse atrobbin' in his neck," Nate answered. "He's burnin' up with fever. Like as not, it's from layin' out all night in the cold rather than his wounds. They don't look to be enough to have him this sick."

"We have no use for these dead braves or that live one. Stand back," Joaquín ordered. "I will finish what the Kiowas started. It will be easier for him and us."

"What's you fixin' to do?" Nate stared at the Mexican.

"I said stand back, *esclavo.*" Joaquín hefted his rifle and thumbed back its hammer. "I am going to send his soul to the heathen gods he worships."

A shiver crawled up Nate's spine, then slithered back down when he stood. Joaquín intended to kill the brave for no other reason than his own amusement. "We could patch up his wounds."

"For what purpose? He is no good to me or to you. Now step aside like I told you. I don't want to waste more than one ball on him."

Nate's right hand tucked beneath the buffalo robe he wore wrapped about him and eased inside his coat as he backstepped. His fingers found and closed around the worn wooden grips of an old Colt Texas tucked beneath his belt. What moved him to defend a fever-ridden Comanche he had never set eyes on before when he had never been able to stand up for himself he did not know, nor was there time to ponder his actions. He thumbed back the hammer while he pulled the pistol free and swung it to cover Joaquín.

"Put the rifle down. You ain't got no need to go killin' him."

Joaquín's squinting eyes went saucer round. A Colt Texas was the ill-balanced, five-shot revolving pistol that Texas Rangers had first made famous. It carried only a .34 caliber load, but that was more than enough to put a killing-size hole in a man—a fact that Joaquín's expression announced he was all too aware of. "What is this Comanche to you? He is of no use to us."

"He means your death if you don't ease that hammer down and lower your rifle." Nate's hand was rock steady while he kept the pistol's muzzle trained on the Mexican. "He's *Kwerhar-rehnuh* and this is Kiowa territory like you said yourself. I want to know what he's doing here. He might know about the women. There's only one way to find out, and that's what I intend to do."

"You are *loco en la cabeza!*" Joaquín's rifle remained nestled against his shoulder.

"Might be I am crazy. But if'n you don't put the rifle away, I'm goin' to kill you as sure as you're standin' there." Nate refused to back down.

For seconds that seemed to drag to hours, Joaquín stood his ground. His eyes shifted between the wounded brave and the slave who held him at gunpoint as though he weighed the possibility of Nate's deciding to squeeze the trigger. With a heaving sigh of disgust and a shake of his head, he lowered the rifle. "There is no way to take him with us, *luto.*"

Nate kept the pistol trained on the Mexican. "Find some branches and build a litter. We can drag it behind one of the packhorses."

"Wood? In this country? Where am I to find branches in a prairie?"

"I don't care where, just find 'em."

Joaquín shrugged and sighed again. "I will not argue with a mad man. I will find the branches and make a travois, but remember well what I say—for your trouble that one will wake one night and slit our throats!"

When the Mexican mounted and rode away in search of wood, Nate returned the Colt to his belt and walked to his mount. He retrieved a full canteen from the saddlehorn to bathe the brave's wounds.

TWELVE

THE MORNING after they discovered the *Kwerhar-rehnuh* warrior, his fever broke. Although Joaquín's frowns and long stares in the Indian's direction bespoke his disapproval, he did nothing to hinder Nate as he went about tending the brave's injuries.

On the second morning the brave proved strong enough to wave off the litter and sit astride one of the packhorses. He rode wrapped in the warmth of a buffalo robe throughout the day, never uttering a sound, although Nate spoke to him constantly in broken Comanche and sign language. The light in the Indian's eyes said that he understood. However, the tight set of his lips

also said that he had no intention of speaking until he was ready
—if ever.

Nate refused to allow the brave's lack of response to dampen
his effort. Nor did he let Joaquín's constant reminders that a
Comanche would never speak to a man who walks without a soul
deter him. For two more days he rode beside the Indian, telling
him of their long search, describing the land they had crossed
and the bands they had visited.

As they made camp the fourth evening, the warrior spoke when
Nate called him a *Kwerhar-rehnuh*. In two quick, grunting sen-
tences he said that he was called Fights-Like-the-Wolf, and that
he was not *Kwerhar-rehnuh,* but a *Kuhtsoo-ehkuh* or Buffalo-Eater, a
member of the Comanche bands that roamed the plains between
the Red and Canadian rivers to the south.

The unexpected pronouncement took Nate and Joaquín by
surprise. Question the brave as they did, Fights-Like-the-Wolf
rolled himself in the buffalo robe, stretched on the ground, and
slept.

On the fifth morning, when Nate handed the warrior a tin mug
of steaming coffee, Fights-Like-the-Wolf began to talk. While
Nate's Comanche was far from perfect, he knew enough of the
Indian tongue to piece together the brave's tale. Last summer
Fights-Like-the-Wolf had been a member of a small *Kuhtsoo-ehkuh*
band that followed the buffalo herds onto the Llano Estacado.
There they had met with traders from New Mexico. When the
New Mexicans returned home, they left the band with more than
the trade goods they had brought with them. They left the spot-
ted sickness.

"Smallpox," Joaquín explained.

All but five of the *Kuhtsoo-ehkuh* in Fights-Like-the-Wolf's band
had died from the virulent disease. Those who lived joined a
Kwerhar-rehnuh band, thus explaining the *Kwerhar-rehnuh* clothing
the brave wore.

Fights-Like-the-Wolf drained the cup and held it out to be
refilled. When Nate complied, the brave stared at the black man.
"I never considered a black white man taking a woman and having a child by her. Because of the kindness you have shown me, I
feel sorrow for your plight. If my words help you find your

woman and daughter, then a portion of the debt that I owe to you will be paid."

The brave explained that last fall a raiding party was raised in the *Kwerhar-rehnuh* camp he now called his tribe. He did not feel that there was enough medicine to follow the warrior who would lead the braves far to the southeast along the Brazos River. "I had heard two owls speaking during the night. This did not portend well for a raid. But twenty warriors of the band painted their faces and their ponies and rode with Buffalo Brother."

Nate had learned enough of Comanche ways to know that there were no war chiefs among the migrating bands. A raiding party was formed when one warrior could convince others that his medicine was powerful enough to lead them against their enemies. It was a brave called Buffalo Brother who had gathered the *Kwerhar-rehnuh* to ride against the farmers on the Brazos.

Fights-Like-the-Wolf said that four days passed before the marauders returned with the captives they had taken. "There was two black white women among the captives, one young and one old."

My Bessa and Mary! Nate's heart raced, but he held himself in rein. This was the first Indian they had encountered who had actually seen his wife and daughter.

The warrior explained that none of the braves in the band wanted the women, but all had heard rumors of the Kiowas who would pay highly for white women. "I was among twenty braves who rode north with the captives to seek these *kiwas.*" Fights-Like-the-Wolf used the word *kiwas* to describe the Comanche allies the Kiowas; it meant rascals or scoundrels.

Through the fall they rode in search of Kiowas who wanted to trade for white captives. Where the Cimarron and Arkansas rivers met they found a small band of Kiowas who promised to lead them to a larger band willing to pay for the captives with ponies, rifles, black powder, and lead balls.

"The *kiwas* spoke in truth," Fights-Like-the-Wolf said, pausing for a sip of coffee. "We rode northward into this land with them and were paid many rifles and ponies for the women."

Before the Comanches could ride back to the Staked Plains,

winter set in. The Kiowas invited the twenty braves to stay in their village until spring. The invitation was accepted.

"Throughout the time of snow and ice, we lived and hunted beside the *kiwas*. All was as it would be between brothers," the adopted *Kwerhar-rehnuh* said. "Then came the first breath of the coming spring. We gathered our rifles and ponies and began the long ride back to our own people."

For four days the Comanche braves had driven their prizes toward the southwest. On the evening of that fourth day, they sought the shelter of a gully for their camp.

"We left only two braves to guard us while we slept, but had all twenty of us been awake that night it would not have been enough." Fights-Like-the-Wolf's face grew as hard as stone. "Every warrior among the *kiwas* rode down on us. Around me I saw my friends die beneath a hail of arrows and lead."

He recounted how he had taken an arrow in his shoulder. While he attempted to pull it free, something hit him in the head. His fingertips probed the red graze wound that ran across his forehead. "I remember nothing after that, until I awoke on your travois."

Nate found it hard to contain his excitement. "Were the two black women still in the Kiowa camp when you left?" He realized only nine days had passed since Fights-Like-the-Wolf and the other *Kwerhar-rehnuh* had started for Texas.

"They remained with the *kiwas* as did the other women we brought in trade," the brave answered with a confirming nod. "The *kiwas* often spoke of trading them to other tribes when spring's warmth came—after they grew tired of them."

Nate refused to consider the horror implied in the Comanche's last phrase. Nine days ago Bessa and Mary had been held in a nearby Kiowa camp. The odds were that they were still there, as well as the other women they had sought for all these months. Their search was almost at an end!

"Joaquín, did you hear him!" Nate turned to the Mexican.

Joaquín held his Walker Colt in his hand; the hammer was cocked and the muzzle aimed at Nate's chest. A thin smile played across the man's lips. "I was wrong when I tried to kill this one.

He has proven to be valuable. And his value will triple when we find this Kiowa camp."

Furrows ran across Nate's brow. "I don't get your drift."

Joaquín chuckled. "It is because you do not think like a Kiowa. I told you they were not to be trusted. This one knows that now. The Kiowas hoped to have the women for nothing. The only way their scheme will work is for all the Comanches to die. If one lives, such as this brave, he will tell of their treachery. The Kiowa allies, the Comanches, will rise against the band and slaughter every brave, squaw, and child. Yes, these Kiowas will pay dearly to have our guest in their hands again."

"You can't turn him over to the Kiowas," Nate protested, knowing now what the Mexican planned. "They'll kill him right out."

Joaquín shook his head. "I have no intention of turning him over to the Kiowas; I am going to trade him for the women. And do not worry about them killing him immediately. The Kiowas will take days before they let this one die for all the trouble he has caused them."

"I can't let you do that." Nate's right hand inched toward the Texas in his belt.

"Do not be stupid, *luto.*" Joaquín's eyes rolled to Nate's belt. "You have no desire to die, not with your wife and daughter so close. What is the life of one *Kwerhar-rehnuh* when those we have come for are at our fingertips?"

Nate's hand halted, fingers mere inches from the pistol tucked under his belt. The Mexican was right; he had to think of Bessa and Mary.

"Take out your gun and toss it to me." Joaquín waited while Nate complied. "Now double tie the brave's arms and legs and toss him over a packhorse. There is a band of Kiowas waiting to trade with us, but they do not know it yet!"

THIRTEEN

THERE WAS A GRIM SET to Joaquín's mouth as they rode northeastward in the direction Fights-Like-the-Wolf had indicated the Kiowas' village lay. The Mexican's dark eyes constantly scanned the rolling prairie around them. Slung from the saddlehorn beside his own rifle was Nate's weapon. Tucked beneath his belt was Nate's five-shot Colt. Joaquín's own six-shot Walker Colt, cocked and barrel aimed toward the Comanche who rode to his left, was in his right hand resting atop the broad horn of his saddle.

In spite of the direction the pistol pointed, Nate realized it was not a solitary Comanche brave, bound hand and foot and slung belly down over the back of a horse like a sack of potatoes, that played on Joaquín's mind. It was the Kiowas. Joaquín's display of bravado when he announced his intention of trading Fights-Like-the-Wolf for the captive women was one thing. The fact that the braves of the very Kiowa camp in which he planned to work that trade had slaughtered nineteen *Kwerhar-rehnuh* warriors was another. The inescapable possibility that those braves would follow after them to steal back the women as they had the Comanches' ponies and rifles was what drew the Mexican's lips into a thin line of determination.

Nate was certain of that. The same thought had darkened his own mind since they had mounted three hours ago. If the Kiowas had exhibited no fear of twenty Comanches, they certainly would not be frightened by a lone Mexican and a black slave. It would be no small miracle if the Kiowas allowed them to leave the camp with their scalps still intact.

Out of the corner of an eye, Nate studied the prisoner with which Joaquín hoped to buy the women's freedom. Fights-Like-the-Wolf made no sound nor did he move. Nate saw traces of moist crimson spreading on the shoulder of his buckskins. The jostling ride had reopened his arrow wound.

The injury was shallow, and the flow of blood offered no danger that the brave would bleed to death, Nate realized. Still, he could not avoid a flush of guilt for the pain the Indian now endured. He was unaccustomed to the barter of human beings, at least from the standpoint of being the one who traded in flesh. The mantle he wore this day ill-suited him. Fights-Like-the-Wolf's plight struck too close to his own.

That this brave was a member of the *Kwerhar-rehnuh* band that had kidnapped his wife and daughter and in all likelihood repeatedly had violated Bessa and Mary during the months they and the other captives had been his prisoners hardened Nate to the burdensome task to which he willingly lent himself. To have Bessa and Mary back, he was ready to trade a hundred Comanches this day—or die trying.

"Smoke." Joaquín drew up his horse and pointed to the north.

Nate's gaze found the fingers of gray, greasy smoke that wove to a sky sprinkled with fluffy patches of cloud. The fires that gave birth to the smoke lay hidden within a bowled depression in the prairie as did any hint of Kiowa tipis. Beside him, Fights-Like-the-Wolf lifted his head and peered at the smoke. For an instant his face went rigid, betraying recognition.

"The smoke comes from no more than five miles away." Joaquín stood in his stirrups and surveyed the terrain. "We will rein to the left and ride in from the west."

Nate had no idea why the Mexican did not approach the village on a direct line, but he did not question the man's reasoning. In their months on the trail together, he had grown to respect but one of Joaquín's traits—his knowledge of Indians and their ways.

Swinging out in a wide arch, Joaquín brought them to the crest of a rolling hill sprinkled with green shoots of spring's new grass. The elevated vantage point provided an unobstructed view of the Kiowa village. To Nate it appeared closer to a city than a village. Two hundred tipis, maybe more, filled what appeared to be the flood plain of a creek that flowed south of camp.

"They will not expect to see us or him." Joaquín tilted his head to Fights-Like-the-Wolf. "They will be stunned by our boldness. I will use that to quickly strike a deal and ride out before they can gather their wits about them."

Nate was not certain whether Joaquín explained his plan, or merely spoke it aloud to bolster his own courage.

"You know that this brave will buy back your wife and daughter, don't you?" When Nate nodded, Joaquín drew a heavy breath and released it. He then passed Nate's weapons back to him. "Keep these in plain sight, but do not go for them unless I tell you. An open show of our firepower will impress the Kiowas."

Two single-shot rifles and eleven rounds in two pistols was not that formidable a display of firepower to Nate, not when confronted with the immensity of the Kiowas' village.

"Say nothing when we reach the camp. I will say all that needs to be said. What is required of you is to stay in the saddle with the horses." Joaquín glanced at the distant village, then back at Nate. "When the captives are brought out, show no sign of recognizing them. I do not want the Kiowas to know that they are the reason we have come to their land."

Nate nodded and clucked his mount after Joaquín as the Mexican started down the rise toward the camp. After the bloody ambush of the *Kwerhar-rehnuh* braves, Nate expected mounted warriors to ride out from the small city of tipis and challenge their approach. Instead the gathering of old braves and squaws who stood and watched them was reminiscent of the first Comanche camp he had ridden into back in the Cross Timbers. The youngest brave he saw appeared at least forty years old, an ancient age for most plains Indians whose deaths were often as violent as their lives. This one limped heavily on his right leg, a harsh reminder of a brush with an enemy or the horns of a bull buffalo.

Joaquín hailed the small group of braves who stepped forward to greet them. That the Mexican spoke Comanche no longer took Nate by surprise as it had the first time they had ridden into a Kiowa camp. The fierce Comanche bands dominated the plains. Even those tribes who did not openly ally themselves with the Comanche, as did the Kiowas, learned their tongue. It was a matter of simple survival.

Nate easily followed the exchange between Joaquín and the Kiowas. It was when the Indians spoke among themselves using their own language that he found he could make neither heads nor tails of the guttural sounds that burst from their lips. Nor did the Kiowas allow their hands to give away their meaning. Nate could not read Joaquín's face, leaving him in doubt as to whether the Mexican understood one syllable of Kiowa, a fact that did nothing to reassure him of their chances of surviving this day.

Nate did notice fear betrayed on the Indians' faces when Joaquín waved an arm to Fights-Like-the-Wolf. His words struck like steel to flint as he told them that the bound brave was what he came to trade. Joaquín made no mention of the price he hoped to extract from the Kiowas.

A hasty inspection of the Comanche appeared to assure the Kiowas the Mexican did not lie. None of their faces hinted that they suspected blackmail in Joaquín's heart as five of the braves led the Mexican into a tipi.

A cold sweat, like nips from invisible needles, prickled over Nate's body while he remained in the saddle as Joaquín had commanded. Unlike the Comanche disinterest he had grown accustomed to over the past months, the Kiowas formed a tight circle about him and the packhorses. Now and then a bold squaw would step forward to jab Fights-Like-the-Wolf in the side or the buttocks with a stick. The action sent a ripple of humorless laughter through the Indians. The Comanche brave endured the humiliation without so much as a grunt.

Unlike the long sessions spent palavering in Comanche camps that were required to strike a bargain, a mere half hour passed before Joaquín and the five braves stepped from the tipi. The Mexican strode to Nate. "Luck sits on our shoulders. The first buffalo herd of the spring has been sighted a three-day ride to the south. All the warriors have ridden from the village to hunt. Only the old and the young are in camp."

"The women?" Nate asked.

"They are here. The old ones are afraid of Fights-Like-the-Wolf. They know the Comanche will slaughter every man, woman, and child in this camp if he returns to his people and tells of the Kiowa treachery. They have agreed to a trade. We get the women, and the brave will die when the young warriors return with the full moon."

The full moon—that was but three nights away. Nate glanced at Fights-Like-the-Wolf. The *Kwerhar-rehnuh*'s dark eyes glared at him, simmering with the knowledge that he had been condemned to an agonizing death at the hands of the Kiowas.

Joaquín took in the Indians crowded about them. "Unload everything you can from the pack animals. Keep as much food as possible and the buffalo robes. As soon as I come back with the women, I want to move out. Fear of the Comanche dulls these old ones' wits. They are too long from the war lance to realize that they could kill Fights-Like-the-Wolf and us if they wanted. I want to be far away before that thought occurs to them."

Excitement pounded in his temples as Nate nodded agreement and swung to the ground while Joaquín followed the braves deep into the village. Bessa and Mary would be in his arms once more in a matter of moments. His hands trembled as he worked. The sacks of cornmeal, flour, coffee, beans, and jerky he repacked on the back of one of the horses. There were not enough provisions to get Joaquín and him back to Texas let alone feed fourteen women and girls during the journey, but it was what they had. They would feed the women as they often fed themselves—by hunting. Game would be more plentiful with the coming of warmer weather.

All the other trade goods, the pots and pans, hunting knives, bolts of cloth, mirrors, tobacco, deer and antelope hides, and a myriad of smaller items chosen to pique Indian interest, he piled on the ground. Beside them, Nate placed Fights-Like-the-Wolf.

The Kiowas edged closer. Nate held his ground, a lone guard keeping the braves and squaws alike away from the small mountain of trade goods and the captive brave.

"Back. Make way," Joaquín's Comanche opened a path through the crowd.

Nate's heart hammered wildly in his chest. This was the moment he had waited for all the long months, the endless miles. Behind the Mexican came Master Turner's two daughters Rachel and Terry. There was Martha, Milt Steward's wife, her face smeared with grime. Next was Tallie Steward, Brewster's wife; tears rolled down the woman's cheeks as she tried to stand straight and proud. And at her heels came Howard Rawlins's daughter Caroline, dark bruises on her left cheek and forehead.

Hand-in-hand walked Denise Newman and her twelve-year-old daughter.

"Get them on the horses and give them buffalo robes to keep them warm," Joaquín ordered. "Every moment we waste here weakens our chances of getting out alive."

Nate's gaze raced over the line of seven women. An ice floe ran through his spine. Bessa and Mary were not among them! Nor was Master Turner's wife, Elizabeth.

"My wife and daughter? Where are they?" He turned to Joaquín, uncertain of what was happening. "Where are Bessa and Mary?"

"They aren't here." Joaquín helped Denise Newman to the bare back of a packhorse and handed her a robe. "There is no time to talk now. We have to ride from here. Move, *luto!* Move! Our lives are at stake!"

Not here? The words hit Nate like a sledgehammer. His brain dazed and his body numb, he did as ordered, helping the women atop the horses. Then at Joaquín's signal, he mounted and rode from the Kiowa village. He looked back only once. Fights-Like-the-Wolf's dark eyes lifted to him, burning with hatred as the Kiowas wrenched him to his feet and dragged him into a nearby tipi.

WITH THE SUN hanging an hour above the western horizon, Joaquín called a halt. For the first time since leaving the Brazos, the Mexican helped Nate build a small fire from buffalo chips. As the fire caught, the women huddled close, still wrapped in their heavy hide robes. None of them spoke while Joaquín gathered water from the stream in two pans and put coffee on to boil.

Nate studied the women's faces and their downcast gazes. It was as though they were afraid to let their eyes meet his or Joaquín's. Nor was their silence unusual. Not one of the women had spoken a word since they had ridden from the Kiowa camp.

That had been six hours ago. Joaquín had led them westward away from the village, then swung to the north, circling wide of the Indians as he backtracked to the east. Once the creek was reached, they had ridden in its shallow waters for three hours.

The Mexican had explained that if the Kiowas decided to follow, the Indians would expect them to ride to the west. He was certain trackers would eventually find their trail, but hoped the stream would throw them off for a while.

Nate prayed that when their trail was discovered several days' ride would separate them from the Kiowas, and that those days would dull the warriors' desire for revenge. Without such an edge, there was nothing Joaquín and he could do to protect the women, or themselves. Two men had little chance of standing against such a large village of Kiowas determined to take their scalps.

"I know you ladies are tired and would like to rest, but I am afraid we will not be able to do so—not tonight." Joaquín explained the danger of a Kiowa raiding party while he passed a sack of jerky among the women. "We will stop here long enough to rest the horses and eat, then we will ride through the night. We will keep to the creek to hide our tracks—"

Nate closed the Mexican out as he poured a mug of coffee and handed it to William Turner's daughters. "Miss Terry and Miss Rachel, drink this. It will help keep you warm."

The older of the two girls nodded without glancing up, took the tin cup, and drank deeply before passing it to her sister. Nate wanted to press them with a barrage of questions about his wife and daughter, but he held back. The fear and uncertainty he saw in their expressions were reflected on all the women's faces. Theirs were not the glassy-eyed, distant stares that had belonged to Mariah Ewell when she had been taken from the Comanches so many months ago. However, Nate was afraid to push any of the women, frightened he might nudge them over the line that separated sanity from madness.

"Your daddy's been worried plumb sick about you two," Nate said, then added, "And about your momma, Miss Elizabeth. He'll be the happiest of men to have you home with him again."

Tears trickled down Rachel's cheeks, but it was Terry who said softly, as though embarrassed by the sound of her own voice, "We ain't seen Momma since before winter. The Comanches kept her. She wasn't brought with us. We don't even know if she's still alive or not."

Nate closed his eyes and repressed a shudder that tried to quake through his body. In none of the Comanche camps they had visited had there been a hint that the women had been divided. "Is that what happened to my Bessa and Mary? Did the Comanches keep them, too?"

"We don't know." Terry's eyes refused to lift to his. She handed him an empty cup. "You should give the others some."

"They don't know what happened to your wife and daughter." Denise Newman spoke. "They didn't see what became of Bessa and Mary. I did. So did Tallie and Martha. We all saw."

Again Nate held rein on himself and the flood of questions he wanted answered. Instead he poured another cup of coffee and handed it to Denise Newman. "You saw what become of my wife and child?"

The woman nodded as she took a tentative sip from the steaming mug. "They were bought by a medicine show wagon about five days' back."

Nate's eyes narrowed. "Medicine show wagon?"

"There was three white men in a bright red and green medicine show wagon. You know, like they sell snake oil from." She paused for a deeper drink from the cup. "They bought Bessa and Mary for two rifles and four jugs of white lightning, didn't they, Tallie?"

The other woman nodded in confirmation as Mrs. Newman passed her the tin cup.

"Medicine show?" Nate sank to the ground, his brain trying to reject what he heard. While he nursed Fights-Like-the-Wolf's wounds, his wife and daughter were being sold to white men.

"The wagon had one of them false bottoms, and it was filled with rifles and whiskey," the woman continued. "I heard the men say they didn't have room for no white women, but they could uses blacks as sla—servants, that they could sell 'em later in Texas."

Nate turned from the women. Bitter tears welled in his eyes. He had ridden through half of Texas, the Indian Territory, and deep into Kansas to help free these women—these white women —from their captivity only to find his wife and daughter had been bought by white men as slaves. *Bought for jugs of rot gut whiskey!*

"At least they're alive," the woman continued. "We seen Harriet Jenkins and Sally Howe hung up by their heels and skinned alive. Don't know what happened to Laura Alsep. She went all crazy like and wandered off one day. None of them redskins even tried to stop her."

Nate nodded. In their own way Indians respected madness. Those touched by insanity were allowed to go their own way. In Mrs. Alsep's case, the woman had probably died from exposure to the elements or starvation.

"Wanda Mueller died of a fever about three months back," Mrs. Newman said almost as an afterthought. "The heathens didn't even bury her, just tossed her body into a gully."

Of the seventeen captives taken in the *Kwerhar-rehnuh* raid, only Miss Elizabeth, Bessa, and Mary remained unaccounted for.

"We heard that the Comanches who brung us to the Kiowas was killed. Is that true?" Nate did not look to see which of the women spoke, but he heard the hatred in her whisper-soft voice.

"It is true," Joaquín answered. "I found their bodies. All but one had been killed. That one I traded for your freedom—and he will die when the full moon rises."

"Dead," another woman said in a venomous tone. "It is too easy for them."

A mumble of approval ran through the other women.

Nate shuddered. He understood the poison in their words. They had suffered the abuse of both Comanche and Kiowa. Yet, their freedom meant nothing to him, not with Bessa and Mary still missing. He had traded a human life, bartered flesh for nothing.

He looked back at the women and tried to tell himself that their freedom did have meaning, that there had been purpose in what he had done. All he felt was a hollow ache. These were white women—three who had watched his wife and daughter sold for two rifles and four jugs of cheap whiskey and done nothing to stop that cruel barter. He had condemned a man, red-skinned though he might have been, to death for them.

"Ladies, the sun is setting, and it will soon grow dark. Our fire will be like a beacon on this prairie," Joaquin stood. "We must travel again."

The women rose and mounted their horses while Nate doused the fire and used the side of a boot to kick its remnants into the stream. There was no need leaving any sign of their passage for the Kiowa trackers to find. With Joaquín taking point, Nate in the rear, and the women in between, they moved into the coming night.

Nate rode silently, his mind plagued by the twisted kinks fate had woven into this day. Try as he did, he could not shove aside the memory of Fights-Like-the-Wolf's hate-filled glare. Nor could he escape the role he had played in trading the brave's life for the lives of women who meant nothing to him. His action made him no better than the men who had purchased his wife and daughter for rifles and jugs of whiskey.

A moon three nights' short of being full rode the length of an outstretched hand above the eastern horizon when Nate eased back on his mount's reins. For five minutes he watched Joaquín and the women continue downstream, none of them aware that he had stopped. He then turned his horse's head upstream toward the Kiowa camp.

TWO MILES FROM THE VILLAGE, Nate halted. South of the tipis loosely ranged a herd of two hundred Indian ponies. In Comanche bands young boys who waited acceptance as full braves by their people were assigned to guard the stock at night. Nate assumed the Kiowas followed a similar custom, although he was too far away to discern the guards from the horses they tended. His hope was that the same was true if the guards had seen his approach.

Dismounting, Nate walked close beside his horse, using the animal's bulk to hide him while he moved toward the herd. As daring as his plan appeared on its face, the truth was the ponies offered the only cover between his position and the camp.

He reached the edge of the herd without sighting a guard or being sighted. Carefully, keeping close to his mount's side, he wove to the edge of the village, then crept toward the tipi into which he had seen the Kiowas drag Fights-Like-the-Wolf. Triple checking to make sure he went unnoticed, he let his horse have its head, reins dragging the ground. As the horse lowered its neck to graze, Nate shot beside the tipi.

His breath came short and shallow when he paused in the shadow cast by the conical arrangement of wooden poles draped with tanned hides. He sucked at his tongue to return moisture to his cotton-dry mouth; it did not help. He scanned the camp, seeking unseen eyes that followed him. Finding none, he ducked through the tipi's flap.

Fights-Like-the-Wolf sat at the center of the hide tent, bound wrist and ankle to a wooden post that had been driven into the ground. The Comanche brave's head jerked up, his eyes wide with surprise and uncertainty. Contempt hissed in his words. "Do you return to make certain that the *kiwa* pigs kill me?"

Nate ignored him. He eased a hunting knife from a sheath slung at his waist.

"Or do you prefer to send my soul to the Valley of Ten Thousandfold Longer and Wider?" Fights-Like-the-Wolf's eyes narrowed to slits. "Only one who mates with a dog would slit a warrior's throat while his hands are tied."

"If you keep talking like an old woman, you will wake the whole village and bring them down upon us," Nate answered in the brave's own tongue. "It would be better if both of us got away from here alive."

Doubt clouded the brave's expression. "Got away?"

Nate used the knife to slice through the rawhide cords knotted about the *Kwerhar-rehnuh*'s ankles. "Unlike the Comanche, a black white man does not sell another man for gold or for other lives."

"A man who walks without a *soul* cannot know the value of *one*," Fights-Like-the-Wolf answered simply.

Nate drew a deep breath and shook his head. "I know enough about souls that I'm saving yours."

The brave stared at him, but said nothing.

"Only a few strides from this tipi are the Kiowa ponies. If you can catch and mount one, you can escape. It's a long way from here to the cap rock, but at least you'll have a chance. And that is better than you have now."

"Far better," Fights-Like-the-Wolf agreed.

Nate severed the cords around the Comanche's wrists. "You'll need a weapon." He handed the brave his hunting knife.

The Comanche weighed the blade in his right hand while he pushed to his feet. "It will be enough."

Without another word, Fights-Like-the-Wolf darted out of the tipi. By the time Nate poked his head outside, the brave had vanished into the herd of ponies. Glancing to both sides, Nate hastened to his own horse, gathered its reins, and began to weave back the way he had come.

A mile from the herd, excited cries returned his gaze to the village. Three Kiowa boys shouted an alert to the village as a lone Comanche drove a painted pony westward into the night. While he watched, several braves ran from their tipis to the herd. Frightened ponies shied and bolted as the Kiowas attempted to catch mounts.

Taking advantage of the chaotic confusion, Nate swung into the saddle, and spurred his horse eastward to rejoin Joaquín and the women.

FOURTEEN

"BOY, you are the craziest nigger I ever met in all my days." Samson Moore shook his head while he ladled a taste of soup from the steaming kettle he had stirred for the past half hour. "Needs a mite more salt."

"I ain't crazy, Samson. I'm just a man who wants his family back." Nate watched the army private take a fistful of salt from a bag and throw it into the kettle.

Moore was a black man, although the light hue of his skin placed him in the category of what most white folks called "high yellow." Samson was also the first free black man Nate had ever met. Born in Pennsylvania, he had never known the chains of slavery. That gave him an odd way of looking at life, at least, as far as Nate was concerned. He gave voice to things most black men were afraid to think.

"It sounds more crazy than sane to me for a man like you to want to go traipsin' way out there in Indian Territory when he could be tendin' to gettin' hisself to the free states." Samson glanced up from the soup and shook his head again. "Most bought and paid for niggers I've knowed would give an arm to be sittin' where you're sittin' right now."

Where Nate sat was in the middle of a U.S. Army camp seventy-five miles from the Missouri border. Two evenings ago Joaquín had accidentally led Nate and the women to a cavalry company bivouacked along the creek they had followed since leaving the Kiowa village.

"My wife and daughter ain't in no free state. Some medicine show men got 'em. And the *Kwerhar-rehnuh* Comanches got Mrs. Turner," Nate explained for the hundredth time since he had met Samson two nights ago.

"Odds ain't with you for findin' none of them. You know that, don't you?" Samson filled a bowl with soup and handed it to Nate. "Best eat that. Whatever you decide to do, you ain't gonna get no cookin' the likes of that for a long time to come."

Nate sampled the soup and nodded his appreciation in spite of the fact that the watery mixture of dried beef, potatoes, and carrots was too salty for his taste. "Odds were against us findin' those seven women over yonder in the big tent, but we found them."

Samson glanced at the headquarters tent that had been used to house the women since their arrival in camp. "You was plumb lucky findin' them, and you knows it. 'Sides, you had that Mexican feller with you when you done it. You'll be goin' at it alone this time. Never met no nigger that knew the first thing about no Indians. Ain't met many white folks that knows either, for that matter."

There was no way for Nate to deny that. This afternoon Joaquín would be riding back to Texas with the women under the protection of a ten-man cavalry escort. It was Nate's own decision to try and find the medicine show wagon and his wife and daughter. Neither Joaquín nor the Army had raised an objection to his plan. Although Captain Clyde Martin and Joaquín both thought him insane; he had seen that in their expressions of disbelief when he announced his intentions.

"I've learned a lot about Comanches and other Indians since I left the Brazos. If they're still alive, I'll find them." Nate wished he felt as certain as he sounded. As the time for Joaquín's departure grew near, Nate's confidence in the decision to proceed on his own dwindled.

"Only thing you need to know is that if you don't change your mind, them Kiowas or them Comanches is gonna cut off your hair." Samson abandoned the soup kettle to check on a bowl of rising bread dough. "The cap'n don't like no biscuits, so I got to fix him fresh bread every day."

Nate swallowed a mouthful of soup. "If I don't go after 'em, ain't nobody else goin' to. Your Captain Martin's done told me that medicine show wagon was too far into Indian country for him to take after—said he'd have to have the whole U.S. Army along with him before he'd go."

"Boy, why you keep callin' that a medicine show wagon?" Samson glanced over a shoulder and frowned at Nate. "I know the cap'n done told you that them men weren't sellin' no cure-all remedies, but sellin' rifles to the Indians. We been lookin' for 'em the last three months now."

Nate nodded as he scooped the last of the soup from the bowl. "A wagon painted all bright red and green like that should help in findin' it."

"Still, if I was in your boots, I'd be headin' east. All you have to do is follow the Missouri down to where it joins up with the Mississippi and the Ohio," Samson said. "Build yourself a raft and float on across to Illinois. Ain't nobody gonna stop a big man like you, 'specially when he's totin' a rifle and pistol the way you are. Get to Illinois, and you're a free man."

"If I find Miss Turner and take her back to Master Turner, I'm a free man," Nate answered.

Samson shot Nate a dubious look. "If you say so, but it seems like the long way of goin' to get something that ain't but a couple of days' east of here. 'Sides a man can always get hisself another wife."

Nate did not get a chance to reply. Joaquín stood in front of the tent containing the women. He waved Nate to him. While Nate stood, ten soldiers leading a string of saddled horses approached the tent. They dismounted when the women exited the tent to help them atop the mounts.

"*Esclavo,* there is still time to change your mind and return to Texas with us," Joaquín said when Nate reached the tent. "No one will think less of you for coming along with us."

Nate's impression was that the Mexican feared that those back home might think less of him for giving up the search and letting a lone slave continue on his own. "No, I've got to go on. We know where that wagon was nine days ago. It shouldn't be too hard to pick up its trail."

"I think it is a foolish plan, but you will need help." Joaquín made a show of rummaging into a pocket. When he was certain he held all the women's gazes, he came up with two twenty-dollar gold pieces that he placed in Nate's hand. "You will need money to buy trade goods to take with you." In a softer voice meant only for Nate's ears, "I will take this from your share of the reward when I get back."

That the Mexican's display of generosity was meant to impress the women, and in turn their menfolk back on the Brazos, did not matter to Nate. He thanked Joaquín. Forty dollars would buy a lot of goods to fill the now depleted packs.

"God be with you as well as luck." Joaquín climbed into the saddle.

Nate nodded, then walked back to Terry and Rachel Turner. "Miss Terry, Miss Rachel, you tell your daddy that I ain't givin' up —that I'm still lookin' for your momma, will you?"

"We'll do that, Nate." Terry smiled at him, but he saw no hope in her eyes.

"And I'd greatly appreciate it if you tell my childrens that you saw me and I was doin' fine. Tell 'em that their pappy misses 'em."

"We'll walk down and see Ben the day we get home," Terry assured him as a blue-uniformed lieutenant at the head of the column of soldiers gave a command to pull out. "And we'll tell David and little Naomi for you."

Nate stood and watched as they left the camp, moving southward toward the Indian Territory and Texas beyond. They were no more than black spots in the distance when he realized Terry had called Eve "Naomi" and Daniel "David." Tears welled in his eyes.

FIFTEEN

THE NICKER of a horse brought Nate from half sleep. He made no sudden moves to announce he had awakened. His eyes opened to slits while his right hand tightened around the handle of his Colt Texas. If Kiowas crept toward his fireless camp, the only advantage he had was surprise. Let them believe he still slept until they were in range of the .34 caliber pistol.

His gaze darted about. There were no Indians with faces painted for war, only a dog sniffing at one of the packs sitting on the ground ten feet to Nate's right.

Dog? Nate's eyes opened wider. The mangy-looking mongrel was not a dog, but a coyote that boldly scrounged for food!

Nate sat straight up, throwing aside the two buffalo robes covering him. "Git! Git away from there you worthless—"

His curse was drowned by high-pitched yipping as the startled coyote tucked a bushy tail between its hind legs and scurried away. Nate watched the animal run across the gently rolling prairie until it disappeared over a humplike knoll a half a mile from where he sat on the ground.

"Damn!" The impact of this curse was lost among the chattering of his teeth while he gathered the robes back around him. That, in turn, brought another string of cuss words directed at the crisp cold of the air. In Texas, March meant an end to winter's freezes. This far north, he was not sure when spring's warmth would finally push the chill from his bones, or if it would at all.

Stretching back out on the ground, he closed his eyes and awaited the return of sleep. It did not come. Instead his ears caught every night sound within a quarter of a mile. His imagination did the rest, transforming the rustle of a rabbit darting through the winter-desiccated grass into a whisper of moccasins slipping over the ground, embellishing the clack of hoof on stone when one of the horses shifted its weight from one leg to the other until it became the pounding hooves of approaching Indian ponies.

Grunting with disgust, Nate sat up and hugged the robes closer. He told himself he was overly cautious because of the moon in the night sky—that ragged sleep had come in fits and starts for the five nights since he left Captain Martin's army camp because of the long years of living in fear of the Blood Moon. He also knew he lied to himself. His inability to sleep stemmed from the sole fact that he was alone.

It tripled his disgust to admit it, but he missed Joaquín. In spite of the Mexican's abuse, he had grown to depend on the man's knowledge of Indians and the land. Joaquín had made every decision since leaving the Cross Timbers, whether it had been choosing the trail they rode or rationing water between water holes, which often were separated by several days' ride.

Those decisions now sat squarely upon his own shoulders. For the first time in his life Nate Wagoner was alone, truly alone. And he was not certain that he liked the situation.

He glanced at the sky. The moon dipped toward the western horizon. An hour, two at the most, remained before a new day broke.

An ironic little smile lifted one side of his mouth as he remembered Samson urging him to flee to the east, across the Mississippi River to freedom. The army cook had been wrong. Nate had found freedom to the west, here on the Kansas prairie. No man could ask for more freedom than he possessed.

Only now while he sat shivering with buffalo robes clutched tightly about him did Nate realize that he and Bessa had lived a lie for all those years along the Brazos. Those twenty-five acres had not removed the chains of slavery as they told themselves and their children. Here, faced with choosing every minute detail of his life, his survival, true freedom was realized.

And it was frightening.

Not for the first time since riding west, Nate considered turning back. If he rode hard, he could catch Joaquín and the soldiers and return to—

His thoughts stumbled when a cold chill that had nothing to do with the weather crept along his spine. As much as he wanted to turn tail and run like the coyote he had scared away from the packs, he could not. Bessa and Mary were still somewhere out there. That they were in white rather than red hands did nothing to lessen his fear. The cruelty of white men to those of black skin had been known for generations before a black ever laid eyes on a Comanche or Kiowa.

Nate recalled the wagon tracks he had sighted on the banks of a stream he crossed a day ago. The deep ruts were several days' old and he had no proof they belonged to the medicine show wagon he sought, but wagons were a rarity this far out on the plains and it was headed west. While he admitted he might be grasping at straws, he was certain it belonged to the three men who had bought Bessa and Mary from the Kiowas.

For a day and a half he had followed the tracks the wagon's wheels cut into the soft earth. The depth of those tracks said the wagon was heavily laden as would be a wagon with a false bottom filled with rifles. In that time he had come across four mounds of ash, each marking where the wagon had stopped to camp. Nate figured two camps per day of travel. The wagon was having a rough go of it on the open prairie, barely covering ten to fifteen miles a day. Even with three fully laden pack animals to slow him down, Nate traveled a full thirty miles from sunup to sundown. It was only a matter of time before he caught up with the wagon.

Only a matter of time, with that reassuring thought, he drifted to sleep.

He awoke to the rough feel of fingers rubbing against his left cheek—and a Comanche brave standing over him. The perplexed expression that twisted the Indian's features was the only thing that stopped Nate from lifting the barrel of the Colt he clutched beneath the buffalo robes and firing the pistol point blank into the brave's exposed belly.

Even though Nate's eyes were now wide open, the Comanche reached down and roughly rubbed his fingers over Nate's right cheek. The brave then studied his fingertips, the confusion on his face deepening. He stood straight and shook his head. "I do not understand. The paint does not come off on my fingers."

"For a mighty hunter, Running White Horse, your thoughts are sometimes as empty as the air."

Nate's eyes rolled to the side, going round. A second brave sat stride a chestnut mustang while he held his companion's pinto pony. Neither Comanche wore the black paint of war, which did nothing to reassure Nate that his position was anything more than precarious. Where there were two braves, more were certain to be near.

"He is a black man. His face is not painted. It is as I said, one can tell by his hair. It is as thick and tangled as the hair of a buffalo's hump." The mounted brave used the Comanche phrase *to-oh tivo* to describe Nate, which translated as black white man. "Such as he is of no concern to us when there are empty bellies in our camp."

The brave called Running White Horse grunted and pointed to Nate's horses. "We could steal his ponies. There are two for each of us."

The mounted Comanche shook his head. "There is no honor in stealing from a creature that has no soul. Who is to say such a being does not raise horses that also are without souls?"

"Who is to say?" the other brave agreed when he turned from Nate and leaped to the paint's back. "You are right. Our women and children's bellies cry for meat and not for ponies stolen from such as this."

Without a glance to the man they left bundled on the ground, the two braves yanked their mounts' heads around and galloped toward the south. Nate blinked several times as he sat up and stared while the Comanches disappeared in the distance. His left hand poked from the buffalo robes and his fingertips rose to touch his left cheek. His lips puckered, and a whistle of relief escaped them. Today the color of his skin had saved his scalp. For the first time in his life, he silently gave thanks that he had been born black.

THE SNOW caught Nate with his pants down.

The buffalo chips sprinkled over the ground drew him into the gulch. His intent was to gather the dried manure for a small fire over which to cook a skillet of beans and a pan of coffee. Since leaving the army camp, he had kept himself alive on jerky and water, fearing smoke would attract Indians. That fear remained, but the sack of jerky he had purchased before heading west was all but empty.

Besides a hot meal would lift his spirits and give the horses a chance to graze. Although he carried grain for the animals, he rationed it, letting the horses forage for grass whenever possible.

Staking the horses out on a promising patch of new spring grass, he had selected several large paddies for the fire when nature demanded his attention. Leaving the paddies in a pile, he walked several yards downwind of his campsite, unlaced his breeches, dropped them around his ankles, and squatted.

The dark wall of clouds that pushed in from the north caught him in that position, still tending his business. When the first snowflakes fell, he was tearing up handfuls of grass to cleanse himself. By the time he hiked his pants back around his waist and relaced them, flakes as big as silver dollars filled the air.

Thoughts of beans and coffee forgotten, Nate gathered his horses and remounted. While he wrapped himself in a buffalo robe, he glanced about the gully that had seemed so promising but minutes ago. A rising wind had already begun to pile snow into drifts along its walls. If he remained here, he and the horses would eventually be buried by the falling blanket of snow. He did not know if there was shelter from the snowstorm to be found on the open prairie, but if there was, he had to locate it elsewhere. He tapped the bay he rode on its sides and moved out of the gulch.

Blizzard was a term Texians applied to any storm that left at least six inches of snow on the ground. A foot of snow covered the plains within an hour after Nate had left the ravine. Another six inches had been added to that when Nate sighted the wagon.

It was not the red and green medicine show wagon he sought, but one with ripped canvas flapping in the wind. It lay on its side, with the rim of a front wheel busted and spokes in its back wheels shattered. The broken-down wagon was the remnants of nameless pilgrims who had tempted to cross the prairie to reach the promised lands of the west, Nate realized. What he did not know was whether its former occupants had been defeated by the elements or Indians.

Nor did he dwell long on their fate. The overturned wagon offered shelter from the storm, one he intended to take full advantage of.

Attaching chains he found on the wagon's tongue to two packhorses, he managed to pull the wagon around so that its bottom broke the north wind. He restretched the torn canvas over the wagon's ribs as best he could. It did not keep all the snow out, but fifty percent was better than none. There was no space for the horses inside. As much as Nate would have preferred their added warmth within the shelter, he could but securely tie them outside and hope the toppled wagon dulled the wind's cutting edge.

Once inside, Nate covered himself from head to toe with buffalo robes and prayed the blizzard's fury would soon run its course.

EDGING ASIDE the robe drawn over his head, Nate peered through a rent in the canvas. Cloudless blue skies met his gaze. Warm sunlight backlit the motionless cloth. Blinking against the unexpected harshness of the light, he threw back the buffalo hide. An action that sent two inches of powder snow flying through the air.

Outside calf-deep snow covered the prairie in eye-squinting white. The white was confined to the ground. Not even a fleecy puff of a cloud drifted across the sky. By the time the sun reached its zenith, half the snow would be melted.

A smile touched the corners of Nate's mouth. The storm had come and gone—and he still lived! While he waited for the sun to do its job, he would strip enough wood from the wagon for that fire and the beans and coffee he had promised himself yesterday.

His smile faded when he turned to the horses. One of the packhorses was gone! The frayed length of rope still tied to the wagon told him all he needed to know. The horse had managed to break the rope during the night and wander away. The falling snow had obscured the animal's tracks. Nate cursed aloud, his breath coming from his mouth in a roiling mist. Without tracks he had no hint which way the missing animal had gone.

Laying aside the prospects of a hot breakfast, he saddled the bay and rose to the saddle. Finding the packhorse was more important than quieting the rumblings of his stomach.

SIXTEEN

RIDING in ever-widening circles that led away from the toppled covered wagon, Nate worked through the snow and then the icy slush that transformed the prairie into muddy muck by midday. He had all but given up any hope of finding the missing pack animal and decided to return to the wagon's shelter for the night when he saw the horse. It stood a mile to the southwest from his position, pawing the ground with a hoof as though trying to get at the grass beneath the slush.

Nate reined beside the animal and picked up its frayed lead, drawing only a disinterested look from the horse. The mud splattered on the packhorse's legs required Nate to dismount and run his hands over the animal's shins and ankles to make certain the horse hadn't been hurt during its night and day of freedom. Satisfied the horse was uninjured, he wiped his hands on the thighs of his breeches and stepped into a stirrup. As he rose back to the saddle, he saw the wagons.

Or the charred remains of what had once been wagons. A mile farther to the southwest the blackened skeletons of what had once been five wagons lay in a narrow draw between two rolling hills.

Nate tugged the bay's head toward the burned-out wagons, and tapped the horse's side with his boot heels. An uneasy churning worked in Nate's stomach when he neared the fire-blackened remains. More than burned wood littered the ground. Twelve bodies lay sprawled about the charred wreckage—the bodies of men and women alike. Clamping his eyes shut and sucking down several steadying breaths, Nate quelled the rising nausea in his gut before moving closer.

Massacre—it was a word Texians often used cheaply. Nate had once heard it employed to describe the murder of two men in the East Texas Piney Woods by four Cherokees. But as he stared at the gruesome scene presented by the dozen bodies, it was the only word that accurately encompassed the horror and repulsion he felt in viewing this wholesale butchery of human beings.

All twelve victims had been scalped, but that was only a minor mutilation of the corpses. Half the bodies, both men and women, had been stripped of their clothing and their flesh sliced time and again by relentless slashes from knife and lance. A sickening shiver shuddered through his body to settle in the pit of his stomach. These six had in all likelihood been alive when each of the wounds was inflicted. Their deaths had not come easy, but had been a lingering, hellish torment.

He saw neither lance nor arrow to indicate whether Comanche or Kiowa had fallen upon these nameless pilgrims. Warriors of both tribes wasted little. When time and situation permitted, they recovered the deadly feathered shafts they employed against their enemies for use on another day. Here in the middle of this expansive sea of grass with no fear of detection, the raiders had ample time to gather spent arrows.

While he pondered how to bury the twelve properly without either shovel or hoe to use, flecks of green and red paint on the charred ruins of the lead wagon caught his eye. Ice that had nothing to do with wintry slush spread over the prairie coursed through his veins. Immigrants to distant Oregon and California did not travel in wagons decorated so gaudily. Dread leadened every muscle in his body when he tugged on the reins and nudged the bay toward the blackened wreckage.

Slight though his ability to read might have been, Nate could still make out distinctive letters in the seared paint and varnish. In a wide arc, the top line read **Doctor Da**—a darkly scorched patch obliterated several letters—**Gordon's.** Beneath was the line **Traveling Medicine Sh**—again the flames had devoured a portion of the letters—followed by a third line that proclaimed **Potions, Elixirs, and Ointments for All Complaints and Ailments.**

Nate's lips formed a silent "no" in denial of what he read. His hands trembled, and his legs threatened to give way beneath him as he stepped from the saddle. This was the medicine show wagon he searched for. He was certain of that. How many other snake-oil salesmen would travel this far into Indian territory?

His head jerked about first to one side and then the other, searching the area around the wagons. Every body he saw was white; he had overlooked none of the dead.

Bessa? Mary? Where were they? His gaze returned to the half-burned medicine show wagon. His eyes widened in panic. Had they been trapped inside?

His head slowly shook, refusing the possibility. Yet, his hands reached out to grasp the burned boards of the wagon, ripping them away. A quavering sigh of relief rushed from his lips. Nothing—there was nothing inside except heat-exploded bottles that had once contained snake oil, or whiskey.

Closing his eyes, he sucked down several steadying breaths to subdue the quivering muscles of his body. Bessa and Mary were not here. If Mrs. Newman and the other women had been mistaken about his wife and daughter being sold—Nate doubted they had misunderstood what they had seen and heard—that meant they were in Indian hands again. *Comanche or Kiowa?*

Nate opened his eyes and once more surveyed the massacre. He found nothing—no Indian sign to identify the attackers.

A glint of metal caught his eye when his gaze shifted back to the medicine show wagon. He brushed aside the jagged-edged fragments of broken, blue-colored bottles. The metallic gleam came from a fist-sized hole burned in the floor of the wagon.

False floor. Nate's lips drew to a thin line as he remembered Mrs. Newman describing the wagon's false bottom and the jugs of whiskey and rifles it contained. The raiders who struck these wagons had been too hasty in their search and overlooked a treasured prize.

Slipping the fingers of his right hand through the hole, he yanked upward. Half the wagon's fire-weakened floor came away to reveal two dozen single-shot rifles neatly lining the wagon's hidden compartment. The weapons had completely escaped the flames. The same could not be said of a dozen earthen jugs that had shattered from the heat.

Packed beside the rifles were bundles of small lead blocks and disks and molds for casting the balls required by the rifles. He saw no casks of black powder, realizing that if there had been powder in the wagon, it would have exploded in the fire and reduced the wagon to splinters.

But rifles and lead without black powder? Nate rubbed a hand over his neck. It did not make sense. What use were rifles without powder? The weapons were useless!

Or perhaps that's exactly what these traders had hoped. With rifles and lead they could have opened a route to Kiowa and Comanche bands and assured that they would be welcomed back when they returned with powder at a later time. What they had not taken into consideration was the possibility of running head-on into a war party before they established themselves with the Indians.

Now all that was left of them and their scheme was to bury their bodies and the bodies of the others they had—

Nate forgot the thought before it was fully formed. He hefted one of the rifles and stared at it. A humorless smile lifted the corners of his mouth. The three men who had driven this wagon into the prairie had meant to trade these rifles. He could do the same—not for profit, but for a lost wife and daughter!

Four rifles at a time, he unloaded them from the wagon's wreckage and carefully secured them on the backs of his packhorses, making certain the weapons were concealed beneath the other trade goods. Although Comanches might ignore him while he rode across the plains, he doubted they would ignore rifles in plain sight.

Before remounting, he gathered the unburned portions of the wagons into a single pile. Atop this, he placed the twelve bodies and set the wood afire. Without a shovel there was no way he could dig so many graves, but he did provide a funeral pyre and a recitation of the Lord's Prayer for the nameless victims of the Indian attack.

A column of boiling black smoke rolled toward the cloudless sky when he mounted and rode westward.

WHITE MEN AND BROWN MEN called them *Yampahreekuh* or
the Eaters of Yap Root. Or they were simply lumped in with all
the other bands of their nation and called Comanches. To themselves, they were the *Nermernuh,* the True Human Beings or the
People. Of the bands of the People, the *Yampahreekuh* ranged the
farthest north and west, their domain stretching from central
Kansas on the east to the Canadian River in the south. The
Arkansas River marked the northern boundary of their lands with
the foothills of the Rocky Mountains to the west.

Those who braved the Santa Fe Trail that ran from Missouri to
New Mexico well knew the *Yampahreekuh,* and they, in turn, were
familiar with the whites who dared to cross their lands. Many of
the scalps hanging from Yap-Eater lodge poles were of men who
had not survived that long journey to Santa Fe. Like all other of
the *Nermernuh,* the *Yampahreekuh* philosophy of the universe contained no place for a man with blue-black skin the ebon hue of
midnight.

When Nate entered a *Yampahreekuh* camp of fifty tipis four days
after finding the wagons and their dead owners, he was received
as he had been in every Comanche village he had entered with
Joaquín DeRosa. He was ignored.

He anticipated the reaction, since among the Comanches only
the *Kwerhar-rehnuh* warrior Fights-Like-the-Wolf had ever spoken
directly to him or acknowledged his presence. More than anticipated, he used the Comanches' denial of the black man to arouse
their curiosity.

Upon sighting the Yap-Eater's village, he approached it without hesitating. Instead of stopping at the camp's periphery and
attempting to talk with one of the braves or draw a squaw's
attention, he rode directly through the village, leading his
packhorses behind him. His gaze remained directly ahead of him
as though the tipis and Indians who inhabited them were invisible
to his eyes.

He stopped after crossing a narrow creek along which the
village had been erected. On the bank of that stream he made his
own camp complete with fire and skillet of beans and pan of
coffee. He had made certain the savory aromas of his supper

would carry to the village on a gentle north breeze. Although he never directly looked at the Comanche village, from the corner of an eye he caught an occasional glance cast by braves and squaws alike as they came to the creek for water. That night he slept in buffalo robes beside his small fire.

Before dawn when the village woke, he rose and took three rifles and three hunting knives from the packhorses. These he placed atop a buffalo robe he spread on the ground. He then cooked a fresh pan of coffee, placed several tin cups by the fire. He sat cross-legged atop his remaining robe and waited, occasionally filling a cup and drinking.

Throughout the day a steady stream of braves found reason to stroll beside the creek. Never once did their eyes lift to Nate, but each studied the rifles and knives. When evening once more came, Nate built a fire, cooked his supper, and slept.

The following dawn greeted the Comanches, and they found Nate still beside his small fire and boiling pan of coffee. They also found the rifles and knives on the buffalo robe had increased to six each.

Throughout the morning, Nate doggedly maintained his vigil, watching the growing interest on the braves' faces as they once again found the creek to be the most interesting portion of their camp. Nate rose from the buffalo robe only when he could no longer endure the pressure of his bladder caused by the constant coffee drinking.

The noonday sun blazed overhead when a brave with strands of silver hair running through his long, dark braids crossed the creek to squat beside the fire.

"It is a clear and far-seeing day. A day that should not trouble a man of the People." The brave studied the western horizon, keeping his gaze averted from Nate. When he spoke, it was as though to himself. "On such a day why should Stealer of Many Enemy Horses, a brave who councils his people in war and peace, be troubled by the smell of coffee when he has not had such to drink since the first ice of winter?"

Nate said nothing. He picked up an empty cup from beside the fire, filled it with steaming coffee, and set it on the ground at Stealer of Many Enemy Horses' feet.

The brave bent down, picked up the cup, and took a tentative sip. He immediately jerked back and blew on the coffee for several minutes before attempting another sip. This one drew a pleased sigh from his lips. Stealer of Many Enemy Horses completely drained the cup before he spoke again, this time as though praying to the sun. "A vision of a new rifle has also filled my mind's eye this day. Why am I tempted so when I only have fine buffalo robes?"

Nate heard and understood the opening. The brave offered robes for a rifle. What Nate wanted was his wife and daughter. Yet, he had learned enough from Joaquín to know that a direct approach with Comanches would only drive them away. He had to earn the *Yampahreekuh*'s trust. That was why six of the rifles lay on the buffalo robe.

Pushing from the ground, Nate walked to his bay and carefully examined the animal. While he inspected the horse, he spoke aloud as though giving voice to his thoughts. "This is a fine mount. It has served me well, but it grows tired of my journey as do my packhorses. They are white man's animals and not the stout ponies of the People that can travel across the face of this land, living only on the grass. A lonely man such as I who searches for a wife who is like him in color should have mustangs for his journey. This horse and a rifle would be a fair trade for two strong and healthy mustangs."

Nate paused long enough for a sideways glance at Stealer of Many Enemy Horses. The Comanche's gaze remained averted, but his head was cocked to one side while he listened. Nate allowed himself the luxury of a smile; his scheme, as slow and indirect as it was, appeared to be working.

"In this vast land of the *Nermernuh* black white women are as rare as buffalo with humps like snow. Only the ponies of the True People are suited to such a search." Nate returned to his seat on the buffalo robe and refilled Stealer of Many Enemy Horses' cup. The brave now knew why Nate ventured into Comanchería, and at the same time Nate bartered for animals that thrived on prairie grass. His supplies of grain needed for his present stock grew short.

Stealer of Many Enemy Horses leisurely sipped at the coffee

while he studied the horizon and then the village across the creek. When he had drained the cup, he placed it by the fire, stood, stretched, and walked back to the camp.

Nate's spirits plummeted. That the brave was only his first attempt to reach the Comanches and the fact that others might prove successful did nothing to break the gloom that settled over him. Since leaving the burned wagons he had merely continued westward without the slightest idea who had captured Bessa and Mary or where they had been taken. He needed some shred of information, no matter how small, that would lead him to his wife and daughter.

The hollow clop of approaching hooves lifted Nate's eyes. His heart pounded, and his pulse raced. Stealer of Many Enemy Horses led two ponies, a sleek chestnut and a dappled gray, to the edge of the stream. The brave paused there a moment as though uncertain how to proceed. He then crossed the creek, let the rope leads around the horses' necks drop to the ground, and stepped away from the animals.

Following the Comanche's earlier example, Nate slowly sipped at his coffee, his eyes occasionally shifting to the offered ponies. Their confirmation was good, and they appeared well suited to his needs.

After judging enough time had passed, he rose, selected one of the rifles from the hide, then retrieved his bay. When he gathered the mustangs' leads, he left the horse and the rifle in their place.

"Were I to hunt a white buffalo this day, I would travel north to the great mountains. Two have been seen traveling that way," Stealer of Many Enemy Horses said as he lifted the rifle and walked away with the bay.

Nate smiled. The brave had told him two black women had recently been seen to the north. Were they Bessa and Mary? He could only wait and hope other braves would come to him to exchange more information for rifles.

They did. Two approached and made their barters that afternoon. The next day brought five more; and four the next until the buffalo robe lay bare. In trade Nate accumulated four mustangs, five buffalo robes, a dozen deer hides, several sacks of pemmican, and five pairs of newly sewn moccasins.

More importantly, he pieced together what had happened to the wagons he had found on the prairie. A raiding party of thirty *Yampahreekuh* Comanches of a band to the far northwest, where the People's land met the territory of the Cheyennes, had ridden south in search of horses. Led by a warrior called Rides Hard in the Night, they came upon the wagons. Having never seen black-skinned women before, the warriors took two captive, as well as five young white girls, and returned with them to their camp near the twin forks of the Arkansas River and Bent's Fort along the northern route of the Santa Fe Trail.

Nate had no idea of how far away the forks of the Arkansas River were nor where Bent's Fort lay. He did know that if he headed north he would eventually come across the river. That was enough. As night ended his fourth day camped beside the *Yampahreekuh* village, Nate loaded his packs onto the backs of his new ponies and girded saddle to the gray. He mounted and by the dark of the moon struck out for the Arkansas River.

SEVENTEEN

A TEN-POINT BUCK and four does cautiously picked their way through reed-covered marsh. Nate slowly lifted his rifle, nestled it firmly against his right shoulder, cocked the hammer, and sighted down the long barrel. He aimed behind the buck's left shoulder, holding his forefinger curled around the trigger until the deer halted, its head lifting to sniff the air, then he fired.

The buck leaped high before it dropped to the ground to stay there. Sensing danger, the does bounded away to disappear over a nearby bluff.

A satisfied smile edged across Nate's lips when he rose from the spot where he had knelt for the past half hour. Immediately he reloaded the spent rifle. A ready weapon in Comanche lands was far more important than venison.

Although, he admitted to himself, roasted back strap seemed very important to him at the moment. In the month that had passed since leaving the *Yampahreekuh* village far to the southeast, fresh meat had been a rarity. Aside from a few rabbits that had had the misfortune of crossing his path, he had kept himself alive on the pemmican he had bartered for at the camp. Nourishing though it was, the mixture of grains, dried berries and fruits, nuts, and buffalo fat was a fare that rapidly grew monotonous, no matter how healthy it was for man.

A hundred yards into the reeds, Nate found the buck. His shot had been quick and clean. The animal had died before it hit the ground.

Hefting the dead animal to his shoulders, Nate hiked a half mile downriver to where his horses stood tied beneath a gnarled oak tree. At least, he believed it to be an oak. The tree grew acorns, but its leaves were unlike the red and pin oaks he knew from the Cross Timbers. He tossed a rope over a low limb, secured one end around the buck's hind legs and hauled the animal into the air, then tied off the rope by wrapping it around the trunk. He went about the task of cleaning and dressing the animal.

The back strap he skewered on his rifle's ramrod, jammed the opposite end of the rod into the ground, and hung the venison over a campfire to roast while he cut several steaks to cook later. He tucked one of the haunches inside an empty pemmican sack and placed it on one of the packhorses. The meat hopefully would keep for two or three days. Regretfully he left the remainder of the buck's carcass on the ground for the coyotes and the wolves. There was no way he could eat the meat before it spoiled, nor was there a smokehouse in which to jerk it.

Flipping the roasting meat, Nate sat on the ground and leaned his back against a trunk. He closed his eyes and—

He jerked upright and stared about. An embarrassed smile slid across his lips. He had drifted into a light sleep. After a quick check of the meat to make certain he had not nodded long enough for it to burn, he settled back against the trunk again with a shake of his head.

Things had definitely changed since those first nights he had spent alone on the prairie. He had actually caught himself napping as though he did not have a care in the world. An attitude like that could get a man killed in this country. He tried to reprimand himself, but he paid his own advice only a perfunctory mental nod.

Whether it was the warm spring day or the savory aroma of the venison, or perhaps a combination of both, he felt good—better than he had felt since—

His frivolous thoughts stumbled. The day the *Kwerhar-rehnuh* Comanches raided his home pushed into his mind. He had not felt this way since that crisp October morning nearly nine months ago.

Lord! His mind reeled back. How far away in distance and time that morning seemed, yet in other ways it had happened but yesterday. Had he not still ached to have his family around him, he could almost believe the events of that day had happened to another man.

Nate's gaze coursed over the rolling plains that stretched from horizon to horizon. How green this land was—how rich the soil to produce such a bounty of grass. At times, after days of gentle rain, his oat field achieved this luxurious hue, but that was only on rare occasions. With a plow a man could make a good life for himself here.

For an instant he forgot where he was, and shook his head again. Since leaving the *Yampahreekuh* camp he had not seen another human being in a month. To be certain he had crossed Indian sign every day during that time, but he had not sighted one Comanche or Kiowa. It was easy to fool one's self into believing that a man was alone and free in this vast land.

A man. The phrase rolled over in his mind while he drew his knife and sliced a sampling taste of the venison. Not a slave, boy, darkie, pickaninny, *esclavo, luto,* or even a black man—but simply a man. He had never thought of himself that way before.

It's the land, he told himself while he chewed the bite of meat, and knew that he lied. He had made that mistake for more years than he wanted to think about. It had taken a Comanche attack to show him how wrong he had been in that belief. A man became a man with freedom and the chance to prove he deserved to be called a man, if only by himself and not the world.

Samson Moore had been misguided in advising him to flee east into the free states. The three months Nate had traveled the plains alone had given him the chance to prove himself. Each day in this land a man earned the right to be here. That Nate still lived in spite of Comanches, Kiowas, and the elements was all the testimony of that fact he needed.

He sliced a thick chunk of venison from the grease-dripping back strap and tore into it with his teeth. Freedom had a taste as sweet as this piece of meat. Having savored its flavor he knew he could not go back to the way it had been.

Soon as I find Miss Elizabeth, he thought, *freedom will be mine forever!*

But before he returned to the Texas high plains for Elizabeth Turner, he had to locate the camp of a warrior called Rides Hard in the Night and, hopefully, find Bessa and Mary.

Slipping the back strap from the ramrod, he skewered the steaks and placed them over the fire. Tonight, when he camped, he would eat them. Cold though they would be, cold meat was better than no meat at all.

HE SIGHTED THE TWO BRAVES an hour after he had doused the fire and resumed his westward journey. They sat astride grass-fattened mustangs atop a knoll a hundred yards to the north.

Nate's pulse quickened not because the pair were Indians, but from the fact that they were the first human beings he had seen for a month. In spite of the urge to approach them, as much to hear the sound of another voice as to question them about the warrior Rides Hard in the Night, he rode on without allowing the gray to break its stride. The braves would come to him, if it suited their purpose.

They aren't Comanche! From the corner of an eye, Nate saw the Indians rein their mounts to the right, paralleling his movement while he continued west along the Arkansas River. They were too tall and slender to be *Nermernuh.* The designs of the beadwork on their buckskin breeches were unlike any he had encountered among the Comanche bands. The breeches themselves bespoke of a strange tribe. With the warmth of spring Comanche braves shed their winter clothing, preferring to go naked with only a breechclout to cover themselves.

A cold shiver trembled up Nate's spine. If they were not Comanches, then what tribe did they claim? Were they Cheyenne or Arapaho? Stealer of Many Enemy Horses had mentioned that both tribes dwelt near the village of Rides Hard in the Night. Except in the *Yampahreekuh* village, Nate had never even heard of these tribes. How did a black-skinned man fit into their view of the world? Would he be ignored as with the Comanches or was a Negro scalp considered a prize trophy to hang from a lodge pole among these unknown tribes?

The possibility of sudden attack rode at the forefront of Nate's mind while he constantly watched the two braves at the periphery of his vision. Keeping pace with his mount, they maintained a hundred yards' distance, never allowing their ponies to edge ahead of or behind him. Nor did they speak or signal with their hands and arms to draw his attention.

For an hour they stayed with him. Then as silently as they had appeared, they tugged their mustangs' heads to the right and rode northward. Nate allowed himself a relieved sigh fifteen minutes later when he again sighted the braves, no more than black dots in the distance continuing their northward ride across the open prairie.

Although the braves had disappeared that did not rule out the possibility that they might return, perhaps with others of their band. Clucking his mount into a faster pace, Nate moved the packhorses into the shallow water near the river's bank. He had no intention of leaving an easy trail should the two decide to pay him another unexpected visit.

THE LINE OF TREES marked a feeder creek that flowed into the Arkansas River. Keeping his mount and packhorses in the shallows, Nate moved two miles up the creek before selecting a patch of grass among the willows and poplars for a night camp. His hope was that if the two braves he had sighted earlier did return and decide to search for him upriver they would never consider he had detoured so far from the Arkansas to camp.

He unloaded the pack animals and hobbled their forelegs. Well acquainted with the nightly routine, the horses dipped their heads to the thick, green grass and began to graze. The gray Nate left saddled and bridled, although he did hobble the animal's legs. The precaution was simple. Yet, should he have need for quick flight during the night, all he had to do was sever the hobble thong, swing into the saddle, and ride. Packhorses, trade goods, and supplies rapidly depreciated in value when a man was faced with the choice of losing them or his own life.

While the last reds of sunset faded to deep purples, Nate spread a buffalo robe beneath a poplar and sat atop the hide. He silenced the rumbling protests of his belly with the two cold venison steaks, washing the meat down with fresh, cool water from the stream. The frosty light of a moon two days away from full brightened the eastern horizon when he stretched out on the robe and folded an arm beneath his head for a pillow. The day had been long and the ride tiring. Not even his worries about the two strange braves could keep back sleep.

The scream, however, shattered it!

Nate bolted upright; his head jerked from side to side searching the moonlit night while his hand found the Colt Texas tucked in his belt and thumbed back the hammer. Nothing! A frown creased his forehead. Had the cry been an imagined fragment of a forgotten dream—the yowl of a nearby coyote?

His gaze lifted to the sky as he sucked down a series of deep breaths to quell the pounding of his heart. The moon hung halfway to the meridian. He had been asleep for two or three hours. Easing the pistol's hammer down, he cocked his head first to the left and then to the right. Still there was nothing. A smile that began at the corners of his mouth died before it was fully born.

The silence surrounding him was unnatural. Strain as he did, he heard nothing—no chirping insects, no cries of night predators on wing above the prairie. Something was wrong—terribly—

A second scream confirmed the half-formed thought. No echoing of a forgotten dream was this, or the high-pitched, yipping howl of a coyote. The scream was human, the tormented cry of a woman, or perhaps a child.

Colt clutched in hand, Nate pushed from the buffalo robe. Another scream rent the night. His head jerked around; his eyes searched the night for the source of the anguished sound.

To the north a glowing dome of orange, its intensity dulled by the gibbous moon, was visible through the trees. It came a quarter of a mile from his position where a sharp bend in the creek abruptly turned westward.

A campfire! Nate blinked, unable to accept what his eyes perceived. No sane man would strike a fire at night this deep in Indian Territory. Only an—

His thoughts stumbled over the realization of who had set the small blaze. Yet another bloodcurdling scream gave the fire its purpose. The Indians who had lit the flames used their light to torture a captive enemy.

Trembling with a sudden weakness, Nate settled cross-legged atop the buffalo robe. He swallowed hard, steeling himself against another wretched cry that brimmed with pain. What Indians did to one another was no concern of his. Comanche, Arapaho, Cheyenne—they could wipe each other off the face of this earth and he would feel no twinge of guilt. Bad luck had perched on his shoulder when he had chosen this spot for a camp. While the Indians, whatever tribe they might be, were occupied with their bloody pastime, he should gather his animals and goods and move on before they accidentally stumbled on him and decided to add another victim to their night of grisly entertainment.

Once more a scream sliced the night's unnatural silence. Nate's lips drew back in a tight thin line. The anguished wail was too high-pitched for that of a brave. It belonged to a squaw or a child, of that he was certain. An image of Bessa and Mary fighting against red-skinned tormenters thrust into his mind. He knew the vision was irrational, but he could not escape it. He neared the land of Rides Hard in the Night's band. As farfetched as it seemed, there was a possibility that his wife or daughter was the victim whose screams filled the night.

Shoving from the buffalo hide a second time, Nate reached out and snatched up his rifle. With Colt in one hand and longrifle in the other, he crept toward the orange glow of the fire.

A hundred yards separated him from the small blaze when he

first discerned the silhouetted forms of four braves moving back and forth in front of the flames. The object of their torments lay on the ground.

Nate crept forward another seventy-five yards before he could see that the object was in fact two young Comanche boys stretched spread-eagle atop the grass, their arms and legs bound with rawhide to wooden stakes driven into the ground. The beadwork on the braves' buckskins was the same as on the two riders Nate had sighted during the day.

Closing his eyes, Nate turned his back on the scene. The boys were not Bessa or Mary. How or why the two had fallen into these braves' hands meant nothing to him. A man intent on keeping his hair knew when to leave well enough alone.

New screams echoed along the creek. Nate swung around, eyes narrowing as he stared back to the fire. The cries came from the boy nearest Nate's position behind the trunk of a willow. Two of the braves bent over him, drawing crosshatch patterns in his bare chest with the tips of their hunting knives.

The other boy was beyond screaming. His body, carved to a bloody pulp, was still. The braves' blades had ended his torture, and his life, with a final cut that had opened his throat from ear to ear.

It was the delighted chuckles that came from deep within the braves' throats that decided Nate. The four took too much pleasure from the anguish they carved with their knives. Indian boy or not, they tortured a child!

Nate came from behind the tree in a full run. The cry of horror and disgust that bellowed from his chest and throat was drowned in the thunder of ignited black powder as he squeezed the rifle's trigger.

The shot meant to frighten the four had a greater effect. One of the braves hovering over the boy jerked rigid, spun halfway around, then toppled to the ground, his body twitching spasmodically.

The three remaining braves swirled to face the unexpected attack. Their eyes were wide as they darted about with uncertainty.

Nate took full advantage of the Indians' confusion. Dropping the rifle to the ground, Nate passed the Texas from his left hand to right. His thumb tugged back the hammer. The guardless trigger dropped from the pistol. He held the weapon at arm's length, took a bead on the nearest of the braves, and fired.

The shot struck the brave in the center of his chest, the impact throwing him to the ground never to rise again.

With two of their number dead, the thought of making a stand fled the remaining two braves' minds. Spinning on the balls of their feet, they turned and ran toward four horses tied to a willow.

Nate's next two shots went wild, but his fourth caught a third brave between the shoulder blades just as he reached a chestnut pony. Like the two before him, he fell as death claimed him.

The last of the Indians managed to swing astride a painted mount, jerk the animal's head around, and spur to the north.

Once more the Colt thundered as Nate fired at the fleeing brave. The shot missed its target. Cursing, Nate stood and watched the lone brave disappear into the night. He had meant to make four clean kills. Now he had to move quickly if he wanted to keep his scalp attached to his head. The escaped brave was certain to return to his village and bring others to avenge the deaths of his three companions.

Curses that reprimanded himself for letting emotion overcome reason spewed from Nate's mouth when he tucked the spent pistol under his belt and walked into the fire's light. The young Comanche boy's eyes were saucer-round when they watched Nate free a hunting knife from its sheath. A frightened whimper pushed from the boy's lips as Nate stepped toward him, then the boy passed out.

Nate blinked and stared at the child, uncertain what had occurred. He placed a palm on the boy's chest and felt the throb of his heart. The young Comanche still lived and at the moment that was all that mattered; he could tend the child's wounds later when they were safely away from this place. Severing the rawhide binding the boy's wrists and ankles, Nate lifted the child from the ground and started back to his camp.

EIGHTEEN

NATE LIGHTLY TUGGED on the reins easing the gray to a gentle halt. The sleeping Indian boy he had held securely nestled between himself and the saddlehorn throughout the long ride moaned softly, but did not wake.

Edging back the brim of his hat, Nate looked overhead. The sun neared the zenith. He closed his eyes and released a weary sigh. As much as he wanted to continue westward, he and the horses needed rest, if only for an hour or two before pushing on again.

With a glance over a shoulder to assure himself that no one rode on his tail, he nudged the gray's sides with his heels, moving the horse from the river's shallows to a broad patch of shade beneath a willow. Carefully dismounting, he eased the buffalo robe-bundled Comanche child into his arms. Another moan escaped the boy's lips when Nate placed him on a bed of green grass, yet the child's sleep remain unbroken.

A smile rode at the corners of Nate's mouth when he rose from the boy's side to gather fallen twigs and branches for a small fire. He had forgotten how deeply children slept. This young Comanche was no different from his own children. The world might be crumbling around them, yet they would sleep unaware of anything but their own dreams, trusting all would be right when they woke.

From one of the packhorses he took a pan, poured in a measure of coffee, then filled it with water from a canteen before setting the pan on the flames. Leaving the fire to do its work, he led the horses, including the three new additions to the growing remuda gathered from the three braves he had killed last night, fifty feet north of the willow and staked them out in ankle-high grass. An hour or two of grazing would not make up for the rest they had been robbed of last night, but for the time being, it would have to do.

Nate's gaze shifted to another buffalo robe bundle lashed to the back of one of the new ponies while he retrieved a tin cup and the venison haunch from the packhorses. There had not been time last night to bury the young Comanche wrapped in the shaggy hide. He silently promised himself that when he was certain he had put enough distance between himself and possible reprisal from the brave who had gotten away last night, he would see that the dead child received a proper burial. Until then, the best he could do was to keep the boy's body away from the coyotes and wolves.

Returning to the fire, Nate seated himself cross-legged on the ground on the opposite side of the flames from the young Comanche he had managed to rescue. The boy still rested deep in sleep. While Nate watched the child out of a corner of an eye, he sliced a half-dozen strips of meat from the haunch, skewered them on his rifle's ramrod, then hung them over the fire. Within moments the venison began to sizzle as the heat brought dripping juices and fat to the meat's surface.

The rich aroma of roasting venison that wafted in the air elicited a demanding rumble from Nate's stomach. To quiet the noisy protest, he filled the cup with steaming coffee from the boiling pan. After blowing over the cup, he took a tentative sip, scalded his tongue and the roof of his mouth, and continued blowing over the surface of the dark-colored brew.

Across the fire, the Comanche youth rolled from his back to a side. The movement brought a pained groan; the boy's eyes flew open. Dark in hue and wide with fear, those eyes darted from one side to the other, eventually locking on Nate.

"It is all right," Nate spoke in the child's own tongue. "It is all over, and you are all right."

"Real?" The fear on the boy's face remained—the same expression Nate had seen last night before the child had slipped into unconsciousness. "You are real?"

"Real as this fine day," Nate answered with a nod.

"And you are a man." The fear faded, replaced by disbelief.

Nate smiled with the realization that the child had fainted last night, not because of the braves who had tortured him, but because of the black-skinned man who sought to free him. "Yes, I am a man. What else would I be?"

The boy's chest rose and fell as a whisper-soft sigh passed over his lips. "I was not certain. I have never seen a man with the skin the shade of a moonless midnight—"

"And when I came running out of the trees last night, ahowling and ascreaming, you thought I was some kind of demon from hell." Nate's smile grew. Living this far west, a *Yampahreekuh*, especially one as young as this boy, was not too likely to run into many black men.

The young Comanche nodded to confirm Nate's words.

"Well, there is nothing to fear. I am a man and no hell-spawned devil."

"I can see that." The boy's reply held a hint of indignation. "I am not ignorant of the world. I have seen a black white woman before. In truth, there is one in my village. She sleeps in the tipi of an old, wrinkled brave called Losing His Teeth."

Nate's heart pounded against his rib cage. *Bessa!* There was a black woman in this child's village! This far away from the white man's settlements that woman could only be his Bessa. *Or Mary!* Nate held a tight rein on the hundred questions that thrust themselves into his head. The boy was speaking openly now, as uncharacteristic of a Comanche as that was. To pelt him with a barrage of questions would arouse his suspicions and drive him to silence. For now it was enough to know that in all likelihood this boy's band was the one Nate sought.

"The Cheyenne dogs would have killed me last night as they did Runs Like a Deer, but you killed three of them and saved me," the boy said. "Why?"

The suspicion Nate feared hung in the child's voice. "You are *Nermernuh* and they were Cheyenne." Nate made no mention of the fact that he had no idea that the four braves had been Cheyenne until the boy mentioned it. "My regret is that I did not arrive soon enough to save the one you called Runs Like a Deer." Nate glanced at the pony bearing the buffalo robe-concealed burden.

The young Comanche's eyes followed Nate's gaze. For several moments he sat silently and stared at the grazing horse. Eventually he nodded in acceptance of Nate's explanation of the rescue. "And now what do you intend to do with me, *to-oh tivo?*"

"While I am a black white man, I also have a name. It is Nate." Nate took a sip of the cooled coffee. "As to what I am going to do with you—first I shall feed you some of this venison. Second I will take a look at your wounds and clean them if needed, and then I will take you to your people."

Nate could see flickering doubt in the boy's dark eyes, but the aroma of the roasting meat won out. "And coffee? Will you give me coffee, too?"

"And coffee," Nate answered when he pushed from the ground and retrieved another cup and two tin plates from one of the packs. He filled the cup with coffee first and passed it to the young boy, then divided the cooked meat with the child. "How are you called?"

"Brother to the Coyote," the boy replied around a mouthful of venison.

"Brother to the Coyote," Nate repeated. "It is a good name. The coyote is a friend to the People."

The boy said nothing while he wolfed his way through two strips of the meat and washed them down with hot coffee. If the latter scalded his mouth Nate could see no indication on his face. He did notice Brother to the Coyote wince several times when he shifted about trying to get comfortable. The wounds the Cheyennes had sliced into his chest had been designed to deliver pain not death. Although Nate had cleaned and doctored the cuts as best he could last night, there was no way to lessen the pain and stiffness of healing injuries.

Chewing on a venison strip, Nate slid the two remaining slices of his portion onto Brother to the Coyote's plate. He then unsheathed his hunting knife again, cut the rest of the haunch into strips and hung them over the fire.

"What I don't understand is how the Cheyennes came to capture two boys like you and Runs Like the Deer," Nate said while he took another sip of coffee.

"I am not a *boy!*" Indignation crept back into Brother to the Coyote's tone. "I am a warrior of the *Nermernuh* as was Runs Like a Deer. Had we not been tending our uncles' ponies when the

Cheyennes attacked our village, the Cheyenne mongrels would have learned that."

Brother to the Coyote spewed forth a string of curses detailing the Cheyennes' mating habits that would have brought a blush of embarrassed red to the cheeks of most grown men had they been able to understand the Comanche tongue. Nate listened silently, waiting for the vehement verbal tirade to pass and for the boy to describe the Cheyenne raid on his village.

"A buffalo herd was sighted an hour's ride from our tipis two mornings ago. The braves mounted their mustangs and rode to the hunt," Brother to the Coyote said. "Runs Like a Deer and I had just reached the grazing horses when the Cheyenne dogs attacked, riding in from the east. There were twenty of them in all and they came directly for the ponies, fearing to attack the village and the braves they thought were there—being cowards like all Cheyennes."

That was all the boy said, but it was enough for Nate to piece together what had happened during the raid. The Cheyenne attackers had come for mustangs. It had been Brother to the Coyote's and Runs Like the Deer's misfortune to be assigned the task of watching over the stock that morning. They had been taken captive by the raiders. Within the village there had been only the very old and the very young, the rest of the *Yampahreekuh,* young squaws included, had ridden to the buffalo hunt. There had been no one in the village to ride after the Cheyennes either to steal back the ponies or rescue the two boys. The price Runs Like the Deer had paid for the Comanche custom of leaving a village unguarded while braves hunted buffalo had been far higher than stolen mustangs.

Given that a full day had passed before the Cheyennes felt safe enough to stop and torture their prisoners, Nate estimated the fleeing raiders had ridden at least forty miles from the village. Nate's head snapped up as he completed some quick mental ciphers. "We're not that far from your village!"

Brother to the Coyote glanced up from the last of five strips of venison and looked around as though noticing his surroundings for the first time. "The river forks like a snake's tongue beyond those hills to the west. The smoke from my village's tipis can be seen to the south from there."

Nate's face lifted to the rolling hills a quarter of a mile from the willow under which he sat. "And in your village is a warrior who is named Rides Hard in the Night."

Brother to the Coyote stared at the ebon-skinned man. "How did you know that?"

"It doesn't matter." Nate shook his head. There was not time for him to explain about another *Yampahreekuh* and a brave called Stealer of Many Enemy Horses and a promise he would find the women he sought among a band who camped near the fork of the Arkansas River.

Pushing from the ground, Nate wiped the grease from his fingertips on the thighs of his breeches. "Finish your meal quickly. It is time to take you back to your people."

NINETEEN

NATE SIGHTED THE BRAVE ten miles from the *Yampahreekuh* village. Like a living shadow the breechclout-clad Comanche reined a sorrel pony fifty yards to Nate's left and fell in beside the black man and the string of horses he led. The warrior held a feather-adorned war lance in his right hand. However, the flint tip pointed skyward and did not dip to menace the unexpected intruder into the lands of the Yap-Eaters.

Nate carefully kept his own hands in plain sight, far away from either the rifle slung about the saddlehorn or the Colt Texas tucked beneath his belt. Having come this far and with the gray columns of smoke rising from the *Yampahreekuh* tipis now clearly visible, the last thing he wanted was for some innocent gesture to be mistakenly interpreted as a threat that would cost him his life.

Brother to the Coyote, who still rode wrapped in the buffalo robe with Nate astride the gray, glanced at the brave. Recognition flashed in the boy's dark eyes. However, the child said nothing.

Nate followed the young Comanche's lead and kept silent, neither speaking nor hailing the brave with sign.

Five minutes after he appeared, the brave abruptly yanked on a single-rein hackamore and swung his mount's head to the left. Digging his moccasined heels into the sorrel's sides, the Comanche urged the pony up a slope of a grassy rise, galloped over the crest, and disappeared behind the hill.

Another five minutes passed before the warrior reappeared—accompanied by five mounted companions. Nate was fully aware of the lances and bows the braves carried, but he also noted that none of the six wore the red and black paints of war smeared on their faces. He sucked in a steadying breath and slowly released it while the warriors divided into two equal groups. Three to each side of him they rode, neither looking directly at nor speaking to the man they ushered toward the village.

With such an impressive escort, Nate was not certain what reception to expect among the *Yampahreekuh*. What he was not prepared for was every brave, squaw, and child within the eighty-tipi camp to abandon their tasks and crowd around him and his stock and stare silently up at him.

"Friends—" Nate's arms lifted so that his hands could repeat the words that came from his lips— "I have come in peace. I bring with me . . ."

Both his voice and fingers fell silent. To his right the braves and squaws parted. A lone warrior, tall for a Comanche, yet at least two inches shorter than Nate's own six feet, approached. His dark eyes shifted between Nate and Brother to the Coyote. Without uttering a sound, the brave walked directly to the gray's side. He held up his arms, and Brother to the Coyote went to him. Still no word, muttered or spoken directly to Nate, passed the Comanche's lips while he tightly hugged the child to his bare chest, turned, and walked away.

As though the brave's action were some silent signal to the rest of the band, the crowd about Nate dispersed. Each brave, squaw, and child returned to the activities they had forsaken but minutes before.

"That's it?" Nate muttered his disbelief in English. Anger and bewilderment roiled in his breast. Unable to contain the mounting frustration, he shouted, "I kilt three Cheyennes to save that boy, and that's all any of you got to say to me? Not so much as a 'thank you' or a 'go to hell'?"

The outburst echoed through the camp. Not one Comanche turned his head or glanced at the black white man who had returned a lost child to the band.

"I come here for a purpose!" Reason told him that the *Yampahreekuh* treated him no differently from the way he had been received in other Comanche villages. He was a man who walked without a soul; he held no place in the world as viewed through the eyes of the *Nermernuh*. Reason did not contain the rage that seethed within him while he watched the brave, Brother to the Coyote still in his arms, disappear into a tipi. "I didn't ride all this way for my health. I got business here, damn you! I got to talk with you—any of you!"

That he spewed his frustration in English did not occur to him. What he saw was a young brave and squaw approach in answer to his cries for help. Although the rugged Comanche way of life lined their faces such as middle age might carve wrinkles into the countenances of civilized men, Nate judged their years at no more than two score. They came toward him without speaking. Their eyes were lifted, and they stared directly at him.

"It is good that you hear my . . ." Nate's Comanche trailed off.

The couple walked past him, their gazes still locked straight ahead.

It was not him they walked to, Nate realized when the couple stopped beside the buffalo robe-burdened Cheyenne pony. These were Runs Like the Deer's father and mother come to claim the body of their murdered son. Silently he watched while the brave untied the ropes and lifted the hide bundle in his arms. As the two had approached, they left, except for the tears now welling in their dark eyes.

Nate's body slumped in defeat as the anger that had raged within him but seconds ago escaped like air through a rent in a bellows. He was a black man, and they were Comanches—that was the way of things. Curses and shouts would change nothing. He had dealt with *Yampahreekuh* on his own before. He could do it

again. It was simply a matter of making them recognize him
without openly displaying that recognition.

"Nate!"

He snapped straight in the saddle. *Bessa!* His head jerked to the
left and right. The voice that called to him was unmistakable—
Bessa. She was here in the village as he had suspected.

There! His temples pounded wildly.

On the southern edge of the village, a brave grabbed the shoulders of a squaw—a black-skinned squaw—and spun her around.
With an upraised hand he cuffed the side of her head. When she
cringed away from another blow, he cursed and used both arms
to shove her into a tipi. The brave cast a hasty glance in Nate's
direction, then darted into the tipi after the woman.

Bessa! Nate's right hand snaked toward the rifle slung from the
saddlehorn. His arm froze when his fingertips brushed the weapon's wooden stock. *What am I doing?* An icy spike of fear drove
into his spine. He snatched his hand away from the rifle as though
the weapon had just been taken from a forge and glowed cherry
with heat. He had come to rescue his wife, not to get the both of
them killed. He had to use his head to achieve that. Not black
powder and lead.

How? His mind went blank except for the image of the Comanche brave striking Bessa and thrusting her into the tipi. *Think!* He
drew three long breaths and exhaled them to calm himself. Bessa's image remained in his mind, but his Bessa, not the squaw-
clad woman he had just glimpsed. If he wanted *that* Bessa back, he
had to clear his mind and think.

These were Comanches. His gaze roved over the village. Not
one brave or squaw in sight appeared to notice him. A direct
approach with these people would never work, not from a man
they viewed as a soulless entity wandering this earth. He had to
deal with this band the same way he had with Stealer of Many
Enemy Horses' village back on the Kansas prairie.

Nate's gaze returned to the tipi Bessa and the brave—Losing
His Teeth, he recalled the name of the old brave Brother to the
Coyote said kept a black woman in his lodge—had disappeared
within. Twenty feet from the front of the tipi three rotund squaws
busied themselves with a smoke-blackened kettle that bubbled

and steamed over a cooking fire. Although a dozen other cooking fires burned within the village, none of them was better situated for Nate's purpose. With Stealer of Many Enemy Horses' band, he had camped outside the Comanche village, here he would set up housekeeping right on Losing His Teeth's door stoop.

Reining the gray beside the fire, Nate dismounted. Imitating the *Yampahreekuh,* he ignored the three squaws while he unsaddled and removed the packs from his horses.

"Bessa, I know you can't answer me now. Don't even try to," he spoke aloud as he prepared a pan of coffee, setting it beside the fire over which the squaws cooked their evening meal. "I just want you to know that you're the reason I'm here, and that I ain't leaving without you. It might take me some time to get you out of that tipi, but I will. One way or the other, I will. I promise you that."

There was no answer, but he did not expect or want one. He spoke only to reassure Bessa that he had heard and seen her, and that when he left, it would be with her by his side.

His stock unloaded, he led the horses to the village's edge and hobbled them so that they could graze until he was ready to ride from camp. He then returned to the community fire outside Losing His Teeth's tipi. Spreading a blanket on the ground, his buffalo robes having gone with the two boys he had returned to the village, he settled beside the flames. He caught an occasional sideways glance from the three plump squaws, but other than that they continued to act as though he did not exist. Nate paid them little heed; his actions were meant to draw the attention of one Comanche alone—the old brave who hid within the tipi with Bessa.

"I've been lookin' for you and Mary ever since the day them *Kwerhar-rehnuh* hit our place." Nate faced the tipi's flap and spoke while he pulled the strips of venison he had cooked earlier that day from a saddlebag. "I found Eve. I don't know if you know that or not. But I found her and took her back home after trading a mule to a band of old *Tahneemuhs* for her. Ben's been takin' care of her and Daniel while I've been looking for you. We done ourselves proud with Ben. You know that, Bessa. He's grown into a fine young man."

While he worked his way through six strips of cold venison and three cups of steaming coffee, he continued to talk. He told his wife of all that had happened since the raid along the Brazos—of Harlan Crouch and Joaquín DeRosa and how he and Joaquín had freed the other women from the Kiowas in Kansas.

"It was them womenfolk that told me about you and Mary bein' sold to them men with the medicine show wagon. I found its trail and followed it west."

Twice he saw a single finger poke out of the tipi's flap and edge the hide back. Although he could not see into the tipi, Nate could well imagine Losing His Teeth peering out at the black madman who had camped on his doorstep. Nate repressed the smile that tried to rise at the corners of his mouth. There would be time enough for smiles later—when Bessa and he rode away from this village. For now it was enough to know that he was getting to the old brave.

"I found them *Yampahreekuh* who raided the medicine show wagon and them other wagons. It was them that told me you and Mary had been traded to Comanches way out here near the Rockies."

By the time he had concluded his tale with recounting Brother to the Coyote's rescue from the Cheyennes, night cloaked the plains. The cooking fires no longer blazed, but glowed a dim red as their embers gradually faded and winked out. The *Yampahreekuh* village slept.

Nate poured the last of the coffee from the pan into his cup. Wrapping the blanket about his shoulders to fend off the high country chill in the air, he lifted the tin cup to his lips and sipped. Tonight there would be no sleep for him, not while there was the chance that Losing His Teeth might try to slip off in the night, taking Bessa with him. He intended to spend all of the night keeping an eye on the tipi that stood before him.

THE VILLAGE awoke with the dawn. Bleary-eyed braves and squaws shuffled from their tipis to slide their breechclouts to the side or hike their buckskin skirts and squat in the dirt to relieve themselves. A bladder swollen from three pans of coffee consumed through the long night was the only argument needed to convince Nate to ignore conventional modesty, unlace his breeches, and adapt to the Comanche way. From all the attention his actions received, his proper, although brief, hesitancy had been a waste of time. The Comanches still ignored his presence in their village.

After tossing several buffalo chips atop the fire he had kept burning throughout the night, Nate prepared another pan of coffee and settled back on the ground to stare at the tipi. Neither Bessa nor Losing His Teeth came outside. As much as he prayed for the old brave's kidneys to fail him, Nate's prayers went unanswered, and Losing His Teeth remained inside throughout the morning.

Nor did the morning bring a change in the *Yampahreekuh* attitude toward Nate. The band's members went about their daily routines without a glance or a grunt to acknowledge his existence. The three squaws who had used the fire when Nate had first made his camp, returned with their black kettle to prepare another thick stew from hunks of buffalo meat, tubers, wild grains, and dried red peppers.

The latter ingredient came from trade with Comancheros, Nate realized, a fact that did not hinder him from dipping his empty coffee cup into the boiling concoction to retrieve his breakfast.

Although the three women made no attempt to stop him from sampling the meal they cooked, the squaw nearest him tightened her grip on a sharp pointed stick she used to occasionally test the stew's meat. Her lips drew back in a thin determined line as though to warn silently that Nate could push his nonentity status among the Comanches just so far before she drew the line and used the stick to skewer more than the chunks of buffalo meat floating in the kettle.

Fully understanding the woman's glowing white knuckles, Nate limited his breakfast to a single cupful of stew. To salve away any hard feelings, he poured a ration of coffee into an empty earthen bowl on the ground beside the squaw. Although the woman never looked directly at Nate or the coffee, he did notice that her grip on the stick immediately relaxed—a signal that the trade was acceptable.

Not until the noonday sun rode high in the sky did other members of the village venture close to Nate's position. These were two braves. Nate recognized the taller as the warrior who had taken Brother to the Coyote from the saddle yesterday afternoon. The second Nate had never seen before. However, it did not take long for him to learn the *Yampahreekuhs'* identities.

Standing beside the now dead fire, the taller spoke first in a loud voice to make certain he was heard by more than the brave at his side. "My brother Spotted Pony, I have been robbed of sleep. As uncle to your son Brother to the Coyote, my mind and soul are troubled."

A pleased smile slid across Nate's lips. Time had come for the Comanches to make contact—in their own manner. The shorter of the two Comanches was Brother to the Coyote's father and the taller his uncle. It was *Nermernuh* custom to place a maturing son in an uncle's care to see that the boy received proper training in all that was required for a boy to become a man.

"And what is it that troubles you, Long Walker?" Spotted Pony asked in a voice equally as loud as his brother's.

His gaze never shifting to stare at the two braves, Nate listened while Long Walker replied, "Our son, Brother to the Coyote, was returned to us yesterday. He has told me of a black white man who killed three of our enemies the Cheyennes to rescue him. It is known to all the People that a black white man is not truly a man and could not possibly have done these deeds. Yet, Brother to the Coyote tells of the great bravery shown by this soulless one."

Long Walker fell silent for several minutes and stood motionless except for the fingers of his right hand, which crept beneath his breechclout and scratched.

Eventually Spotted Pony spoke again. "I see your problem, my brother. One with so much courage should be rewarded for his acts. But how can the People reward one who does not truly exist in this world?"

"Or speak to him if such a soulless man did exist?" Long Walker added with an exaggerated shake of his head. "It is a dilemma that hurts the head and robs a brave of rest."

Spotted Pony nodded and pursed his lips. "I would not desire to have this burden."

"Nor would I wish my troubles on you," Long Walker said. "It is advice I seek. In what manner would you remedy this situation, if you stood where I stand?"

Again the two braves fell silent for long, heavy minutes. It was Spotted Pony who broke the silence after giving his head a wag to emphasize his inability to aid his brother. "I have no advice. But were this my burden, I would listen to the wind. Perhaps it carries an answer in its song."

Spotted Pony and Long Walker had given Nate the means by which to speak to them. Quietly Nate sat and stared at Losing His Teeth's tipi and waited. When the first breeze stirred the air he began to sing. There was little or no tune to his song, merely a fluctuation of his voice that slid between a grinding bass and a high-pitched whine. The tune, or lack of it, was unimportant.

What mattered were his words. As he had spoken to Bessa yesterday, now he sang in Comanche of his long journey in search of a lost wife and daughter, of how he had eventually come to the fork of the Arkansas River, only to find his wife in the tipi of an aging brave who would soon only have his gums with which to chew his food.

"It is my wish to have my wife returned to me and to be told how I may find my daughter," Nate concluded his hour-long song.

For another fifteen minutes Long Walker and Spotted Pony stood by the cold fire without speaking, then the two turned and walked away.

Two hours passed before Spotted Pony and Long Walker returned—not to the campfire, but to Losing His Teeth's tipi. They came leading seven mustangs and carrying three blankets and two buffalo robes in their arms. Four times they called out before Losing His Teeth opened the tipi's flap and stepped outside.

The old brave, his weathered face lined with crevice-deep wrinkles, suspiciously eyed the two younger men, his gaze occasionally darting to the black man who sat at the entrance to his tipi. From his dour expression, Nate was certain the ancient

Yampahreekuh had overheard every word that had passed between Spotted Pony, Long Walker, and himself.

"We have come seeking a solution to a problem that troubles my brother," Spotted Pony spoke. "The wind has spoken to us. It has whispered your name, saying that only the brave the People once called Knife with Two Edges could lead us to that solution."

Losing His Teeth's chest expanded when Spotted Pony mentioned the name that had once honored him. A slight smile slid back his leather lips to reveal the snaggled teeth that were responsible for his present name. "Solutions to problems are not easy to come by. Many bowls of tobacco should be smoked, but my tobacco pouch has been empty for two passings of the time of ice and snow."

"I have brought tobacco enough for us." Spotted Pony handed the old brave a bulging pouch. "Within is tobacco to bring visions for many comings and goings of the moon."

Losing His Teeth's smile faded while he studied the beadworked pouch; his sour expression returned. Whether or not he possessed tobacco within the tipi, Nate could not say. But he sensed the old warrior had used a lack of tobacco as an excuse to keep the younger braves out of his lodge. Now there was no reason for Losing His Teeth not to invite Long Walker and Spotted Pony inside.

"Come"—Losing His Teeth nodded while he held open the flap to his tipi— "we will share a pipe and talk."

Nate tried to see within the hide tent, but glimpsed only darkness. He spoke aloud again. "Bessa, nows the time to be sayin' your prayers. The two young braves have come to barter your freedom for me."

He knew nothing else to say. Cocking his head from one side to the other, he strained to hear what was said within the tipi while he whispered his own prayer. Now and then he caught a word or a phrase. Neither was enough for him to piece together what passed between the three *Yampahreekuh*. All he could do was close his eyes and trust to the one to whom he prayed—and to the father and uncle of Brother to the Coyote.

THE SUN sat a hand's length from the western horizon when Nate's eyes opened. His pulse quickened. Someone stirred within the tipi. A moment later Long Walker stepped outside, stretched and rubbed at his eyes. For a moment, just the briefest of moments, his gaze met Nate's, then he looked at the seven mustangs tied beside the tipi.

"You are good mounts that my brother has taken from our enemies," he spoke to the horses. "You are a fair price for having Brother to the Coyote returned to us."

Nate's heart leaped. A bargain had been struck. The gifts of horses and blankets Spotted Pony and Long Walker had brought were acceptable to the old brave!

Losing His Teeth pushed the tipi's flap aside and stepped outside. He walked to the mustangs, took the animals' rope leads, and led them away.

Nate pushed to his feet when the leather flap moved aside again. Spotted Pony walked out, and behind him came Bessa. She hesitated when her gaze alighted on her husband, uncertainty furrowing her brow.

"Bessa." The name came from Nate's lips in a reverent whisper. Then a smile moved across his face growing to a beaming grin of unashamed joy. He threw his arms open wide. "Bessa!"

The doubt, the hesitancy vanished. Tears rolled down Bessa's cheeks when she ran to him, her own arms wide. "Nate, my sweet Lord, Nate! It's you! Beautiful Jesus, it's really you! I didn't think I'd ever see you again. I thought that we'd both be dead and in the ground before we ever—"

"Shhhh," he gently hushed her while he gathered her close, tears streaming down his own cheeks, and showered her face with kisses. "It's all over now. I've come for you. I've come to take you home again."

The soft shuffle of moccasins edged back his elation. Spotted Pony and Long Walker moved away and strode into the village. For a moment Nate had forgotten that he was among the *Yampahreekuh.* A man could lose his life by such an oversight.

"Bessa"—he eased his wife from his embrace—"we got to be movin' on 'fore one of these bucks decides I ain't got no right to you. You understand? We got to get out of here and put some distance between this village and ourselves."

Bessa nodded. "I understand. Take me away from here, Nate. Take me home."

"That's just what I mean to do." He grinned and lightly kissed her lips one last time before he turned to the task at hand.

As quickly as he could without displaying the fear and dread that filled his chest, he saddled the gray and threw the packs onto the backs of the other animals. He helped Bessa onto the gray, then climbed astride the back of a strawberry roan he had taken from the Cheyennes. When he clucked the horses forward, he reached out and took Bessa's hand. Eastward, away from the Yap-Eaters' village they rode hand in hand. Time and again, he glanced over a shoulder. None of the Comanches followed them.

TWENTY

NATE MOANED SOFTLY in protest when Bessa edged back the blanket and started to roll away from his side. His arms tightened around her waist, drawing her close so that she pressed warmly against the length of his body. He nuzzled her neck, his lips lightly kissing an ear.

"Nate Wagoner, what's got into you?" There was no irritation in her whisper. Her tone was somewhere between a delighted girlish giggle and a womanly purr of contentment. "You're actin' like a young buck in spring!"

"Ain't nothin' got into me, 'cept you." His lips teasingly crept down her long neck and worked upward to find her lips. "Ain't no need for you to go gettin' out of this bed. It's chilly out there."

"Hummph! This ain't no bed, just a couple of blankets thrown on the ground." Bessa twisted her head to the side, avoiding his lips when they sought her mouth. "I got things to tend. 'Sides you do too!"

He used his fingertips to turn her chin to him and kissed her with all the passion he felt. The soft sigh that escaped her throat when they parted pleased him as much now as it did the very first time he had heard it more years ago than he wanted to count. "The *Nermernuh* have a wise sayin'—the night is for lovemakin' or sleepin'."

Bessa smiled and shook her head, then tried to inject a stern streak into her tone. "And you're talkin' foolishness. You done had your lovemakin', and it ain't night. That's the sun over yonder that's about to poke its head up."

She wiggled from his arms and rolled from beneath the blankets. "Lordy, Nate Wagoner, I truly don't understand what's got into you. You just had your lovin', and you're askin' for second helpin's!"

Nate rolled to his back, tucked his arms beneath his head, and grinned up at his wife as she stood. "Woman, I don't know of it bein' written down nowheres that says a husband and wife got to go and put a number on their lovin'. You're supposed do what you feel—and I got a powerful feel for you this mornin'."

She gave her head a little reprimanding shake, but he saw the pleased flash of her eyes in the soft glow of predawn. "And you're gonna have a powerful hunger in a half hour or so if we don't do something 'bout breakfast."

"In all the time I was searchin' for you, I learned to ignore my stomach's rumblin's when there weren't no food to eat," he said. "But I never did learn to get along without you." He paused, his expression and tone dead serious when he said, "Bessa, I love you. I know I ain't one for puttin' my feelin's into words, but I love you."

The smile returned to her face and her voice softened. "And I love you, Nate Wagoner. Sometimes it's hard to remember a time that I didn't feel that love." She knelt and tenderly caressed his cheek with her fingertips. "But that don't change the fact that the sun's nigh on up, and we've got to move on."

His groan went unnoticed as Bessa rose and walked to a three-foot-wide puddle yesterday's rains had left in a shallow depression in the prairie. She slipped a light blue dress over her head and knelt naked beside the water to wash the garment. The dress and a yellow one of the same design she had sown from bolts of cloth he carried to trade with the Comanches. She wore one until they found water, then she washed the soiled dress and changed into the other.

In the week following their departure from the *Yampahreekuh* camp at the fork of the Arkansas, she had worked on the dresses with the determination of a madwoman. Once they were completed, she had stripped away the rawhide dress she wore and threw it into a campfire. While the flames devoured the leather, she announced, "Now I ain't no heathen squaw no more. I'm a Christian woman again."

Nate had said nothing. He simply gathered her in his arms and held her close while she softly wept. In the four weeks they had been together that had been her only mention of her long months among the Comanches and Kiowas. Whether she kept her silence to spare him a recounting of all the indignities that had been heaped upon her, or to protect herself from reliving the horrors, he did not know. Nor did he ask. She was his wife and he respected her reasons, whatever they might be. When the time came for talking, he would be there to listen and to hold her while the tears came anew.

Spreading the wet dress atop the grass to dry beneath the morning sun, Bessa returned to the puddle and began to bathe herself in the water.

Nate's gaze lovingly caressed the lines of her body, delighting in the way the golds and pinks of sunrise danced along the rivulets of water that cascaded down her bare back and willowy legs. There was a God in the heavens; Nate was certain of that. And that God was a good and gentle God. He had to be to have created such a woman and then given her to Nate so that they might share their lives.

"How much farther until we come upon the Antelope band that's got Mary?" Bessa dried herself with a scrap of burlap.

"It's hard to reckon time or distance on these plains." Nate shook his head. "I don't rightly know. I found you by just ridin' till I came to where you were. We'll do the same till we find Mary."

A month had passed since he had led his wife away from the tipi of Losing His Teeth. Bessa had seen the *Yampahreekuh* sell their daughter for five ponies and a cloth pouch of rifle balls to a brave called Mangus Amarillo. She knew nothing more about the warrior except that he was young and came from a Comanche tribe to the southeast.

So it was that Nate had traveled to the southeast as they left the Rocky Mountains. None of the three Yap-Eater bands he and Bessa came across had heard of Mangus Amarillo.

Six days ago they had ridden into the New Mexican town of Santa Fe. There from Comancheros Nate had learned that the brave he sought was a fierce young warrior of a *Kwerhar-rehnuh* band who was gaining a reputation as a powerful war chief upon the Llano Estacado. He also learned that Mangus Amarillo was the name given to the warrior by the priests in Santa Fe because of the white man's yellow shirt he often wore. The name translated to Yellow Sleeve or Yellow Shirt.

From Santa Fe, hides and buffalo robes traded for fresh goods, they had ridden directly into the rising sun, back onto the cap rock and the high plains of Texas. Although Indian sign was plentiful on these flatlands, no *Kwerhar-rehnuh* band had been spotted. Nor, as best as Nate could determine, had they been seen by the Comanches.

"You might consider usin' a little of this here water." Bessa's voice brought him from his thoughts. His wife tugged the yellow dress over her head and nodded to the puddle. "It's been three full days since we left that creek. You ain't started smellin' like a rose in that time."

"You're a hard woman, Bessa." Begrudgingly Nate abandoned the blankets, realizing Bessa had no intention of returning to his arms.

"And you was the one who was tellin' me how soft I was no more than fifteen minutes ago." She smiled and winked at him.

"That was fifteen minutes ago." He chuckled while he rolled and tied the blankets in a tight bundle. He walked to the shallow water, skinned off his clothes, and began to wash himself from head to toe.

"You might also think about shavin' that face of yours," Bessa said while she piled buffalo chips for their breakfast fire. "You nigh on rubbed the skin off my cheeks this mornin' with all your kissin' and huggin'."

Nate rubbed a hand over his chin. The stubble felt like a stand of prickly pear. He turned to retrieve a razor from his saddlebags. Before he took a step toward the saddled gray, his head snapped back around.

To the south, sitting right on the horizon, a slender finger of gray smoke rose to the sky. This far from the white man's frontier, that thin column could mean but one thing—Comanches.

"Bessa, look." He jabbed a finger toward the smoke.

His wife's head came up, and she stared to the south. Fear flashed in her eyes—the same fear he had seen every time they approached a Comanche village. Although she said nothing, he could well imagine the remembered terrors that flooded her mind. The long months among the plains Indians had left unseen scars.

"Will they be an Antelope band?" she asked.

"Here on the Staked Plains, there ain't no other kind of Comanche," Nate answered.

"Then we'll ride to the south today." Her head gave a determined tilt toward the column of smoke. "Mary might be with them."

Nate's chest swelled with pride. Bessa had always been a strong woman, but until these last four weeks, he had not realized the depth of her strength. Time and again, she put aside her own fears and rode into Comanche villages to search for their oldest daughter. Had he suffered as she, Nate was certain he would have run screaming from even the thought of seeing another Comanche.

Returning to the puddle with razor in hand, he studied the smoke while doing his best to scrape the whiskers from his face without aid of soap or mirror. "The camp ain't that far away. No more than fifteen, maybe twenty, miles. We should reach there by noon. That is, if them *Kwerhar-rehnuh* ain't on the move."

"Nate, you and me have got to talk."

Something in Bessa's voice diverted his eyes from the smoke. Worried lines deeply creased her brow. Her gaze shied from his while she poked at the campfire with a twig.

"There's something you should know," she said softly.

Nate felt his own forehead knit with uncertainty. "We've always been ones to talk to each other."

"This is different." Bessa's pursed her lips, and her face appeared as though she were in pain. "I missed my time of the month, Nate."

"Wha—" He blinked, her meaning slowly sinking in. Uncertainty vanished from his face, replaced by an ear-to-ear grin. "A child? Are you sayin' you're with child?"

She nodded, her eyes still avoiding him.

A glowing ball of pride expanded in his chest until it tingled through his arms and legs down to his fingers and toes. "A baby! Lordy!" If possible, his grin grew wider. "I reckon it's to be expected. We've spent every night for the past month bundled together in those blankets."

"It ain't the first month I missed my blood, Nate." Her head turned, and she stared at him. "It's the second month."

For several moments his mind refused to work. He swallowed when he finally grasped her meaning. He was not the father of the child growing inside her. Losing His Teeth or another nameless Kiowa or Comanche brave had planted his seed within her.

Bessa turned away, staring at the growing flames. "I'm sorry, Nate. All these weeks, I've tried to tell you, but I couldn't. Soon I'll be showin', and I didn't want you believin' that this baby was yo—"

"Shhhhh." He placed the razor aside, walked beside his wife, and wrapped an arm around her shoulders. He squeezed her tightly. "Bessa, it makes no never mind what happened. That's all over now. The child you carry is ours. No man will ever say different."

Bessa's dark eyes rolled up to him. "Are you sure, Nate?"

"Sure as I am of that sun comin' up each day." He lightly kissed her forehead. "You and I are husband and wife. That means any baby growin' in your belly is ours. We will be its ma and pa."

Throwing her arms around his neck, she clung close to him and wept. His own arms encircled her trembling body, his huge hands tenderly stroking away her fear.

A COLLAPSED WALL of stone and dirt led down into a canyon that sliced deeply into the plains. Nate estimated they rode a full eight hundred feet down the steep incline to reach the canyon floor. A mile from the collapsed wall stood thirty *Kwerhar-rehnuh* tipis, raised beside a narrow creek that ran red with muddy water.

As with the other Comanche camps they had entered together, both braves and squaws ignored their presence. Although Nate noticed that he went more unnoticed than Bessa. Here and there he caught the gazes of braves studying his wife. However, no one in the village approached them as they crossed the creek and set up camp as had become Nate's habit when dealing with Comanches. Together Bessa and he lit their campfire, put on a pan of coffee, spread the blankets, and covered them with trade goods. They then sat cross-legged by the blankets and waited for *Nermernuh* curiosity to overcome their belief that black men did not exist.

It was the afternoon of the second day that Bessa whispered urgently to her husband, "Nate, look!" She nodded toward the other side of the creek. "It's Miss Elizabeth!"

Nate's gaze darted back and forth along the line of squaws who gathered water from the muddy stream. Twice his eyes passed over a squaw dressed in beaded buckskins before noticing the color of her long, grease-slickened, braided hair.

Red! Nate's pulse quickened. No natural-born Comanche had red hair.

The squaw lifted her face and stared at the black man and woman across the creek. Her eyes narrowed, and her head cocked from side to side.

In spite of the sun-darkened hue of her skin and the dirt smudged on her face, there was no mistaking a woman Nate had known for most of his adult life. The squaw was Elizabeth Turner, Master Turner's wife!

Dragging a water bag from the water Elizabeth Turner corked its mouth and hefted the heavy burden to a shoulder. She turned, took three steps toward the tipis, then halted.

Nate squinted, attempting to discern what happened with the woman; he could not tell. He looked at his wife. Bessa's gaze shot to him for a moment. The same questions he held were reflected in her eyes.

Abruptly Elizabeth Turner swung around. Boldly she strode to the creek, standing directly opposite the husband and wife. For moments she stared first at Nate before gazing at Bessa, then her eyes shifted to Nate and then returned to Bessa.

There was no doubt in Nate's mind that she recognized both of them. The perplexed expression on her dirty face vanished and surprise widened her eyes—for an instant. In the beating of a heart her astonishment vanished, replaced by a twisted look of grief and pain. Her mouth opened and her lips trembled as though she intended to speak. She did not. Instead she twisted about and scurried back to the village.

"She knew us, Nate." Bessa stared after the woman. "She remembered us. I saw it in her eyes. There were tears in her eyes. I've been where Miss Elizabeth is. I know. A woman has to push everything she was and had away from her mind, forget them—if'n she wants to stay alive. To remember the past is the way to madness. So you learn to live each day as it comes, never thinking about what your life used to be like or never wonderin' what the morrow will bring. It's like bein' a field nigger. All you do is what you're told—nothin' else."

She turned to her husband. "Then something comes along to remind you of the woman you were before you were stole away. There ain't nothing a body can do to stop the memories then. They come rushin' back, afillin' your head. They hurt, Nate. They hurt like nothing else in this world, 'cause you can see what you was and what you are now, and there ain't no way to hide from it. No way at all."

Nate reached out, took his wife's hands in his own, and squeezed them. There was no way he could ever feel what Bessa and Miss Elizabeth had felt. But he could imagine what it was like to have every fiber of dignity stripped away from a soul and still live on. Crouch and Joaquín had taught him that.

"We got to get her free, Nate." Bessa's voice and eyes pled with him. "We got to. No woman should be forced to live like she is.

We got to buy her free and take her back to Master Turner and her girls."

"We will," he assured. "We'll take her home."

ON THE THIRD DAY in the *Kwerhar-rehnuh* village the temptation of keen-edged knives, sparkling glass beads, polished copper pots, and bright bolts of cloth could no longer be resisted. The first brave wandered across the creek. In the convoluted manner by which the Comanche spoke to a man without a soul, a bargain was struck for five of the twenty Bibles Nate carried with him.

The Comanche's fascination with the Bible, an item Joaquín DeRosa always packed for trade, Nate quickly learned had nothing to do with a desire to grasp the message contained in the Good Book. It was the thin paper on which Bibles were printed that warriors prized so highly. The pages were torn from their bindings, crumpled, and stuffed between the two layers of dried buffalo hide employed by the *Nermernuh* in making their war shields. Far more effective than the dried grass usually used to fill the space between the leather coverings, tightly compressed, packed paper had been known to stop a rifle ball from penetrating a shield. Such powerful medicine always brought the finest hides and buffalo robes in trade.

More importantly the first *Kwerhar-rehnuh* supplied Nate and Bessa with the name of the brave who kept Miss Elizabeth in his tipi—Eats Turtle. The name stemmed from the brave's habit of dining on that taboo meat whenever game grew scarce on the high plains.

By the end of the day, piecing one garnered bit of information with another, Nate learned that Eats Turtle, an aging warrior who would soon be too old to ride with war parties, had bought Miss Elizabeth after the death of his wife. The younger women of the village and their fathers avoided the brave. Eats Turtle's mounting years and dwindling number of horses placed him at the bottom of the heap when it came to prospective marital material.

A month ago, during a raid on a town below the Rio Grande River, Eats Turtle's brother was killed by Mexican bullets. Eats Turtle suddenly found that his tipi—unable to attract a single

Kwerhar-rehnuh squaw a few months back—was filled with women. Eats Turtle, as was the Comanche way, inherited his brother's three wives. Neither of the three squaws appreciated having to share their new husband with a captive white woman. The brave had attempted to sell Miss Elizabeth and remove the irritation that threatened to destroy the harmony of his woman-rich lodge. However, no man in the village was interested in taking the unwanted captive off Eats Turtle's hands.

Nate left subtle hints with each of the *Kwerhar-rehnuh* braves who visited him that he would be willing to alleviate Eats Turtle's burden by purchasing the unwanted captive. Then he waited.

Two more mornings came and went. Each day Miss Elizabeth visited the creek and stared at Nate and Bessa. Though none of them risked speaking, it was more than clear from her expression that she begged them to free her. On the afternoon of the fifth day, the opportunity to do so presented itself. Eats Turtle, with Miss Elizabeth walking behind him, crossed the creek.

"I have brought this strong woman." The brave ignored all Comanche customs and spoke directly to Nate. "I will trade her for three ponies and six buffalo robes."

Nate caught himself before his lips could utter an acceptance. To strike a quick bargain was not the Comanche way. He had no desire for Eats Turtle to know how important Elizabeth Turner was to him. Setting aside the cup of coffee he sipped, Nate glanced up at the woman and studied her for several minutes. He then picked up his coffee and took another sip without saying a word.

"I paid five ponies for her less than a year ago." Eats Turtle settled in front of Nate when Bessa poured coffee into a cup and placed it at the brave's feet. "She is a hard worker and does not complain."

"One horse for her," was Nate's offer.

Eats Turtle did not reply until he had leisurely sipped his way to the bottom of the tin cup. "Two ponies, five blankets, and six buffalo robes would be a good price."

So it went for an hour, two, three. Only when the sky ran with the reds and golds of sunset did Eats Turtle accept an offer of a single pony, two steel-bladed knives, three wool blankets, and an equal number of buffalo robes.

While the brave carried away his goods, Bessa led Miss Elizabeth beside the small campfire, poured her coffee, and held the cup to her lips so that she might drink. The woman took two sips before she broke down, her whole body wracked by sobs while tears streamed from her eyes. Bessa gathered the woman into her arms and held her, rocking back and forth as though she comforted a child.

"It's all right, Miss Elizabeth. It's all right now," Bessa softly whispered. "You're safe now. You're safe with Nate and me. Ain't nothin' gonna hurt you."

Nate wearily rubbed a hand over his face and pursed his lips while he stared at the two women. Bessa's words were filled with gentleness and good intentions, but they were lies. There was the whole Comanche nation here on the plains that could hurt them. He had relied on the color of his and Bessa's skin to protect them as they wandered from Indian camp to Indian camp. Miss Elizabeth was white. That protection was gone. It would be suicide to attempt to continue.

Mary filled his mind. He steeled himself to the image of his oldest daughter as a captive in the tipi of a *Kwerhar-rehnuh* brave called Mangus Amarillo. For now he had to abandon the search for her. Bessa carried a child in her belly and Miss Elizabeth's presence endangered them all. It was time to return to the Cross Timbers.

While Bessa continued to comfort Elizabeth Turner, Nate dowsed the campfire, saddled and packed the horses, then helped the women onto the gray. As darkness shrouded the canyon, they rode eastward, Nate constantly scanning the terrain for attack and Bessa holding tightly to the still sobbing woman. They would travel throughout the night and all the next day before resting. Nate wanted to put as much distance between the *Kwerhar-rehnuh* village and themselves as quickly as possible.

TWENTY-ONE

NATE HELD UP A HAND to signal a halt. Shifting his weight in the saddle, he glanced around at the two women who rode behind him. "We're gettin' close to home."

"Home?" Bessa and Elizabeth Turner chorused from the backs of a gray and a paint.

"Up yonder." Nate jabbed a finger to the east. "Can't be more'n three or four miles up there, right beyond that hogback ridge. We should make it in another hour."

Rather than delight, horror washed over the women's faces. Nate blinked, uncertain whether or not to believe his eyes. "What's wrong with you two?"

"Ain't nothin' wrong, 'cept neither me nor Miss Elizabeth realized we was gettin' so close," Bessa answered with a shake of her head. "We ain't ready yet."

"Ain't ready yet?" Nate's confusion grew.

"We ain't dressed for it," Bessa answered.

"Ain't . . ." His words trailed off and he shook his head. He had no idea what his wife was talking about. "Bessa, what in the world's got into you?"

"We can't go ridin' in to see our childrens dressed like this," Bessa explained. "It's been nigh on a year since we been home. We want to look our best."

Nate's confusion remained. The very time they had been away would be enough reason, at least to him, to be spurring their mounts ahead at a dead run. He started to speak.

Bessa cut him off. "Don't you worry none about what I'm sayin'. Just you go off up in those woods and keep your back to the river and don't look back till I call for you."

"Bessa, you're not makin' no—"

"Hush now," his wife ordered him. "Just do like I said. Go on now. Up into them woods."

Nate gave up; Bessa had no intention of explaining herself. He tapped his heels to the roan's sides and reined toward a dense stand of red oaks fifty yards from the bank of the Brazos River.

"Nate," Bessa called to him, "where's that bar of saddle soap I saw you packin' away last week?"

He halted the roan and looked back to point to a bay pack-horse. "In that pack."

Without another glance in his direction, Bessa waved him on as she dismounted. To Miss Elizabeth, she said, "Now this ain't no proper soap for a lady, but we have to make do with what we got. It will wash away the dust and dirt. Now you . . ."

Nate smiled. During the two weeks that had passed since leaving the *Kwerhar-rehnuh*'s canyon, Bessa had worked a miracle with Miss Elizabeth. Like a mother nursing a sick child, Bessa had brought the woman out of the shell she had used to fortify herself against her time among the Indian bands—brought her back to the world of the living.

Without Bessa, he would have been unable to handle Miss Elizabeth, he realized. Master Turner's wife would now be as lost and dazed as he remembered Mariah Ewell after her rescue from the band of old *Tahneemuhs.*

Reining around the red oaks, Nate stepped from the saddle. A smile touched his lips while he gazed about the stunted forest. How familiar it all was. He and Ben often hunted along this portion of the river. This was home. Just standing there breathing in the smell of the woods made the last two weeks of hard riding and cold camps all worthwhile. *Home,* the word repeated over and over in his mind. After the long months, he was home.

The sound of splashing water and laughter came from the river. Nate started to turn to locate its cause. He caught himself, remembering Bessa's command to keep his back to the river. It did not take a genius to realize what use the women had found for the saddle soap; they were bathing—a dunk-your-whole-body-soap-and-suds bath!

He glanced down at himself and hiked a critical eyebrow. He could do with a bath too, but it would have to wait until this evening. He was too close to seeing his children again to let a little trail dust slow him down.

However, he thought, *womenfolk is another thing.*

His gaze returned to the oaks and junipers that covered the hill rising before him. Much of the underbrush and weeds had gone to seed. As strange as it appeared to his eyes, it was to be expected. It was mid-August. The Cross Timbers had seen winter and spring come and go. Now, summer was nigh on gone—and he had missed each changing of the seasons.

Nearly a year had passed since he had ridden from his home, Nate realized. He slowly drew in a breath to help fill the hollowness that emptied him. A year come and gone—all his babies had watched their birthdays pass without either a mother or father beside them.

Except my little Naomi. He closed his eyes to stem the tears that blurred his vision. Even after all these months the memory of Naomi's twisted and broken body brought more pain than a man should be expected to endure.

And Mary? He swallowed hard. How had his oldest daughter spent her birthday? She was fourteen now. Bessa had been but fifteen when she had been first brought to him.

He opened his eyes to drive away the fear that thrust into his mind. It would not be driven away. Many girls were of the age to bear children at fourteen. And he had no doubt for what purpose Mangus Amarillo had bought his daughter. He shook his head and drew another deep breath. White or red, the color of a man's skin did not alter his use of black women.

The woods around him lost their sweetness. He stood here so close to his home, and Mary was out on the Llano Estacado a captive in the tipi of a Comanche brave called Yellow Shirt. Guilt welled within him. How could he feel contentment when his daughter was so far from her family? How could any man—

"Nate!"

He jerked straight when the voice intruded his dark reflections.

"Nate!" It was Bessa. "You can come on back down now. We's ready!"

Stepping into the saddle, Nate reined his mount around and headed out of the trees. His eyes widened when he saw the women.

"Don't stand there gawkin' like a fool what ain't got no tongue." Bessa grinned up at him. "Tell us what you think?"

"I think I done died, and the angels have come to take me up to heaven." He forced himself to return the grin and nod with approval, in spite of the images of Mary that filled his mind. "I never did see no prettier-lookin' women in all my days."

The clean fragrance of saddle soap wafted in the air. Both women's faces, scrubbed clean, were aglow in the afternoon sun as they stared up at him. Even their still damp hair which clung to their heads did nothing to detract from their beauty. Both wore new dresses they had sewn during the nights the lack of a moon allowed for a campfire. The two dresses had been cut from a bolt of yellow cloth Nate carried to trade with the Comanches.

"Never even seen a field of Mexican Hats that looked so bright and beautiful," he added. He caught himself before he said, "Your children won't recognize you."

The new dresses were not for him, but for those children who waited ahead. The bright yellow hue was a disguise to conceal the fact that both women had spent months among Comanches and Kiowas. It was Bessa's and Miss Elizabeth's attempt to reassure their families that they were unchanged, remained the same women they had always been. It was a thin veil they draped over the truth.

"We've spent enough time here," Bessa said, glancing at Miss Elizabeth and receiving a nod of agreement. "It's time you took us on home."

"Well, I reckon I'll do just that, soon as you ladies climb back onto those ponies." Nate grinned and waved a hand to their waiting mounts.

THE WOODS FELL AWAY, opening onto a wide valley between a forest-covered mountain and a shorter rise. Within that valley stood a house, barn, and smokehouse—the Turner place.

"Smoke's comin' from the chimney." Nate turned to Miss Elizabeth and pointed ahead. "Like as not everybody's inside havin' dinner."

The joy he expected to find on the woman's face was not there. She stared at the farm, her color gone ashen with fear.

"It'll be all right." Bessa reached across and squeezed Miss

Elizabeth's hands as they rested on her mount's neck. "You'll see. Everything's gonna be all right."

The woman's eyes remained locked on the farm as Nate moved forward, reining between rows of broad-leafed squash plants. He drew to a halt in front of the soddy and called out:

"Master Turner! Master Turner, if you're inside, you'd best come on out. This here's Nate Wagoner. I brought somebody you'll be wantin' to see."

A few seconds later, the home's door opened halfway. William Turner, rifle in hand peered out. Behind him, his daughters Terry and Rachel crowded, trying to see around their father.

"Nate? Nate, is that you?" Disbelief filled the farmer's voice.

"Yes, sir." Nate nodded and grinned. "It's sure enough me. I brought someone with me." Nate eased back on the roan's reins to allow the man to see the women beside him. "It's Miss Elizabeth. I brought her back to you like I said I would."

"Elizabeth?" The rifle slipped from Turner's trembling hands and fell to the floor of the house when he stepped across the threshold. "Oh, God! Elizabeth, it's you! Sweet Lord, it's really you."

He came from the house on hesitant legs that moved forward in an uncertain shuffle. Each step quickened with gained confidence. Behind, his two daughters followed, their heads moving from left to right as though they were unable to accept what their eyes saw. "Momma . . . oh, Momma!"

Then they were beside the bay and Turner's arms rose to lift his wife from the horse. The three of them were hugs and tears while they tried to gather Miss Elizabeth into their arms all at the same time.

The tears that now flowed down the woman's cheeks had nothing to do with fear or terror. They stemmed from joy and relief. Her arms reached out, embracing husband and daughters one after another, time and time again.

"These people need to be left alone." Nate turned to Bessa. " 'Sides we've children of our own waitin'."

The doubt he had seen earlier in Miss Elizabeth's expression was now on his wife's face. He reached out, resting a hand atop hers. "Come on. It will be all right. Everything's going to be just fine. You'll see."

Together they rode from the Turner farm and over the rise. Ben, Daniel, and Eve were all working the oat field. Their heads came up, and they stared at the approaching riders with uncertainty. Two heartbeats later the doubt vanished. A whooping chorus burst from their mouths, "Ma! Pa!"

Tossing aside their hoes, they ran through the fields as fast as their legs would carry them. Then they were there crying and kissing and hugging, and kissing and hugging some more as though it were impossible to get enough of touching their parents.

Nor was the homecoming welcome one-sided. The months had been long, and the love stored away during that time broke free in a rushing flood. Nate and Bessa filled and refilled their arms with their children. They squeezed each one tightly and kissed their faces again and again. Their own tears streamed as freely as those of Ben, Daniel, and Eve.

Nate's eyes shifted to Bessa's for a moment while he swept a little Eve, who was at least two inches taller than he remembered, into his arms. The fear and doubt had vanished from his wife's face. His grin widened. They were home; at last, they were at home.

NATE WALKED OUTSIDE feeling as well fed and pampered as a city dog. Ben, Daniel, and Eve had refused to let either Bessa or him help with supper, even to set the table. With obvious pride, they had prepared cornbread and squirrel stew. The squirrel, to Nate's surprise, had been provided by Daniel.

"I remember you teachin' me how to handle a rifle the day I turned eleven," Ben said to his father over the supper table. "So I done the same for Daniel. He's got a better eye than me. Almost as good as you."

Daniel beamed with obvious delight, but said, "It ain't nothing but two old squirrels. I was wantin' to find one of them wild turkeys that you can hear down by the river early in the mornin'."

Nate settled on the ground, leaning back against the house. Daniel's newfound ability was not the only change he had noticed in his children. Eve, at nine, was quite the woman of the house. When she ordered the boys to do something, her brothers snapped to without arguing or bickering. She had supervised the preparation of both the stew and cornbread, occasionally glancing at her mother as though to say silently, "Look, I learned to do it right by watching you."

And Ben! Nate's head moved from side to side with amazement. Although he had called his oldest a man, in his mind he had still thought of him as a growing boy. No more. One glance at the small farm was testimony to Ben's manhood.

When Nate had last seen his children, Ben had spoken of building a lean-to to shelter the stock. A full-fledged barn, every bit as sturdy as its predecessor, now stood in place of the one the Comanches had burned. Beside it was a pen containing a sow and five piglets. The new addition to the livestock was part of a winter barter Ben had made with a nearby farmer.

Casting a critical, fatherly eye to the oat field and the garden, Nate found no fault. Ben had done better than Nate had expected, perhaps better than he could have done.

But the biggest change was the house itself. Ben had cut sod and completely enclosed the home. The only exposed wood was the windows and door. Nate needed no explanation for the sod. Dirt and mud did not burn. Ben had learned his lesson after one Comanche attack.

Nate's gaze lifted to study the deep blue that spread out of the east toward the red glow of sunset. Night lay but a half hour away. In the morning, he would—

"Pa." Ben's voice wedged into his thoughts. "Pa, I need to talk with you."

Nate glanced up. His son stepped from the house and settled to the ground beside his father.

"I was just lookin' at this place, feelin' proud of all you've done." Nate squeezed his son's shoulder.

Ben ignored the praise. "Pa, you're going back after Mary, ain't you?"

"Yes." Nate nodded. "Reckon, I'll be headin' out tomorrow or the next day. The sooner the better the way I see it. The high plains ain't no place to be when cold weather sets in. The wind out there is like a knife. It whips out of the north with an edge that'll cut a man to the—"

"Pa, I want to go with you," Ben said before Nate finished. "Mary's my sister, Pa. I got this place back into shape like you wanted. Now I want to go with you and help find Mary."

"Ben, I don't—"

Ben would not let him get a word in. "There ain't that much to do until harvest, and Daniel and Eve could bring in the oats on their own if need be. With Ma here to watch over them, there ain't no need of me. I want to go with you. I want to get Mary back where she belongs."

"Ben," Nate started again.

This time three approaching riders interrupted him.

"It's Master Turner," Ben said.

Nate recognized Jeb Ewell and Seth Alsep beside him. Trying to ignore the old uneasy feeling that came when white men rode toward his door, Nate pushed from the ground. His rifle was inside the house. To duck in for the weapon would be too obvious with the three so close.

"You go on inside and tell your momma we got company," Nate told Ben. "On the way out, put my rifle by the door." As his son stepped toward the door, Nate added, "And, Ben, you make sure it's carryin' a load. Understand?"

Ben nodded and disappeared into the house. Nate drew a steadying breath and exhaled it. He could think of no reason why there would be trouble, but for the first time in his life, he realized that he was prepared to deal with it, even if it required using the rifle.

Bessa and Ben stood in the doorway when Turner and the other two drew to a halt in front of the house. The three men tipped their hats to Bessa, then looked at Nate. Turner spoke:

"Nate, you rode off today before I could talk with you. We've got some unfinished business between us."

"Business, Master Turner?" Nate was not certain what the man meant.

"Last fall, I made you a promise," Turner answered. "I'm a man of my word; I intend to keep that promise." He reached into a pocket and pulled out a piece of folded paper. "This here's your papers. Jeb and Seth have witnessed my signature. You're a free man, Nate."

Fingers atremble, Nate reached up and took the paper from the farmer. He unfolded it and stared at the written words. He could read only a handful of them, but it did not matter. Bessa would read it to him later. What mattered was that he was free, truly free! And he had all but forgotten Turner's promise.

"And this," Turner continued, "is the title to these twenty-five acres, just like I promised, Nate."

Turner passed him another piece of paper while Seth Alsep dug a pouch from a saddlebag. "This here's what the Mexican left for you—three hundred dollars. Your part of the reward for bringing back the womenfolk."

Nate accepted the coin-jingling pouch, enjoying the weight of it in his palm. In truth, he had expected Joaquín DeRosa to find some way to make off with all the reward.

"That's about it," Turner said, lifting the reins from his mount's neck. He paused and added, "Except to say, all of us appreciate what you done, Nate. Now, I 'spect you'll be wantin' to get back to your family."

The three men tipped their hats to Bessa one more time, then tugged the heads of their horses around and rode off.

"Nate!" Bessa bounded from the door and threw her arms about his neck and covered his mouth with a loud, smacking kiss. "A freedman! You're free! Nate, you're free!"

"And this land is ours, Bessa." Nate held up the two pieces of paper Turner had given him. "It's ours, really ours. We got it down on paper, Bessa."

"Come on inside and sit by the fire." She took his hand and led him toward the door. "I'll read them aloud so we'll all know what it reads like to be a free man."

BESSA NESTLED into the hollow of his shoulder. Her breath tickled through the hairs of his chest while she pondered all he had said. Nate remained silent; he had said his piece. He knew she expected this, but he was certain she had not anticipated it coming so soon.

"Tomorrow?" she asked softly.

He nodded, his hand gently caressing her side. "It would be best."

Again she fell silent. The only sound in their dark bedroom was the rhythm of their breathing and the high-pitched cries of cicadas outside.

"I'll stay longer if you want," he said, but his heart was not in his words.

"No," she shook her head. "You're right. You and Ben should leave as soon as possible. Our daughter is still out there. You have to bring her home."

Nate said nothing, but he noticed that she had given approval to Ben accompanying him to the high plains. "In the mornin' I'll take fifty dollars and ride to the store. We'll need supplies and goods for tradin'. I'll take a couple mustangs, too, and trade them for another rifle. You'll need one here."

"Ben'll need a pistol," Bessa said. "A rifle ain't enough out there among the Comanches."

Nate had not thought of that. He would take three of the mustangs to trade. "I'll leave the rest of the money in our hidey-hole by the fireplace in case y'all need it while we're gone."

"We won't be needin' nothin'," Bessa assured him. "But it will go a long way to buyin' Ben a wife when you get back with Mary."

A smile crept to Nate's lips. It had been a long time since he had thought about finding his oldest a wife.

"Now, you'd best get your sleep," Bessa whispered. "You'll want to be gettin' an early start tomorrow mornin'."

"I'd rather be lovin' you," he said as he leaned down and kissed her lips. "It'll be quite a spell 'fore we lay together again."

She returned his kiss, then opened her arms as he came to her.

TWENTY-TWO

THE STORM caught Nate and Ben on the rim to the canyon. A mere hour ago, fluffy white clouds had been floating across a field of deep blue. The winds came first—ragged gusts that tore across the high plains like invisible hands that sought to rip father and son from their mounts. The ominous clouds, blue-black mountains that towered toward the very heavens, rose along the northern horizon. They rolled and boiled as they raced downward to blot out the sky.

Dismounting, Nate and Ben turned their backs to the coming storm, sat cross-legged on the ground, and covered themselves with buffalo robes while they clutched the reins and rope leads of their stock. Then they waited.

Lightning like grotesquely malformed spider legs danced across the plain in actinic flashes. Thunder ripped the air, tearing it asunder. And the rain came. In wind-whipped sheets it fell to wash across the flatlands.

Nate cursed under his breath while he hugged the buffalo hide closer and glared at the torrents that hammered the land. Rain that had been so scarce here on the Llano Estacado during the summer months was a daily occurrence since the coming of September. Showers and raging storms alike appeared from nowhere to drench the water-starved prairie, leaving the sandy soil a mire of mud.

The rain and chill it left in the air, Nate could handle. It was the mud that he could not abide. It was not only that it seemed to find its way into everything from his hair to his food; it was the fact that the rain and mud seemed to conspire to erase every Indian sign from the plains. He and Ben came across a trail left by mustangs and decided to follow it in the hope that they would eventually lead to a *Kwerhar-rehnuh* village. Then the rains came, leaving only mud.

Closing his eyes, Nate wearily shook his head. Since reaching the cap rock, he and Ben had found six Comanche camps. None had been the one they sought. Their trade goods had purchased buffalo robes, antelope and deer hides, and two additional mustangs. However, they had not seen or heard of a brave called Mangus Amarillo nor the captive black girl he kept in his tipi.

A week ago, they had come upon a campfire with three Mexicans gathered around the flames. The three, with their line of six packhorses, had journeyed from Santa Fe—Comancheros come to trade with the *Kwerhar-rehnuh*. While the men shared their coffee and beans with the father and son, they had spoken of a large Antelope band to the north camped in a canyon they called Palo Duro. The men had shied from the village, fearing the band's numbers. They said, according to what they gathered from other *Kwerhar-rehnuh* braves, the village consisted of over two hundred lodges.

"Too many Comanches," Juan Hidalgo, the sixty-year-old leader of the three, had said with a shake of his head. "Going among so many Antelope-Eaters would be the same as putting a knife to one's throat and giving it a strong jerk. I have not lived these long years by being so stupid."

Before bidding the men a farewell, Nate bartered hard and long for the six rifles he now carried bundled in oiled leather on the back of one of the pack animals. The weapons had cost him most of the hides Ben and he had accumulated, but rifles, even without powder and lead, were far more likely to draw a Comanche brave's attention than were bolts of bright red, yellow, and blue cloth.

Ben had eyed him suspiciously when he had traded for the weapons, but said nothing. The boy—young man, Nate corrected himself—learned quickly that this was not the Cross Timbers. The rules by which a man learned to survive were different. He either adapted to those rules quickly, or he died. There were no in-betweens.

"It's lettin' up," Ben said at Nate's right.

"We'll let it pass 'fore movin' on." Nate peered at the sky. A raindrop splattered into his left eye. He jerked his head back under the buffalo robe. "Ain't no need gettin' any wetter than a man has to."

Another half hour passed before the rain drizzled out, and the sun broke through the gray clouds overhead. Shaking out their robes, they remounted and rode westward along the canyon's edge. The sun rode on the horizon when they sighted the village below. Nate's heart pounded like a runaway bass drum as he stared down on the tipis stretching along a rain-swollen creek. Juan Hidalgo's information had been wrong. More than three hundred Comanche lodges lined the stream's banks!

"Pa, what do we do now?" A hint of the child Nate had known for so many years crept into Ben's question.

"We find us a way down," Nate answered. "And we see if we can find out anything about your sister."

Ben swallowed hard, but he followed after his father.

IT TOOK FOUR DAYS and three of the rifles for Nate to learn that this was indeed the village of the young war chief Mangus Amarillo, and that he and Ben had set up their camp on the opposite end of the immense village from Yellow Shirt's lodge. Applying the strategy he had used to free Bessa from the *Yampahreekuh* Losing His Teeth, Nate broke camp, rode right through the Comanche village, and made a new camp outside Mangus Amarillo's tipi.

Unlike the Yap-Eater, the young brave displayed no distress at finding two black white men on his doorstep. Nor did he ignore the black-skinned men as was *Nermernuh* custom. He came and went, haughtily glaring at Nate and Ben. And at his side was Mary!

Only once did Mary call to her father and brother and try to run to them. For her effort, Mangus Amarillo grabbed the neck of the fringed doeskin dress she wore, jerked her back, and repeatedly slapped her face while Nate and Ben watched.

Nate's right arm snaked out, grasped his son's shoulder, and threw him back to the ground when Ben scrambled to his feet to aid his sister. "Let it lay. You'll get us all killed. We'll handle this the way I've always done."

When the young warrior disappeared into his tipi, dragging Mary after him, Nate began to sing at the top of his voice—a song that told his daughter to be patient, that her father had come to return her home, and would not leave this village without her. He steeled himself to the cries that came from within the tipi. A few slaps to the face had not been stern enough punishment for Mary's boldness, Nate realized. Mangus Amarillo now beat his captive.

Again Nate had to restrain his son from going after his sister. "It's hard, boy, but it's the way it has to be. Give me time. I know what I'm doin'."

Ben turned from his father and stared at the ground when Nate began to sing again. However, Ben stayed on the ground, which was all that Nate wanted for now.

THE MORNING of the third day outside Yellow Shirt's lodge, the warrior stepped from his tipi. Mary walked a few feet behind him, her head bowed, but her eyes darted between Nate and Ben. Moving directly before Nate the brave stared down at the black man who sat on the ground. Mangus Amarillo edged aside his breechclout, then urinated on Nate's crossed legs. An amused smile hung at the corners of the Comanche's mouth when he said:

"The whole village knows why you've come to the lands of the *Kwerhar-rehnuh*. But your songs are carried away on the winds, unheard by *Nermernuh* ears. You have no place here. Mount your ponies and leave."

He turned and signaled Mary to his side with a flick of his wrist. "Tonight, before the whole village, I will take this one as a wife. She is not your daughter, nor has she ever been. She belongs to me and my tipi."

With that Mangus Amarillo pivoted and walked away. Mary's gaze rose to her father. Nate saw no sign of hope in his daughter's eyes when she slowly turned and followed at the young warrior's heels.

"What did he say?" Ben stared at his father.

Nate waved his son to silence as he pushed from the ground. Without a word, he walked to the creek to clean himself and his clothes. When he returned to Mangus Amarillo's tipi, Ben pointed to four braves who rode away from the camp.

"Yellow Shirt," his son said. "Mary has not come back."

"Then we'll wait until she does." Nate settled beside the small fire they kept burning and poured himself a cup of coffee.

"Pa, why'd he do what he did?" Ben eyed his father.

Hanging in his son's question was another question—why did you let him do what he did? Nate tried to answer both. "We're gettin' at him, Ben. He wants us gone from here. He told me he intends to take Mary as his bride tonight. As far as he's concerned that's the end of it—there ain't nothin' left that we can do."

"Married?" Ben stared after the mounted braves who rode from the canyon.

"But there's always something a man can do, if he puts his mind to it." Nate fell silent, hoping his mind would work as quickly as his mouth, because at the moment he had no idea how to stop Mangus Amarillo.

TWENTY SQUAWS worked through the chaparral that surrounded the village. They brought forth the dead limbs of mesquite, scrub oak, and cottonwoods that leeched the moisture for life from the creek. Near the edge of the line of tipis, they piled the wood, tossing the buffalo chips they found atop the growing mound.

Nate and Ben watched them, neither certain what the women did or for what purpose they intended the woodpile. As the sun began its long, sinking journey toward the western rim of the canyon, Nate began to understand. Mangus Amarillo and the three braves returned. Each of the warriors carried the limp bodies of two pronghorn antelopes thrown over their ponies.

"A weddin' feast." The words came like a curse from Nate's lips.

Moments later, he was proven right. Mangus Amarillo and his companions drew their mounts to a halt and tossed the antelopes to the ground beside the wood the squaws gathered. Clutching a bow, Mangus Amarillo held his right arm high and called to the village:

"The People will fill their bellies tonight! Come all and celebrate the marriage of Mangus Amarillo. Come and share my happiness!"

Nate did not have to explain the words. From the expression on Ben's face, he knew his son understood. The question that ate at Nate's mind was how to stop the feast and the wedding Yellow Shirt had planned? No answers sprang immediately to mind.

Nor did an afternoon of watching the squaws dig pits in the ground and raise spits above them bring inspiration. He had run out of ideas. The luck that had sat on his shoulder for months was played out. All he could do was sit and watch as the braves and squaws of the village wove their way toward the fires over which the roasting antelopes were turned. With them came his daughter Mary, clad in a bead-adorned doeskin dress and surrounded by young squaws who led her toward the feast fires.

Beneath the fiery reds and glowing oranges of sunset that streaked the sky, Mangus Amarillo walked toward the approaching young women. They parted, allowing him to take Mary's hand. He then led her beside the fires where he paraded his wife-to-be before the clan.

"This is Shadow of Night," he called to his people. "I found her running across the plains that lay at the foot of the great mountains to the west. The night breeze whispered that she was to be my bride."

Nate could not endure it any longer. He shoved from the ground and moved to the gathering. The Comanches did not open a path for him as they had for Mangus Amarillo. He did not mind; he elbowed his way through the braves and squaws, stopping only when he stood directly before the young warrior. Mangus Amarillo's eyes narrowed to slits when they fell on the black white man.

"Shadow of Night. Is it a joke Yellow Streak Down His Back tells the people?" Nate asked the question at the top of his lungs, but his gaze remained locked to the young warrior. "The girl is my daughter. Her name is Mary. Yap-Eaters stole her and her mother from wagons in the north plains. It was not the whispering wind that brought her to Yellow Tongue's tipi, but two ponies and a sack of rifle balls!"

Nate risked a quick glance at the Comanches gathered around the fires. While he knew they heard his words, he could not judge whether they listened to their meaning.

However, apparently Mangus Amarillo feared that they did. "A black white man has no voice, yet this one does speak! But why should any of the People believe his utterances? Can one such as this but mock the ways of true men? Each sound that passes his lips can be no more than a lie."

The warrior looked at the braves and squaws circling the fires. "It was the night breeze that brought Shadow of Night to me. She has no father except the earth who was also her mother."

"No!" Nate cried out. "I am her father. And I, as her father, have not granted permission for this marriage. Where are the ponies Yellow Liver has paid for her hand?" Nate glared at Mangus Amarillo as he continued to taunt him with a string of names that bespoke of his cowardice. "Where are the gifts a warrior of the *Nermernuh* brings to the family of his bride? Is Yellow Heart unaware of the customs of the People? Or does he shun them out of contempt?"

Hatred sparked in Mangus Amarillo's eyes. He jerked Mary's arm high and turned her to the people of the village. "This is a woman of flesh and blood! Can a creature who has no soul father such a woman? A black white man does not exist. This thing is not real. He is a trick of our eyes and ears. He is like a bad nightmare that haunts our minds. In time he will fade and vanish in the wind like smoke from our cooking fires."

"I will not disappear," Nate answered. "I am a man the same as white, red, and brown men. The girl is my daughter, and I have come to claim her."

A murmur wove through the Comanches. It took but a glance at the faces lit by the flickering fires to see that the braves and squaws no longer listened to him, but nodded their approval to Mangus Amarillo. Nate's heart sank. His ploy had been bold and smacked directly into the face of *Nermernuh* custom. And it had failed. Nothing short of drawing the Colt tucked beneath his belt and killing Mangus Amarillo would stop the brave.

And in the next heartbeat, Mary and I would both be dead, he thought, knowing the *Kwerhar-rehnuh* would never allow them to live after he had thrown down on a warrior who did not carry a gun.

"The black white man is real. His body is not the dream stuff of nightmares, but flesh and blood like that of the People." A male voice called out from the Comanches crowded around the feast fires.

Mangus Amarillo's head snapped from side to side, his face twisted in rage. Nate slowly turned in a full circle, trying to locate the voice's owner.

Near the fire on Nate's left the squaws and braves parted. A warrior with long braided hair adorned with eagle feathers stepped into the light. Nate stared, feeling he had seen the brave before, but finding himself unable to place the familiar face. In his year on the plains he had seen thousands of Indians. Their faces quickly ran into one another, leaving only a blurred, featureless image.

The brave turned to Mangus Amarillo, then looked at Nate. "This is the real black white man I told of when I returned from the northern lands of the Kiowa. This is Walks Without a Soul, whose medicine brought me back from the realm of the dead."

Fights-Like-the-Wolf! Nate's head spun in disbelief. The warrior had managed to escape the treacherous Kiowas and make his way back to the high plains.

"You go too far!" Mangus Amarillo's tone was an unveiled threat. "Fights-Like-the-Wolf, be careful where you walk."

Fights-Like-the-Wolf's voice brimmed with defiance when he turned to face his fellow warrior. "I walk the path of friendship. This black white man acted as would a brother while I was a captive among the Kiowa dogs. It was his own knife that cut my bonds—the same blade that he placed into my hand so that I might escape from my enemies. This is Walks Without a Soul, who allowed me to return to my people and tell of the bloody treachery of the Kiowa. Without this man, this brother to the *Nermernuh*, we would not have been able to ride north and extract vengeance for our braves killed by the cowardly Kiowa."

Again a wave of murmurs rolled through the gathered Comanches. This time they were accompanied with nods of approval for Fights-Like-the-Wolf.

The brave took advantage of the shift in sentiment. "Is this the way the People repay one who befriends them? Do we rob him of his own daughter—for this girl *is* his daughter!" Fights-Like-the-Wolf thrust a pointing finger toward Mary.

Mangus Amarillo released Mary's hand with a jerk of his arm. His own right hand dropped to his waist and closed around the bone handle of a hunting knife sheathed there. A flick of the wrist brought the blade free. Light from the fires licked along its silvery length. "You have chosen the wrong path, Fights-Like-the-Wolf. Your *Kuhtsoo-ehkuh* heart is showing. Perhaps it is time that I cut it from your chest."

When Mangus Amarillo took two menacing steps toward

Fights-Like-the-Wolf, Nate stepped between the two braves. "No!"

The wicked smile that crept to Mangus Amarillo's lips told Nate that he had made the wrong move.

"You are right, soulless one." The tip of Mangus Amarillo's blade sliced invisible circles in the air. "It is not Fights-Like-the-Wolf's heart I should take, but yours." For an instant the brave's dark eyes dipped to the pistol beneath Nate's belt. "But a soulless creature would not face one of the People as a man with only a knife to defend himself. He would use a pistol that speaks many times."

"Stand aside, my friend," Fights-Like-the-Wolf ordered from behind Nate. "Mangus Amarillo challenged me."

"No." Nate's head moved from side to side. "Mary is my daughter."

"Then lay aside your pistol," Fights-Like-the-Wolf said. "You must face him with your knife—man against man."

Nate swallowed hard. A hunting knife was something to be used for cleaning and dressing game. He had never fought with one. Now, he had no choice. With thumb and forefinger, he reached down, eased the Colt from his belt, and tossed it aside.

Mangus Amarillo launched himself forward, not waiting for Nate to free the hunting knife that dangled in a scabbard from his belt. A yipping cry, like the bark of a coyote, tore from the brave's lips as he jerked back his right arm and slashed out.

Luck more than skill saved Nate from the blade and a sudden end to the fight before it began. So startled was he by the warrior's abrupt movement and war cry that he jumped back. The tip of Mangus Amarillo's knife hissed harmlessly through the air a mere inch from Nate's throat. That inch was as good as a mile; he still lived! Backstepping farther, he managed to find the blade on his hip and yank it from leather.

"You are quick, soulless one." A smile of amusement returned to Mangus Amarillo's lips. "But not quick enough to save your life."

The warrior's right hand snaked out, jabbing his blade straight for Nate's knife hand.

Again it was surprise rather than plan that moved Nate's body.

He jerked his arm away from the silvery fang of steel. He was not quick enough to avoid the abrupt little twist of the brave's wrist that redirected the knife. The honed edge sliced across Nate's left forearm. The sleeve of his cotton shirt opened in a smooth rent; blood oozed from a matching cut in his flesh.

"Quickness is not enough, soulless maggot!" Mangus Amarillo's smile widened to a pleased grin. "I will kill you slow and hard. Piece by bloody piece I will cut from your body until only your black bones remain!"

The warrior lunged. His arm and wrist danced out.

This time Nate was prepared. His own knife slashed up, intent on biting deeply into the Comanche's exposed forearm. He winced as burning pain ignited his left cheek. As fast as had been his reaction, he had not been fast enough. The brave's knife had found his face, nipped his flesh, and darted back before his own blade could find a target.

A humorless chuckle pushed from Mangus Amarillo's throat. "How easy it is!" His knife flashed again, kissing lightly against Nate's right cheek. "Your dying will be long and painful. I will see to that. And when you beg for a quick end to your sufferings, I will let the squaws have you to do as they please."

Nate saw the muscles of the warrior's arm stiffen as he prepared for another attack. He sidestepped when Mangus Amarillo lunged. Once more he was not quick enough. The edge of the Comanche's knife slid across the knuckles of his right hand. He groaned, gritting his teeth against the hot pain. Warm, sticky blood flowed between his fingers, turning the handle of his hunting knife slippery.

"Where next will my knife kiss?" Mangus Amarillo slowly circled. He halfheartedly jabbed the knife at Nate, laughing when the black white man jumped away from the blade. "Maybe an eye, or the tip of your nose?"

Nate sucked in a steadying breath and repressed the urge to throw himself onto the brave. That was a sure way to find Comanche steel in his heart. He had to bide his time and wait for an opening. He was no match for the *Kwerhar-rehnuh* and both he and Mangus Amarillo knew that. His only hope was that the warrior would grow overconfident and make a mistake.

"Maybe your throat?"

In a wide arc the brave's blade lashed out. Nate ducked beneath the steel meant to carve a second mouth in his neck. The knife hissed through empty air above his head. He leaped to the left beyond the range of a wicked backlash, and then to the right as the warrior raked out with his knife again.

"You dance well, soulless mongrel." Another chuckle pushed from the Comanche's throat. "But how long can you dance?"

Again and again Mangus Amarillo jabbed out with his knife. Nate wove, ducked, and dodged barely avoiding the tempered steel that nipped at him. The brave's chuckles were echoed by the braves and squaws who gave the two fighters wide berth. They knew what Nate suddenly realized—Mangus Amarillo played with him. Like a cat with a mouse, the warrior was toying with his prey. It was only a matter of time before the Indian grew bored with his game.

Three more times the brave's knife struck. Nate bobbed away from the first two, but misjudged the third slash. A burning brand of white-hot pain seared into his left shoulder as the knife sank a full inch into his flesh.

"Fights-Like-the-Wolf was right about your flesh and blood." Easy victory flashed in Mangus Amarillo's eyes. "You can be cut, and you bleed red. Of what use is flesh and blood when it is an empty shell without a soul?"

Nate had judged the warrior wrong. There would be no mistakes, no overconfidence—just slow, methodical butchering. If he were to have any chance of surviving this night he would have to do so on his own—make his own chances.

Once more Mangus Amarillo lunged, his blade sweeping out in a wide arc. Nate dropped beneath the knife. Instead of leaping to a side, he threw himself forward. He tucked chin to chest and rammed his head into the Comanche's solar plexus.

A surprise rush of air gushed from Mangus Amarillo's lungs under the unexpected attack. He stumbled back on rubbery legs. Shock widened his eyes.

Nate took advantage of the brave's momentary confusion; he leaped forward. This time his hunting knife and not his head struck. In a fluid upthrust, he slammed his blade into the warrior's midriff. The tip bit just beneath the rib cage. There was a split second of resistance then the knife drove upward toward the heart as the length of steel sank all the way to the hilt.

Mangus Amarillo jerked back, yanking the knife from Nate's blood-slickened hand. His eyes rolled down, and he stared with disbelief at the knife protruding from his belly. His own blade dropped from his hand, and he reached down, his palm closing about—

He never completed the attempt to free the deadly steel. His eyes went blank, rolling back in his head. His legs folded beneath him, and he collapsed face down in the dirt.

Nate stared at the fallen warrior, uncertain that it had ended. He saw no hint of life, but expected the brave to leap up.

"He is dead." Fights-Like-the-Wolf walked to Nate's side. "It is over."

Nate glanced at the brave he had befriended so long ago.

"Take your daughter and return to your home," the Comanche said. "There is no need for you to remain in the land of the *Kwerhar-rehnuh* any longer."

Nate nodded. Like a man in a daze, he slowly turned. The faces of the *Kwerhar-rehnuh* around him were a blur. It seemed like hours dragged by before he found and focused on his daughter. He held out a hand to her. "Mary, it's time I was takin' you home."

TWENTY-THREE

"IT'S ONLY A HALF MILE AHEAD," Ben said, turning to his sister. "Just beyond that turn in the river."

Anticipation brightened Mary's face. "Only a half mile to home?"

"Only a half mile," Ben assured her.

"Race you there!" Without warning, Mary dug her heels into the side of her sorrel mustang. The pony bolted forward.

Ben glanced at his father, watched Nate nod approval, then urged his bay after his sister.

Nate watched his children, a pleased grin on his face. It was a time for foolishness. After all, they were home—finally they were home.

Home to a real home that belongs to me! His grin widened, he let out with a joyous whoop at the top of his lungs. He was a free man with twenty-five acres to his name. And he had all his family back. No man could ask for more.

To be certain he did not know if Mary carried a child, but it did not concern him any more than did the baby growing in Bessa's belly. The only thing of importance was that his family would be together again.

The roan eased around the bend in the Brazos. Nate's heart leaped as his gaze caressed the farm and its field of oats that stood ready for harvest. A year had passed since he had left his crops unharvested in the field. This year would be different; his own hands would bring in the fall oats. He clucked the pony to a quicker pace, tugging on the rope lead of the pack animals and mustangs he had traded for.

"Pa!" A cry came from within the house. It was Ben. Then Mary's voice echoed, "Pa! They ain't here!"

His son and daughter darted out the front door. "Pa! Ma and the kids ain't here! They're gone!"

Nate urged the roan to a gallop, quickly covering the distance to the front of his home. Distress lined the faces of his son and daughter.

"Nobody's inside," Ben said. Mary added, "The house is a mess—things strewn everywhere."

Handing Ben the rope lead, Nate dismounted. "Take the animals to the barn and tend them. Mary give your brother a hand."

They hesitated. Nate waved them on. "Go on with you. Do like I say."

When they turned toward the barn, he stepped inside the house. His heart hammered in his chest when his eyes roved over the interior. He thrust aside his immediate conclusion; the house was in too good condition to have been hit by a Comanche raiding party. Mary's description of "mess" was accurate. Chairs were overturned and flies buzzed around bowls of half-eaten cornmeal mush. He tested one of the bowls with a fingertip. The mush was still soft without a dry crust. The food had been served that morning.

Moving deeper into the house, Nate searched Bessa's and his room first. The bed was unmade. His wife usually tended to such chores after breakfast. The rumpled bedcovers coincided with the uneaten mush. What had happened had occurred during breakfast.

A rough-hewn standing closet Nate had carved for Bessa stood with door ajar. Her two dresses that had hung there were gone. Nate's head jerked around, studying the room. Gone, too, were his wife's personal things, her combs and brushes.

"All Daniel's, Eve's, Ben's, and my clothes are gone too." Mary stood in the doorway to the bedroom, fear in her eyes. "It's like they packed up and lit out."

"Ain't likely." Nate shook his head, although he could find no reason for the state of the house or the missing items. "It don't make no sense. This ain't like Bessa."

Mary stepped back, allowing her father to pass. Nate's gaze moved over the house's main room again; he saw nothing new to indicate what had happened.

"Pa?" Ben waited outside.

"I don't know." Nate drew a heavy breath and shook his head. "It looks like they've gone—got up and left smack dab in the middle of breakfast. I can't make heads or tails out of it."

"They wouldn't up and leave like—"

Ben did not complete his words. Mary stepped from the house, tapped her father's shoulder, and pointed to the rise that led to the Turner place. "Riders comin'."

Four men crested the hill and reined toward them in an easy lope. Nate recognized William Turner, but he had never seen the three men with him. Nate's hand crept to the Colt in his belt, then eased away from the handle. The weapon was there should he need it. For the moment, that was enough.

"Nate." Turner tilted his head in greeting as the four drew to a halt in front of the house. "I saw you ridin' this way from my stoop. I reckoned there weren't no need puttin' this off longer than need be. Elizabeth and me want to pull out by midday."

"Pull out?" Nate's brow furrowed. "What do you mean?"

"That it's been hell for Elizabeth since you brought her back. She can't look out a window without fearin' to see Comanches ridin' down on the house. It's drivin' her mad. She can't live here no more," Turner said. "Which is why I've sold my land and stock to Howard Rawlins. The rest of my property's gone to these men from Fort Worth."

"You don't owe no nigger your reasons, Turner." A bearded man with a sweat-stained hat drawn close to his eyes pulled a long-barreled revolver from beneath his coat. He aimed the weapon's muzzle directly between Nate's eyes while he thumbed back the hammer. "Toss down that gun in your belt, 'less you want me to put a hole in your head."

Nate froze. Turner's meaning penetrated his brain. The "other property" he had spoken of were Bessa, Daniel, and Eve. Turner had sold them!

"Nigger, I ain't got no want for trouble, but if you don't ease that old Colt out of your belt and throw it 'bout a half mile from here, I'll kill you dead," the bearded man threatened.

Nate forced himself to do as he was ordered, repressing the urge to draw on the man. To do so would have been certain suicide.

"That's good and smart." The bearded man smiled. Without taking his eyes off Nate, he said, "Duwayne, Clint, get that girl and young buck up on them horses with you, and we can put 'em over with the others in Cal's barn."

Nate's mind rushed. The only Cal along the Brazos he knew was Cal Jenkins. Bessa, Daniel, and Eve were being kept there.

As the two strangers dismounted Ben and Mary backed away. Ben's hands balled into fists, ready to fight if pressed.

"That ain't smart, boy." The bearded man jabbed his pistol at Nate. "You and that sister of yours get up on the horses, or I'll blow the hell out of your daddy's skull."

Ben and Mary glanced at their father; Nate nodded. "Do what he says. I don't want you gettin' hurt."

"Or yourself, eh, nigger?" The man behind the pistol chuckled while his companions helped Ben and Mary onto the horses, then mounted behind them. "You boys go on. I'll catch up with you in a piece. I want to make sure this darkie ain't got no fancy ideas 'bout comin' after us."

The two men reined away, riding eastward along the river toward the Jenkinses' farm. The bearded man then glanced at Turner. "Ain't no need of you waitin' 'round, Mr. Turner. You and your family can be on your way to the Piney Woods back east."

Turner glanced at Nate and then at the man on his left. "Payden, I don't want him hurt. He's a freedman. He ain't no field nigger."

Payden lowered his pistol, but kept it pointed at Nate. "I ain't gonna hurt him none, I just want to explain the way things is. I've met freed niggers before. Sometimes they got a funny way of seein' things."

With another glance at Nate, Turner yanked the head of his mount around and rode back over the hill.

"Free niggers?" Payden shook his head and laughed. "Men like Turner don't know what they're doin' sometimes. A strappin' buck like you would bring top dollar along the coast. Damn shame him givin' you your papers like he done. But"—Payden drew out that single syllable—"the law says a free nigger can't stay within the borders of this state for no more than six weeks, then he's just like any other darkie. The man who catches him owns him. I intend to catch you if'n you're still around these parts come six weeks from now, nigger."

Nate was not certain if the man spoke the truth or merely attempted to intimidate him. He feared the first, but felt the latter.

"But what concerns me right now is how you're takin' havin' that woman and kids taken from you." Payden rested an elbow on his saddlehorn. "I 'spect that you're thinkin' about comin' after me, Duwayne, and Clint. Don't even let it enter your black mind. We've been in this business for nigh on fifteen years. Last buck come after us, we cut him the way a man gelds a colt. We'll do the same to you—maybe worse to them kids you fathered. Understand?"

Nate nodded. He was only too aware of what a white man could do to a black in Texas.

"Good." Payden grinned. "If I was you, I'd forget all about that woman and kids—even this here country—and head back to them red-skinned niggers you've been livin' with. Find yourself a good squaw."

Keeping his pistol trained on Nate, Payden backed his bay away from the house. Abruptly he jerked the horse's head around, and rode down the river in a full run.

Nate came alive the moment the man wheeled his mount. He darted for the barn and found the rifles Ben had leaned against the wall. Tugging back the hammer on one of the weapons, Nate ran back outside. He cursed; Payden was out of range.

"No!" A moan like the cry of a rending soul tore from his lips. "No, my lord, no!"

Rage, anger, fear roiled within him, churning into a helplessness that leeched the strength from his body. His legs folded beneath him, and he collapsed to the ground on his knees as tears streamed from his eyes.

It could not end this way, not after the long months, the endless miles he had ridden. He lied to himself. It could end this way. All he had fought for, all he had earned, his freedom and this land, meant nothing. Time and again he had deceived himself into believing that he was a man—a man who had earned the right to live his own life. But Texas would not—

He caught himself. No longer could he lie to himself. It was not Texas, the land, or the Comanches who cast his chains. It was those who traded in human flesh, who placed a price on a man's soul, who refused him and his family their rightful place in this world.

No longer, he thought. *It ends here. It ends here and now!*

NATE HALTED the mule-drawn cart inside a cedar brake a half a mile from the Jenkinses' farm. He slipped the Colt from his belt and left it in the cart beside the three loaded rifles and Ben's pistol. The temptation to use a pistol was too great. Tonight he carried only a hunting knife; if needed, a knife struck in silence.

Climbing from the wagon, he carefully tied the mule's reins to the branch of a stunted juniper, then he moved toward the Jenkinses' barn. In the moonless night, he easily discerned Payden and his two companions. They camped behind the structure that stood fifty yards to the right of the Jenkinses' farmhouse. Nate feared dogs more than the three men. A dog's bark would alert the men of his approach.

There were no dogs. As quickly and as quietly as he could move, he worked his way beside the farmhouse, then squatted in the shadows, waiting. Nor did he have long to wait. Less than an hour passed before the three men crawled into their bedrolls and closed their eyes. By the movement of the stars overhead, Nate waited another hour before slipping from the house to the front of the barn.

The barn's single door was not locked, but held in place by a simple board. This he quietly slipped from its niches, and opened the door enough to slip inside. "Bessa?" he whispered. "Bessa?"

"Nate? Is that you, Nate?" his wife answered him from the darkness.

"It's me, and I got the mule and wagon tied out in some trees," he said. "I want you and the childrens to slip out the door as quiet as mice and make for the cedar brake west of here."

"We can't," Bessa replied, her voice whisper-soft. "They've got us tied."

Tied—that meant ropes. Nate could handle that. He slipped his hunting knife from its sheath. "Keep talkin' quiet like so I can find you."

He followed Bessa's voice back into the barn. His family was tied in a hay-filled stall. He freed Bessa first, then his sons and daughters. "It's a half mile to the wagon. Go quickly, but stay quiet. Them three is camped behind this barn. A cough or a sneeze will wake them."

With that he led his family into the night. He was certain that the pounding of his own heart was loud enough to alert Payden and his companions, but ten minutes after ducking from the barn, Bessa and the children were in the wagon.

"Ben, take the reins," he ordered his son. "I want you to drive this mule west along the river. Don't stop for nothing. Just keep going. I'll catch up with you as soon as I can."

"Nate?" Bessa's head turned to him. He could not see her expression in the darkness, but he heard the concern in her tone. "Where are you going? You can't leave us alone."

"I won't be gone long. There's some things I've got to gather together." He lightly kissed her cheek. "You'll be all right. Ben can handle what needs handlin'." He then turned to his son. "Ben, get goin'."

Taking up the reins, Ben turned the cart and rolled from the cedar brake, moving westward toward the Brazos.

Nate watched his family depart for several moments, then he darted from the junipers, running toward a twenty-five-acre farm that had never truly been his.

TWENTY-FOUR

NATE UNHITCHED THE MULE and harnessed a pinto to the small wagon. The rope and leather rigging was a far cry from a Comanche travois, but the pony appeared unconcerned by the strange harness. Running a soothing palm along the animal's neck, he handed the pony's reins to Daniel. "Keep him steady, son, while your brother finishes up."

Daniel nodded, but Nate noticed his youngest son's eyes kept darting to the east. He knew what the eleven-year-old boy expected to find. He squatted beside Daniel and rested a hand on his shoulder. "It'll be all right. Them three ain't even up yet. Like as not, they'll have themselves a cup of coffee 'fore they even check on the barn. By then it will be too late."

"You sure?" Daniel stared at his father. "I didn't like them men none."

"I'm sure." Nate squeezed his son's arm and stood. He was almost as confident as the sound of his voice. They had put at least twenty miles between themselves and the Jenkinses' barn. He wished it were more, but it should be enough—he prayed it would be enough.

His own gaze shifted to the east. The grays of predawn pushed back the blackness of night. To the north he discerned a hint of clouds building near the horizon. *Rain clouds,* he thought. Rain would be good; rain washed away tracks.

Turning, he led the mule into the shallows of the Brazos River. There Bessa sat astride a bay mustang, holding a string of three fully laden packhorses. Beside her Mary and Eve rode another paint while they clutched the reins of two more ponies—one for Ben and Daniel, and one for Nate himself. The Indian horses and the supplies they carried were why Nate had returned to their home after freeing his family from the Jenkinses' barn. He had followed after his family, keeping in the river's water to make certain he left no tracks. No one in the Cross Timbers knew how many horses he had gathered while among the *Kwerhar-rehnuh.* On that fact rested his whole plan.

"Don't you think we should keep that horse rather than this mule?" Bessa asked when he handed her the animal's lead. "One of the boys could ride the horse."

"They can ride the mule, too, when it's rested," Nate answered with a shake of his head. "The mule's too valuable. Ain't nothing a Comanche likes for supper more than a mule when he can't get buffalo. With winter close, this mule just might come in handy if'n we have to make a trade."

Shuffling through the water, he gave the three packs on the horses one last check. Half the animals' burden was supplies, the remainder was trade goods left over from his and Ben's journey to the Llano Estacado. The latter he hoped would provide food for his family when they came upon Indian villages. If not, there was game on the plains and prairies. He had lived off the land for almost a year. He could continue to do so until they reached their destination.

"Pa, how's this?" Ben called to him.

Nate walked from the water and examined the rocks his oldest had piled inside the wagon. "Put another couple big ones in and that should do it. We want them wheels to cut deep into the ground. When Payden and his men come, I want to make certain they got a trail to follow."

Ben nodded, bent to select three additional rocks from the bank, and placed them in the wagon. Nate walked around to the front of the wagon and took the reins from Daniel's hand. "Go mount up. And be sure to keep that rifle dry. Wet powder ain't goin' to do any of us any good where we're headin'."

While Daniel obeyed, Nate tied the reins to the front of the wagon, making certain the pinto's head had plenty of slack. He glanced back; Ben was clear. Turning the pony to the north, he slapped the animal on the rump. The horse came to life, lunging against the harness. The driverless wagon creaked forward, its wheels turning faster with each step the mustang took. Nate watched the horse and wagon trundle northward over an open field of grass for several moments.

"How far you reckon that pony'll go before it gets tired of luggin' them rocks?" Ben asked.

"The farther the better." Nate turned back to his family. "He'll probably do a mile or two before the grass gets his attention, then he'll wander as he grazes. Might do up to five miles 'fore the day's out."

All the while leavin' a false trail for them, Nate thought. During that time, he and his family would be riding westward, sticking to the water of the Brazos to hide their tracks.

"Let's move on out." Nate stooped and picked up the rifle he had placed on the ground. "It'll be sunup in a few more minutes. We got a lot of ground to put under us today."

Wading back into the water, Nate swung astride the roan, then took the packhorses from Bessa. With one glance back at his children, he looked at his wife and tilted his head forward. Together, they nudged their mounts into a walk.

"Nate, how far we got to go to reach the free states?" Bessa asked.

"A far piece," he answered, explaining that they would ride west, deep into Comanche territory, before swinging northward. "From there we cut to the east, cross the Mississippi on a raft, and we're in Illinois. That's a free state. A man named Samson Moore told me about Illinois. We got months of ridin' ahead of us."

He glanced at his wife, noticing she clutched their Bible in her left hand. He smiled. "I'd be careful with that and keep it hidden. Comanche warriors got a likin' for Bibles. Use 'em to pack their shields."

Bessa stared ahead, a distant look in her eyes. "It seems like a long way for a body to go. How can we hope to make it—to escape them men back at the Jenkinses' place?"

"Hope is all we got, and the fact we got black skin." He told her of a man called Walks Without a Soul and his ability to move among the Comanche bands as though he were invisible.

Her head turned to him. "You've told me this before."

"I just wanted to remind you that I'm the man who walks without a soul out here. We're black-skinned, Bessa. Odds are the Indians won't bother us," he said.

"And them behind?"

"They'll follow us a piece, then they'll turn back 'cause of the Comanches. A white man ain't welcome in *Nermernuh* lands. They don't live long." He edged the roan closer to Bessa's bay and reached out to take her hand. "I know what we got ahead of us won't be easy. But with the good Lord watchin' over us, there's a chance—a good chance we'll make it. And that's all a body ever gets—a chance."

Her hand tightened around his. "And we if don't make it, then we die—die free."

Nate did not answer; Bessa spoke the gist of it. There was nothing more he could say.

"Pa, the sun's coming up," Daniel called from behind them.

Nate glanced back at the yellow orb that pushed above the trees and hills. The dawn of their first day—their first day together, truly together, he thought. How many sunrises would they see before his family and he set foot on free soil? He could only guess, and guessing would bring nothing. His gaze turned westward along the Brazos. They would handle the long months ahead as they always had, meeting each dawn as it came.